Praise for Darren Owens

"... hard to put down. I was actually rooting for Victor in the end. Nice twists. Highly recommend." -N Dunkle

"I've never heard of or read a story from this perspective. Victor Powers is a true psychopath, and as terrifying as it is, this book gives a glimpse inside that nightmare of a mind."- K Cutright

"Suspenseful thriller. A must Read." -Kanda

"Perfect love/hate relationship with the villain. Once I started I couldn't put it down."-Amy N

"Intriguing!! A must read."-Sue B

"Wow Loving psychological thriller books and this one does not disappoint!...the whole book gets you hooked as soon as you start it. I can't wait to read more from the author. Great Job!!!" - Dre'

DEMONS

DARREN OWENS

DEMONS is a work of fiction. Names, characters, places, and incidents either are the product of the author's imagination or are used fictitiously. Any resemblance to actual persons, living or dead, events, or locales is entirely coincidental.

Copyright © Darren Owens; 2022,2024

All rights reserved. No part of this book may be reproduced in any form, by an electronic or mechanical means, including information storage and retrieval systems, without permission in writing from the publisher, except by a reviewer who may quote brief passages in a review.

2024 Edition

Edited by: Tammy Olson
Cover Design by: Mark Kinzley
Final Edits by: Jake George

ISBN - 979-8-9874754-3-0 (paperback)
ISBN - 979-8-9874754-1-6 (hardcover)
ISBN - 979-8-9874754-2-3 (ebook)

Connect with the Author on Facebook @darrenowensauthor

This book is dedicated to my children, pick your dreams and follow them, no matter how farfetched, or outlandish. You'll get there, and you'll ROCK IT! Mom and I couldn't be more proud of you.

To My Beloved, for your never-ending faith in me. For putting up with but not taking all my... stuff, for helping me with this little project, for teaching me patience and acceptance, thank you. You truly saved me.

To My Editor Tammy, thank you, thank you, thank you. This would not have been possible without you. One day, we'll be in the same room.

My Friend Mark who is a genius when it comes to graphic design. Thank you for the encouragement, and for designing the artwork for the cover.

A Special Note of thanks to Jake George. Thank you for paying it forward. Thank you for having the patience of a saint. You have my word that when the time comes, I will repay in kind.

To Everyone That read this before it was completed, and offered their encouragement, critiques, and ideas. I can't tell you how much it means to me.

To My Brother Marines whose words of encouragement, and well wishes kept me going throughout this process. You are an inspiration to us all. Semper Fi & Semper Scarface!

DEMONS

1

She won't stop laughing even as the hammer comes down on her face. The laughter just gets louder and harder.
 She is mocking you... Hit her again!
 He swings again full force. The blow lands on the bridge of her nose, but to no avail; laughter still permeates through gurgling blood. Straddling her torso, he raises the hammer once more; it comes down her chin, destroying her lower jaw. Broken teeth scatter on the floor beneath him. Still... only laughter. It's louder, more manic than comical now. He drops the hammer in exhaustion and covers his ears. His hands, slick with blood, smear his face as he looks around the room.
 The portrait of her hanging above the sofa is so drenched with blood and gore that it seems to melt from the wall. The face peering through laughs hysterically, taunting him. In a violent rage, he hurls the hammer. It strikes the portrait's center and the wall bursts into flames. The mangled face below him, still laughing, spits, **YOU NEVER COULD DO ANYTHING RIGHT!**

Filled with desperation, he musters one last burst of energy and pounds what's left of the mangled pulp with his fists; the blood and gore splashing on his bare body feed his frenzy...

Victor's eyes snap open. The woman's laughter is still ringing in his ears as he tries to assess his surroundings. For a moment, he's not sure where he is. His heart pounding in his chest, which heaves with each ragged breath; the sweat on his forehead is running down his face. All his senses are hyperalert. Still frozen, his eyes search the darkness, attempting to scan the room. No moonlight shines through the window. It's dark outside... pitch black, silent, nothing is moving. A soft glow from the bathroom night light streams in from the hallway. He is straining to detect the slightest sound and is startled when the air conditioner kicks on, but immediately welcomes the relief of the cool air flowing from the vent. His wife, lying next to him, breathes with ease, her arm is draped across his chest. He hears the faint sound of his daughter's gentle snoring coming from her bedroom across the hall. Kona, the family dog, who is snuggled in her bed, whimpers and stirs in his sleep. Victor now finds his bearings and realizes it was just a dream. Threat assessment... *Zero.*

Everyone has their demons. Victor is no exception. His demons used to haunt his sleep. Vile and violent were his dreams. The images he saw shook him to his core. They were so terrifying that he dared not speak of them. These dreams revealed another side of him, a dark side, a killer lurking within. There was no rhyme or reason to his calling. He could not justify the killings by saying they were bad people; that the world would be a better place without them. He killed because he felt compelled to do so. His dreams were back and the demons with them.

2

He knew they would come from the moment he saw her that day. No matter how hard he tried to suppress them, or how he prayed they would stay away, he could feel them trying to claw their way out. *Why now?* They hadn't come in years. He tried to force the girl's image from his mind as he drove, but it was useless. She had been chosen. It would be done.

He stopped at the store on his way home and bought a salmon filet, a bunch of asparagus, makings for a salad, and a bottle of wine. Once home, he and his family fall into their routine, making dinner as a family. Taylor Swift's latest song, his daughter's current favorite, is blasting through Alexa's speaker. She is a perfect combination of her parent's looks. Her hazel eyes inherited from her father are accented by her mother's dark brown hair and angelic face. He hopes her eyes are all that she has inherited from him.

He is tending the salmon sizzling on the backyard grill, while his wife, Lindsay, chops vegetables for the salad. His daughter sets the table and sings along, a bit off-key, to the music. He catches his wife looking at him through the kitchen window, and he gives her a wink. She smiles her best smile and returns the wink. The girl intrudes on the moment... she's still there, still in his head, still engulfing his mind.

The fish is grilled to perfection and is complemented by the grilled asparagus and light citrus dressing that Lindsay made for the salad. He pours them both another glass of wine as Shelby rambles on about her day filled with all the dramatics a first-grade girl can muster. After dinner, Lindsay clears the table and takes the glass from Victor's hand with a smile and a slap on his ass as he walks by. Meanwhile, Shelby goes on about how Tommy had pulled Lisa from the swing during recess and had gotten kicked in the shin for his troubles.

Later that evening, while unwinding in the living room, Lindsay talks about her day. Victor is only half listening as she describes the latest drama going on in her office between the front desk and the back-office staff—*heart-shaped smile, flipping hair, red nails*... she won't get out of his head... *PUSH HER OUT!* —He's drawn back, momentarily, to a conversation that he's heard many times before. It amazes him that half the businesses out there are still afloat with all the inner office turmoil.

It's a temporary job. Lindsay had gone to school for television journalism and had a few promising interviews before fate stepped in, and they learned they were pregnant with Shelby. Victor was secure with his job, so they decided Lindsay would put her career on hold and be a stay-at-home mom until the baby was old enough to start school.

After tucking their daughter into bed, something they both relish, knowing it won't be long before she no longer allows it, they lay in bed, watch some mindless show on TV and try to unwind. Still restless, they make love. After, as he drifts into sleep, the girl's face flashes through his mind. His last cognitive thought, before falling asleep, is *Please no*...

He's awakened, a little later, by a dream and knows that he will never get back to sleep. His inner clock tells him it's close to two in the morning. He looks at the clock on the bedside, 2:13am. He gets up and heads to the kitchen to make coffee. Kona hops from Shelby's bed and follows. After letting the dog out, he makes coffee and turns on the TV in the living room for background noise. He stares absent-mindedly at the screen waiting for the coffee to finish brewing and thinks back to the moment he saw her the day before.

His appointment had gone better than he had hoped. He would still return the following week to wrap everything up, but the sale was in the bag. He had stopped for lunch at a downtown bistro and was considering calling it a day when he heard her. She was waiting on a customer at the neighboring outdoor café. It was her laugh that had initially grabbed his attention. It was almost musical. When he looked up, he recognized her instantly though he had never seen her before. A twisted urge washed over him. She had shoulder-length chestnut hair, coffee-colored eyes, full lips, and a slim, yet curvy figure that revealed a hint of a tan. She was a natural beauty with almost no makeup except for mascara and red lipstick that matched her nails. Her lips parted into a genuine, heart-shaped smile as the guy whose water glass she was filling flirted with her. There was an air of confidence about her without being sassy. Every primal instinct came alive as she flashed an easy smile over her shoulder and walked away.

He liked her. She terrified him. Panic set in. He suddenly became anxious and felt the need to leave. He was getting up to go when his server appeared with his lunch.

"Everything okay?" he asked.

"Yes," Victor replied, "I just need to wash up. Where's the restroom?"

The server, gestures and says, "Inside and to the back."

"Thanks," Victor replied and headed in that direction. He looked up from the sink into the mirror. Water dripping from his face, he asks himself, "*Is it her?*" The sinister reflection smiling back at him answers the question. Now he knew what he had to do, but there were rules.

He choked down his chicken salad sandwich with a swig of tea and tried to remain calm when asking for his check. He paid with cash. He tipped an even twenty percent. Not too much, not too little. Don't be memorable, he reminded himself.

The coffee is ready. He walks to the kitchen and pours a cup. His mind is racing. Had he made any mistakes? Had she seen him? *No.* Had anyone seen him looking at her? He doesn't think so. Did he seem out of place? *No.* He is terrified and repulsed by thoughts of what he is going to do to her, yet part of him is excited too.

It has been over eight years since his last calling. He believed he had it under control. He never would have tried for a normal life by getting married and having a family if he didn't think so. Far too risky… but part of him always knew that his demons were still there somewhere and trying to ignore them now would make matters worse. He sips his coffee and grimaces. *Cold?* Looking at his phone, he's surprised to see that it's five in the morning. He's lost almost three hours. Accepting what is going to happen is easier than fighting it. He will no longer ask himself why or try to rationalize it.

He just accepts it. His demons remind him of the rules for killing. Time to get moving. Normalcy is a must.

He hears Lindsay stirring in the bedroom and pours her a cup of coffee. She walks into the kitchen wearing his shirt from yesterday, and her dark hair is pulled back in a sloppy ponytail; it's a look that always drives him wild with desire.

"How'd you sleep?" she asks, as she takes the coffee with a grateful smile.

He kisses her forehead. "Not great. I had a bad dream and woke up at about two."

A look of concern pours over her face. "I'm sorry. Are you okay?"

"Nothing to worry about. Just a dream," he says, kissing her lips this time. "I turned on the TV in the living room and fell back to sleep." He kisses her again and says, "Gotta get going," as he heads for the shower.

3

One of the best things about his job is if he's productive, he's left alone. He arrives at the office that morning for the monthly briefing and sits through Jarod Comber, giving his rundown of how things are going and what's expected to go in the future. It's a RAH-RAH meeting. Jarod, his immediate supervisor, and regional manager is giving kudos to the team because sales are up, production is up, and the higher-ups are sitting pretty although we could, 'always do more,' and they are 'cutting the budget,' again. Typical. Any other day, Victor would head to his office, make his calls, set up appointments, and complete customer follow-ups. Based on his customer reviews, he is the man to call for all their needs.

Today's meeting ends with Jarod saying, "Vic, I need to see you. Everyone else, have a good day." Victor looks up from his tablet, eyebrows raised. *The boss wants to see him?* This strikes him as unusual. He follows Jarod to his office, who sits behind his desk.

"What's up, boss?"

"Have a seat, Vic."

He sits, wondering what this is about. He's always thought Jarod to be an asshole. His name is Victor. He despises being called Vic, but Jarod has always called him Vic for whatever reason. He laughs to himself and thinks, mother would have put you in your place. She always insisted that his name was Victor, not Vic. 'If I'd wanted my boy to be called Vic, I'd have named you Vic, but I named you Victor.' He'd heard it more times than he could count as a child.

Jarod begins, "You have been making quite the name for yourself for the last couple of years now. Your numbers are phenomenal, and your attention to detail and customer service has been very impressive. I'm letting you know that I've recommended you for the regional manager position that's going to be opening in about a month."

Victor is surprised by this. "Uhm, why would you recommend me for your job?"—*coffee-colored eyes, easy heart-shaped smile, musical laugh...* BACK OFF, NOT NOW!

"I'm taking a job at Corporate," Jarod states.

"Wow! good for you." Vigilant as always, Victor has noticed changes in Jarod's looks, behavior, and mannerisms over the last six to eight months. Subtle, but changes just the same. He's lost some weight, and he has a tan. Had he had a facelift? Victor had figured he had a girlfriend, but perhaps he was just kissing ass for a promotion.

"Yeah," he says. "Shitty thing is that we've got to move to Boston."

Interesting, wondering what's happened that would cause Jarod to pack up and move his family twenty-five hundred miles away.

...red nails... GET OUT!

"Anyway, as I've said, I recommended you as my replacement. I got the word yesterday; the job is yours if you want it. Of course, it comes with more responsibility. You will have a team of fifty-eight statewide and will oversee several projects at once. It's a lot of road time, Vic. I won't lie to you, your salary will, of course, go up twelve percent to start, plus bonuses, and you'll get a company car, this office, and one upstate, not to mention a company credit card. There are other benefits that HR will go over with you once it's official."

"Effective when?" Victor inquires.

"June first."

"Wow!" he says, "I had no idea." Dumb thing to say, he knows. He and Jarod aren't friends; the look Jarod gives him says as much, but he doesn't know what else to say.

"Congratulations, Vic," Jarod says as he extends his hand.

Just take it and say thank you, he tells himself. He does and adds, "Of course, I'd like to talk to Lindsay about it before I accept the job. It'll mean a lot of changes in our lives."

"Sure," Jarod replies. "Take the rest of the week and let me know on Monday."

And then it occurs to Victor that he will no longer have anyone looking over his shoulder.

4

The city has been revitalizing the downtown area for about two years. Dozens of sidewalk bistros, outdoor cafes, coffee shops, toney bars, and even a steakhouse have replaced the tattoo parlors, pawnshops, and dive bars that had lined Arizona Ave and Center Street in years gone by. There's a little park, which is named after one of the city's founding fathers, in the Town Square that offers everything from outdoor yoga classes, during the cooler months of the year, to farmer's markets and craft fairs during the summer. There is plenty of parking, and it is a perfect spot for reconnaissance.

The place where she works is called The Edgy Egg. He has driven by a couple of times and finally sees her working her tables on the outside patio.

Gotta be careful now.
Don't be noticed.
There are rules.

An hour later, Victor walks by the Edgy Egg. This time, he is close enough to smell her perfume as she serves a Cobb salad. Lilacs... An hour and a half later, he is sitting at another patio restaurant right across the street, "reading" a book and sipping iced tea.

She is beautiful. More so than he remembers. The easy smile is still there, and she's tanner since he last saw her. *She needs to be careful in the sun. She burns easily, but if she is out in moderation, she tans.* He glances down at his watch. Learning her schedule, he expects she will be getting off soon.

The smell of lilacs drifts towards him as she walks right past him. She has changed out of her work uniform into a yellow sundress and white sandals. A large beach bag is slung over her left shoulder. She appears to be window shopping as she moves towards wherever it is she's going. He gets up, leaves a ten-dollar bill on the table, and follows, making sure he is no closer than a half-block behind her. She is not rushing. The way the hem of her dress sways with her hips as she walks is mesmerizing. Several men turn their heads as she walks by. Even a few women admire her. She doesn't seem to notice. She turns into a mom-and-pop market, and he continues past. He goes around the block intending to pick up her path when she comes out. He comes around the third corner in such a rush that he almost knocks her over as she exits the market.

"Excuse me," she says, still smiling but stepping back in surprise.

"I'm so sorry, pardon me," he stammers. "Are you okay?" He's face to face with her. His nostrils flare when hit with her scent, lilac combined with Double Mint gum. It is heavenly.

"I'm fine," she replies with a smile and more than a hint of a southern drawl.

"Are you sure?"

"Yes, I'm good," she says.

"Again, I'm sorry. Have a good day."

"You too," she chimes, and probably out of habit, she adds, "See you later."

Sooner than you know, watching her walk away, enjoying everything about her. He takes it all in. The way her toes work in the sandals she is wearing, the way her hair bounces on her shoulders as she walks, even the tiny bruise on the top of her left calf. He stands there for a bit, debating on whether to follow her again but knowing he cannot. He has been seen. There are rules, and he's out of practice.

She turns into the apartment building across the next street. Scanning the building for cameras and seeing none, he heads back to his car. Now the waiting begins. *Is it her place, a friend's, or a family member's? She doesn't wear a ring... boyfriend, perhaps? It's too soon to tell... Maybe.* He will watch and learn; he will get to know her habits and routines. He does not care about her as a person. He doesn't even care to know her name, though he knows that will be inevitable. All he knows is that she has been chosen. He will answer the call... he always has... but right now, he must go. He has been here too long. He has been seen.

5

He has some shopping to do. There are rules, after all. Always wear brand-new clothes and boots. Never use or wear anything unique. Never stand out in a crowd. He walks into Walmart; he will get most of what he needs here. Not all at once, of course, and just items that can be purchased anywhere. Pushing the cart down the aisles, he appears nonchalant, not a care in the world. He grabs a couple of new pairs of jeans, not store brand, name brand, a few long-sleeved work shirts, new cotton socks, Caterpillar work boots, New Balance running shoes, and an Arizona Diamondbacks ball cap. Then, he heads over to the food aisles to get a few things for dinner and pays with cash at the checkout.

Victor has spent the last thirty days watching her as much as he can without attracting attention. He uses buses and the Light Rail train system to get to the downtown area. Sometimes he gets off a few stops early and walks, but he never drives. He alters his appearance using glasses, hats, and different clothes, stalking 101. Her name is Riley Duncan. She has a car that she keeps parked in her assigned parking spot in the complex, but she walks almost everywhere she goes. There is no indication that she is dating anyone. She lives alone unless you count the cat. Her work schedule varies.

Since it caters to the downtown businesses, The Edgy Egg is closed on weekends. Every other day she works breakfast, the next day, lunch. She is typically home by three in the afternoon, then heads for the pool where she reads for about an hour. Her apartment is on the ground floor, on the right side, and just past the stairs. There is a back-door fire exit at the other end of the hall. There are no cameras in the building, and as far as he can tell, the closest one is a traffic camera on a corner half a block away. Perfect in every way.

He has been watching her almost nonstop for the last two days. Tonight's agenda has been decided for about a week now. He's confident that he has learned as much about her as he can. It won't be long now.

6

The promotion at work could not have been timed better. It has given him an excuse to not visit Lindsay's parents for the week as they had planned. Lindsay and Shelby are disappointed but decide to go, anyway.

"Give Mom a hug and a kiss for me and tell her again how sorry I am," kissing Lindsay on the cheek at the airport.

"I will," she replied with obvious disappointment hanging on her words. "This is supposed to be a family vacation, Victor."

"Babe, I know, but what would you have me do? Not accept the promotion?"

"No, of course not. It just won't be the same without you."

"We'll make it up soon. I promise," kissing her again and bending down to give Shelby a hug and kiss.

"I'm sure going to miss you, baby girl," squeezing her tight.

"I'm going to miss you too, Daddy," returning his embrace. "It's just a week, right?"

"Yep, just a week and you'll be home," he whispers, still holding her tight.

She pulls back and looks him dead in the eye with sudden seriousness. "Please don't forget to feed Kona."

He smiles, "I won't, baby."

"And walk him!"

"Don't worry, sweetie, we'll be fine. Now, go see Grandma and have fun," he says, standing up. Lindsay watches the entire exchange between father and daughter with a smile. She loves how they love each other so much. It makes her love him that much more. She grabs the front of his shirt with her fingers and pulls him to her again.

"I love you." Kissing him one last time before turning and heading to their gate.

"I love you too!" he calls and raises his hand to wave.

Shelby looks back over her shoulder and waves back, "I LOVE YOU, DADDY!"

"LOVE YOU TOO, PUMPKIN! HAVE FUN!"

7

His heart is racing, and his chest is heaving as he enters the building unseen. *Get it under control or go home,* he thinks, knowing that it is too late to do anything but follow through. As he walks down the hall, he pulls the kitchen gloves over his sleeves, puts a hairnet on under the ball cap, and pulls the hammer from his waistband. Closing his eyes, he takes a couple of deep breaths to get his breathing under control and wills his heartbeat to slow. Now, approaching the door, he sees that the dab of petroleum jelly that he used to smear the peephole a couple of days ago is still there. This means one of two things; either she does not get many visitors, or she doesn't use the peephole. He rings the doorbell and hears her voice from the other side of the door.

"Coming!"

He feels the heft of the hammer in his hand as he raises it. The door swings open, he steps through the opening, takes in as much detail of the room as he can, and brings down the hammer, striking her claw first in the middle of her forehead with a satisfying THUNK. Her expression goes from faint recognition to curiosity and then dead in a millisecond. Her coffee-colored eyes take a moment to glaze over as she falls in a heap on the floor. Leaving the hammer embedded in her skull, he walks further inside, steps over her body, and closes the door.

Head wounds bleed a lot, and this is no exception. Blood is already coming from her nose and mouth, pooling on the laminate floor as he drags her farther into the living room by her arms. Victor stands up and looks around. Her apartment is clean and decorated as tastefully as her budget will allow. Then he sees it, a suitcase standing by the couch, and at the same moment, he hears the shower turn off. *A visitor?* he thinks as panic rushes through him.

"Rye? Who's at the door?" A male voice calls from the bathroom.

He has some time, he thinks, trying to calm himself. Whoever it is, will have to towel off, and at the very least, pull on a pair of shorts before coming out, but it's not enough time for him to get away clean. He shrugs and thinks to himself, *In for a penny, in for a pound.* There are rules. He has only brought one hammer. No time to re-use it. He looks around. The cutting board and kitchen knife are on the counter where Riley had been cutting vegetables for a salad. He grabs the knife and quietly steps behind the wall that separates the hallway from the kitchen entrance, then waits.

Brad Duncan never knows what kills him. He steps from the bathroom, sure that he heard the doorbell, but he doesn't hear voices coming from the living room. He finds it odd that his sister had not answered him, but he figures she was distracted by whoever stopped by. This is his first trip to Phoenix. He'd just arrived about an hour ago. It was his birthday, and he wanted to surprise Riley, hoping they could spend it together. He never expects to be ambushed in her living room, to have his head jerked back by the hair, a kitchen knife shoved, to its hilt, upward into his skull, under his ear, behind his jaw. He, like his sister, never sees it coming as the life in his eyes fades out.

There's work to be done. He goes over it in his mind. Have there been any mistakes?

Do you mean other than the surprise guest?

Not his fault. He has followed the rules so far. He hadn't panicked, and was able to improvise, making sure there were no witnesses left.

He drags the body of Brad Duncan beside his sister's, careful to not step in the blood, as he looks down on them. Their resemblance is unmistakable. Same parents, without a doubt. He focuses on her for a moment. Even in death, she is beautiful. Her expression, though slack, is still one of curiosity. His... surprise. Victor turns the AC as cold as it will go. He has no illusions that the bodies won't be found, but he wants to prolong it for as long as possible. It is June in Phoenix. They will ripen soon enough. He touched nothing but the thermostat and the knife, which is still stuck in Brad Duncan's head. He is careful not to step in the blood.

Leave no trace.
He needs to go.
He has been there long enough.
Time to get out.

He looks at them once more, smiles, and does something he has never done before. He takes the time to play with the police a bit. Breaking one rule but following another, he places them side by side, puts her hand in her brother's, and then turns their heads to face each other. He'd seen this done in a movie once. It had made him chuckle out loud, much to the shock of his wife.

Pulling the telescoping hook and magnet from his inside pocket, he sets the chain, locks the door behind him, and is out the back exit within minutes.

"Walk out like you belong here," he says under his breath. He follows the alley for half a block, stops behind the dumpster, pulls the New Balance running shoes and headband out of the gym bag, and strips down to the running shorts and Hawaii t-shirt that are underneath the jeans and work shirt, which he quickly stuffs into the gym bag. The hairnet is stuck to his head from hairspray. He'll take it off at home. He puts on the shoes and headband, slings the bag over his shoulder, and now he is just a guy running at night when it is cooler. Just like a ghost in the wind, he's not seen and not remembered. He runs all the way home, reliving the events over and over. Other than her brother being there, he had executed his plan perfectly. He tries not to second guess the brother showing up. He couldn't have known. Life happens after all. Even with the brother, Victor is proud of his performance. In a heartbeat, he had improvised his plan, adapted to the new situation, and overcame the obstacle. He smirks to himself, *"It's almost like I've done this before."*

8

It's sloppy, and sloppy will get you caught, rings in his head as he stands under the steaming shower, rethinking the night's work again.

You should have known about the brother.

"There's no way I could have known," he replies in defense.

What if he hadn't been in the shower and was in the kitchen with her?

Victor has never been afraid of getting caught. He has convinced himself that if he follows the rules, getting caught will never happen.

"I'd have dealt with it," Victor smiles.

Being sloppy IS against the rules...

Victor wonders if he can make it stop again. He had done it before. Over eight years ago, he had discovered, more by accident than anything else, that he could keep the demons at bay by self-medicating with whiskey and cocaine. The booze dulled the demons into submission while the coke, in moderation, kept him semi-sensible. He will not let his life spiral down that rabbit hole again. For one, he has a family now. Spending his nights in a bar drunk and high will not go over with Lindsay, and he knows it. Although, that was him when they had met.

⁂

She'd been out with a few friends, and they had come into 'Lefty's', a neighborhood pub trendy enough to draw the college kids during the weekends to pregame, before continuing downtown, but established well enough to keep the regulars happy throughout the week. Victor was there because it was his hangout. He saw her across the room. It was her hair that he saw first, dark brown and curled so that it bounced on her shoulders when she walked. She had natural beauty which was enhanced by her modest makeup and dark eyes that flashed when she smiled. She was truly mesmerizing. He went over to talk to her when she went to the bar to get another drink.

"Hi," he'd said, as he approached her trying to smile.

"Hi," she said back. Her smile was genuine.

"Listen, I'd like to talk with you, but to tell you the truth, I'm drunk, and don't want to make an ass of myself. Can I get your number so that I can call you tomorrow?" he asked with a slight slur in his speech.

"I'm not sure," she teased. "You haven't even told me your name. Why would I give my number to a drunk guy in a bar who hasn't told me his name yet?" Her dark eyes were sparkling and playful.

"Of course," he replied. "Victor is my name."

"Well Victor, at least you're sober enough to know when to not speak. I'll think about it," she said as she took her drink from the bartender.

"Put it on my tab," he said.

"Thank you, Victor, who knows when he's too drunk to carry on a conversation," she flirted and turned back towards her table.

"Wait!" he called. She turned with a dazzling smile on her face. "You didn't tell me your name."

"No, I didn't," she teased and turned back to her friends.

He'd gone back to his table, utterly confused, not sure how that had gone at all. This was not the norm for him. He was usually confident and quite charming when he needed to be. Handsome is not a word most people would use to describe Victor. Not that he's unattractive in any way. He's tall, he's fit, and has a slightly crooked smile that gets more pronounced when he's drinking. It's more his natural and honest charm that he can turn on and off like a switch that makes him appealing. He's never had trouble with the ladies. This was the first time in a long time that he had not even gotten a name. He sat back down at his table as his buddies asked him how it went.

He shrugged and said, "I have no idea," then ordered another drink. They all laughed.

An hour later, the coke was kicking in and he was feeling more clear-headed when he thought about taking another shot at it, but when he looked over, her table was empty. He smirked and thought to himself; *I guess not*. Just then, he felt a tap on his shoulder. He turned around and there she was in all her beauty. She pushed a bar napkin into his shirt pocket, turned, and walked away without a word. He watched her walk out of the door with a drunken smile and retrieved the napkin from his pocket. He opened it, and there, in the most delicate handwriting he'd ever seen, was a phone number with the name Lindsay underneath. Beneath her name, after 5pm was underlined twice. The Demons had been asleep at that point for over a year.

9

The bodies of Riley and Brad Duncan are found a week later. It is the lead story on the six o'clock news the morning he picked Lindsay and Shelby up from the airport. The pretty blonde newscaster reads the headline from her teleprompter, giving her best "serious look" while doing the newscast "bobblehead" into the camera.

"Coming up, police make a gruesome discovery after being called to perform a welfare check at a downtown Phillips apartment after the resident hadn't shown up to work and wasn't answering her phone. Stay tuned for more details after the break."

Victor isn't worried. He'd left nothing behind except the hammer he bought, with one purpose in mind, from Home Depot a month prior, along with a box of nails, a few project boards, and paint. Once he got home, he scrubbed it clean, and never touched it with bare skin again. He dropped the gym bag containing all other evidence into the foundry at the copper recycling plant, of which he was the new regional manager.

This was yet another unexpected benefit of the new job. He had full access to the mill, "the shredder," the foundry, and every recycling plant in the area owned by Little General Recycling, the largest recycling company in three states. No questions were asked, and no eyebrows were raised when he asked for a tour of the facility shortly after accepting the new position.

He turns off the TV and walks out the door. He tries to find the story on the car radio but can't. No big deal. He will catch it on the evening news. The dreams have stopped since the killings. His demons seem to be sated for the time being.

10

"DADDY!" Shelby shrieks as she flies full bore down the terminal with her arms reached out and held high over her head. Victor waits for her to crash into his open arms and envelopes her, lifting her off her feet and spinning her around in place. "I missed you so much, Daddy."

"I missed you too, baby. Did you have fun?"

"Yeah! Grandma and Grandpa got a new puppy!" she screams, unable to contain herself.

"They did? What's his name?"

"Jack."

"Jack is a great name for a dog," he says. "What kind of dog is he?"

Shelby brings her finger up to her lips, struggling to remember the breed of her grandparents' new dog. "I forget. I think it starts with a C," she replies as Lindsay catches up.

"He's a Border Collie," exclaims Lindsay, as she catches up to them while blowing a stubborn strand of dark hair upward out of her face.

"Hi Beautiful," swiping the hair from her face and tucking it behind her ear before kissing her and reaching for her carry-on, which she gives up gladly. "I sure missed you," he says lovingly.

She stares upward into his face and with a furrowed brow, she teases, "Did you now?"

As they are walking out of the airport and across the concourse to the parking garage, a horn comes blaring out of nowhere. Victor instinctively reaches out and grabs Shelby, who is about a step and a half in front of him and pulls her back from the curb. Lindsay shrieks in surprise as a taxi driver, a robust black man, flips them off through the rolled-up window and mouths, "FUCK OFF!" as he blasts past them. Lindsay frantically pulls a pen and paper from her purse, and with shaking hands, starts writing the cab's medallion number and company phone number down. Victor eases his hand to hers, knowing how upset she is, and stops her rage by asking if she's okay.

"I'm fine!" she replies, near tears. "Did you see that asshole...?" She bends down to give Shelby, who is more shocked by her parents' reaction than by her near-death experience, a once over.

"Yeah," he says. "I saw the medallion; I'll call them tomorrow. Is she okay?"

"She's fine. She barely noticed."

"How about you?"

"I'm fine," she says, holding back her tears. "Just shaken up a bit. Did you see him? He almost—"

"Shhh," he wraps his left arm around his wife, pulling their daughter into their thighs with his right, forming a three-way family hug. "I told you, I'll take care of it."

That night, The Demons return, and Victor dreams about an angry black man driving a taxi.

11

Detective Pete Tucker sips his coffee and grimaces. *Cold.* He swallows anyway while going over the case file in front of him. *This guy is smart,* His gut tells him this is not the first time this guy has killed, and more than likely, it will not be his last. Riley Duncan had been a beautiful young woman just getting started in life. Her younger brother had the bad luck of being in the wrong place at the wrong time.

"Whatcha thinking Tuck?" Roni asks.

Tucker looks up across his desk into the face of his partner of almost twenty months. After eighteen years with the Phillips Police Department, Veronica Novetti is his current partner. Her looks are deceiving. She has dark curly hair that sweeps the top of her shoulders. Her smooth olive-colored skin and strong nose expose her Jewish heritage. When she smiles, she is the picture of innocence. Wherein lies the deceit. Roni is tough, cunning, and sees through whatever bullshit is being fed to her. She is confident in her abilities and yet she is still compassionate. She genuinely cares about the job and the people she serves. Roni is the best partner Tucker has ever had.

"You're reading the same report I am. What do you think?"

She dives right in. "This guy... he's no virgin."

Tucker just stares at her, letting her go, letting her process it.

She closes her eyes, thinking out loud more than talking to him. "He's careful. This was planned."

"Keep going," he encourages. "What else?"

"The brother surprised him, and our guy didn't hesitate."

"How do you know?" he asks as he picks up the crime scene photos and flips through them.

"The suitcase for one, and the knife he used to kill him was hers. He had to get in, do his thing, and get out. He brought the hammer with him for her. According to his bus ticket, the brother had only been in town for two hours before our guy killed him." She opens her eyes as she finishes.

"Good, I just wanted to make sure we're on the same page," Tuck says as he drops the crime-scene photos on the desk and starts pacing.

"Then he posed them," Roni says.

"We'll get to that. Let's start from the top and go all the way through it."

Jenkins from the lab interrupts, bringing in the lab report. He hands it to Tucker, who glances through it quickly before handing it to Roni. "What do ya got, Mike?"

"Not much," the lab tech replies. "Most of the prints inside are hers. The brother also has a few. Nothing seems out of place."

"Except for the dead bodies holding hands in the living room," chimes Roni.

"Yeah, except for that," Jenkins replies somewhat embarrassed as he walks to the door.

"Okay," Tucker says, coming around the desk and flipping through the crime scene photos. "Baby brother shows up. Does she know he's coming? Does it matter? He's here, from Baton Rouge. He has a beer with his big sister, but it's been a long day, so he asks if he can take a shower, then grabs his bag, and heads for the bathroom. Meanwhile, Riley makes dinner. She's happy that her baby brother is there, or maybe not. Regardless, she's distracted, and someone is at the door." Tucker's pacing grows faster than his theory as he continues. "She opens the door and in comes our guy, who BAM, buries a hammer in her forehead. Does he notice the suitcase and realize they are not alone? We think he was in the shower, because other than the bodies, there is no sign of a struggle, so maybe the shower turns off? Who knows?" His thought process continues to flow. "What does he do now? Why doesn't he run?"

Roni answers, "He doesn't know how much time he has, and our guy does NOT want to be seen."

"Right!" Tucker exclaims. "So BADDA BOOM, he doesn't hesitate. He adjusts his plan right there on the spot. Whoever is in the bathroom must die. Tough luck Buddy. Our guy grabs the knife off the counter… Does he go into the bathroom? No, he waits. Where does he wait?" he asks while flipping through the photos. "Bingo. Right here in front of the refrigerator. He waited for Brad to come down the hall. Then he jammed the knife into his head. But why her? He's not there to rape her. She was not sexually assaulted, and he's not there to rob her. She's a twenty-four-year-old waitress, for fuck's sake. There is nothing to steal. He's there to kill her. Nothing more. Brad was a bonus."

"But he posed them." Roni states.

"Why though?" Tucker replies. "It's gotta mean something, even though it wasn't part of his original plan."

He picks up his jacket from the back of his chair. "Let's go," he says.

"Back to the apartment," Roni replies, more to herself than to him.

Tucker nods, giving his approval of her ability to read him.

12

Victor is about to turn the channel away from the news. It's the typical story of late. It has an attention-grabbing headline, but no real meat to the story. In short, the police were called to perform a welfare check on a young woman who hadn't reported to work in over a week and wasn't answering her phone. The landlord let them inside, and the bodies of a young woman and an unidentified young man, later determined to be her brother, were discovered.

The newscaster, a good-looking man in his early forties with a "made-for-TV face," turns his head to another studio camera and continues the broadcast. Victor has never met him but thinks that he is a bit too pompous when on the air and assumes that he is the same in real life.

"In other news, a taxi driver who was found murdered in his taxi earlier this week, in downtown Phoenix, has been identified. Jonas Jackson was found on Monday. Police were called to an alley near

Thirty-Second Street and McDowell after a homeless man found his body in his taxi. The investigation is ongoing."

The next day Lindsay asks him to swing by the grocery store on his way home from work and grab a few things. Shelby was having a sleepover with Abby, the neighbor girl, this weekend, and they would need a few things. "Popcorn, soda, ice cream, candy, you know, the basic junk food," she rambled off while standing on her tiptoes to kiss his cheek.

His head is buried in the ice cream freezer, and he's reaching for the last carton of Mint Chocolate Chip when he feels her walk up. He grabs the ice cream and turns straight into a tanned, thin girl wearing cut-off jeans, that are a bit too short but accentuate her long legs. She has on open-toed brown sandals. Her feet are narrow and boney. Yellow nail polish accents her toes. He follows her thin frame to her face, which is long, even for a girl of her height and weight, making it seem more angular. Her eyes are the most beautiful shade of emerald, green that he's ever seen. Her thin lips are almost severe. Her mousy-brown hair is pulled back in a long ponytail that reaches the middle of her back. Victor inhales the scent of her vanilla body wash while she waits impatiently for him to get out of the cooler.

At that moment, he realizes he is staring into a youthful version of his mother. He is so startled he almost drops his ice cream. His heart pounds in his chest, blood is ringing in his ears, and his breathing becomes labored as he falls back against the cooler.

A look of concern crosses her face. "Are you okay?"

It's not her. Pull yourself together!

He knows that this woman is not his mother. That would be impossible. He had killed her fifteen years ago.

"Yeah, I'm fine," he said, fighting to regain control of his breathing. *Good Lord, the resemblance is remarkable.* "You just startled me."
Stop staring at her like a moron!
He chuckles, "Are you okay? I didn't mean to frighten you."

"I'm fine," she said. The look on her face moves quickly from concern to the irritation of a twenty-year-old's sense of entitlement.

"Anyway, I hope I didn't frighten you," he repeats.

"I was afraid that I gave you a heart attack," she smirks much like his mother would have.

"Are we related?" he asks, out of genuine curiosity.

Thinking this is an extremely poor pickup attempt, she rolls her pretty green eyes, huffs, and walks away without her ice cream.

Trying to recover and force himself to a calmness he doesn't feel, Victor puts the ice cream in his cart with the rest of his items and goes to the checkout, and he waits in his car for her...

No, get out! You'll see her soon enough.

"I have to wait. I need to know where she lives."

No! you made a scene. You need to leave now!

Suddenly aware that he's sitting in his car talking to himself after having caused a commotion in the store, he realizes he needs to go.

He starts the car, pulls out of the parking lot, and heads home breathing deeply the entire way to calm his nerves. As he pulls into his driveway, he sees Abby's bike in the garage, and can already hear the girls laughing, giggling, and shrieking as only six-year-old girls do. Victor collects the bags of groceries from the back seat, takes a few more deep breaths, pushes the earlier events to the back of his mind for later, forces a believable smile, and goes inside.

Lindsay is standing in the kitchen, looks up and greets him with a genuine, loving smile as he walks in. Placing the bags on the counter, he leans down to kiss her cheek. She beams at him, gushing as he pulls away. He looks at her quizzically, with eyebrows raised, and a devilish grin now spreading across his face.

"Later," she mouths, then yells, "Girls, come get your pizzas!"

Shelby and Abby come running into the kitchen, still giggling, and continuing their conversation as if Victor and Lindsay are not there. Abby opens the pantry to get the DiGiorno pizza crust, while Shelby roots through the refrigerator for the toppings. Never pausing their conversation, they move in rhythm with each other as they place the ingredients on the counter. Lindsay opens the pizza sauce and leaves the girls to it while Kona lays, ever so patiently, waiting for the girls to get careless with the pepperoni, or sausage.

Lindsay comes around the counter to where Victor stands and wraps her arms around his waist. She presses the side of her head into his ribs as he puts his arm around her.

Pulling back, she looks up into his face. Her eyes are beaming as she says, "Angie and I had lunch today."

Angie Keller, the pretty blonde who anchors the Channel 4 Morning News, and Lindsay have been friends since college. Angie, the forever single professional woman, accepted her position about the same time Lindsay found out she was pregnant.

"Oh, how's Angie doing?"

"She's good. She started dating someone new a while ago."

"Really?" he asks, eyebrows raised.

"Yeah, I invited them over for dinner next Saturday."

"Oh? What's the occasion?"

She leads him by the hand over to the sofa to sit while the girls continue piling toppings on their pizza. "It's a celebration of sorts."

"Celebration? What, that Angie has kept a guy around for more than three or four weeks?" he chuckles.

Ignoring the joke about her friend's love life, she whispers, "Victor, I got the job," she beams, tears of joy welling in her eyes. "I got the job!" She is almost squealing now with girlish glee as she grabs his hands and shakes them.

"The job? At Channel 4? Babe, that's great!" he says, taking her into his arms. He is honestly happy for his wife. She squeezes him tightly as she sobs and laughs into his shoulder.

"It's finally happening," she says as tears flow freely down her cheeks. The smile of pure joy grows wider on her face.

"Mommy, what's wrong?" Shelby asks as she steps into the living room from the kitchen. Her face is full of concern for her mother; Abby and the pizza are temporarily forgotten.

"I'm okay, baby. I'm just very happy."

"Why are you crying if you're happy?" she asks, the confusion clear in her voice.

"Mommy is going to be on the NEWS, baby," Victor explains.

"For what?" she asks, stepping further into the room, her dilemma growing more prevalent.

"What Daddy is saying is that Mommy got a job at Channel 4. Sweetie, I'm going to be reporting the NEWS! Isn't that great," Lindsay gushes.

Shelby's eyes widen, and her mouth drops open. "YOU'RE GOING TO BE ON TV?"

Lindsay smiles through her tears and nods, "Yes baby, I am."

Shelby runs from the room. "ABBY, ABBY, MY MOM'S GOING TO BE FAMOUS!" her voice echoes from the kitchen as the girls squeal with delight.

Victor grabs Lindsay up from the couch, wrapping their arms around each other as they stand in the living room entwined.

With her face turned slightly against his chest, she whispers, "It's finally happening."

Victor rests his chin on the top of his wife's head, takes a deep breath, and blows out, "Yeah..."

13

Tucker is at his desk, going over his interview notes from Riley Duncan's coworkers, boss, and neighbors when Roni comes into the squad room with the forensic report from Riley's apartment. She drops a copy in front of him, crosses to the desk, sits down, without a word, and picks up reading where she left off in the elevator.

"What do we got?" he asks, putting his notes down and scooping up the forensic report.

She doesn't answer, but instead holds up a finger, asking for another minute.

He takes a sip from his coffee mug and grimaces. *Cold. Becoming a habit*, he thinks as he gets up and goes to the coffeepot for a fresh cup. He returns, as Roni finishes reading the report. "Well?" he asks.

Roni looks at him, brow furled, and says, "Nothing much." She tosses the report on the desk. "No prints on the hammer, only hers on the knife."

"Okay, he wore gloves. What else?"

"He wears size thirteen and a half boots based on impressions left on the carpet. He's about two-hundred to two-hundred-twenty pounds and the imprints on the linoleum in the kitchen show no wear pattern."

"No wear pattern?"

"Nope."

"This guy's smart," Tuck says under his breath. Knowing her answer before he asks, "Think he's still got 'em?" She just looks at him with her chocolate-colored eyes. "Yeah, not a chance," he says. "What else do we have?"

"Well, he wears hairspray," she says with a smirk.

"Oh?"

"Yep, they found traces on the wall in the kitchen, where he waited for Brad. They also found petroleum jelly smeared on the peephole of her door."

"Okay, again from the top. What do we know?"

Roni paces the room as is her habit when she's talking through her thoughts. "We know he's smart. He's a planner. Riley was chosen, but why? What was his reason?"

"Not now," Tucker chimes. "Stay on track."

She looks at him as if he had just materialized, in the room, out of thin air. "Right... He's meticulous, so he leaves nothing behind," she continues.

Tucker enjoys watching her when she's in her zone. He remembers he had not been so happy when she was first assigned to be his partner, and he had said as much to his lieutenant. She was "... too green, too pretty," and he would not carry her through the rough stuff if she couldn't hang. He wasn't being chauvinist. Homicide detectives see the worst society has to offer. "I have no problem with her being female as long as she can do the job."

She had shown him on the first day that he had nothing to worry about when Buddy Laird, a local crackhead, and one of Tucker's CI's that they had gone to shake down for information, had screwed up and called her Sweet Cheeks.

"It's Detective Novetti," Roni said with a serious glare.

"Yeah, whatever Sweet Cheeks," Buddy chuckled.

She met his nonchalance with equal ferocity and responded by slamming his head against the trunk of their car, "It's Detective Novetti Asshole. Now you try."

Laird, surprised at being spun around, bent over, and slammed face-first on the trunk of the car, uttered, "Eat shit Bitch!"

Tucker watched with amusement as Roni then wrapped the fingers of her left hand into Laird's hair, banged his head against the trunk again, while her right-hand shot straight to his crotch, found its mark, and squeezed. She then whispered almost seductively and ever so sweetly "My name is Detective Novetti, limp dick, and you are going to repeat that with respect, or I am going to twist these little cheese curds that I've got here until they pop, and then, I'm going to put them in my pocket. Now, let's try this again," the knuckles of her right hand turning white. "What's my name?"

With sweat running down his face and near tears, Laird spat, "Detective Novetti!"

"Are you sure?" she asked him sweetly, but still squeezing. "Try it once more. I don't want you to forget."

"DETECTIVE NOVETTI!" he screamed.

"You sure?"

"God, yes! I'm sure. Just let go!"

She let him go and stepped back to the curb as Buddy Laird, attempting to get up, fell into the gutter and curled into a ball.

Roni simply leaned against the car as Tucker got the information he wanted. Laird, being sure to keep Tucker between himself and Detective Novetti, and carefully monitoring her, answered Tucker's questions with no attitude at all.

"Who was that for?" Tucker asked as they were having lunch afterward.

She looked up from her sandwich, eyes wide, and covered her mouth with her fingers. "Why, Detective Tucker, whatever do you mean?" she says with a passible southern belle impression The feigned look of innocence on her face shifted slowly into an icy, blank glare.

"Point taken." He said, meeting her stare with one of his own. Taking a sip of his Coke, he said, "Call me Tuck." They had been good ever since.

"Neighbors saw nothing, heard nothing, of course," he says, flipping through his notebook. It's not because they don't want to be involved. This isn't New York.

"No, it's because this guy doesn't make a scene," she replies. "He blends into the background as if he belongs."

Tucker knows Roni is right. "This guy is no virgin. He posed them. Why, what's he trying to say?" Experience tells him that killers don't do these things for no reason. Everything means something. But something does not seem right here. Normally, posing the victims is a statement. Brother and sister holding hands and looking at each other might suggest an extremely close relationship between them. "Do you think our guy knew them?"

"Statistics say yes. People are most often killed by someone they know. It's doubtful our guy knew the brother. Cell phone records show that Riley had called Brad, earlier that day, to wish him a happy birthday. Checking his voicemail confirmed that, but, other than a few texts every other week, they didn't seem to have had a lot of contact. Their parents were the only shared contacts on their phones, but maybe he knew her."

Their investigation suggested that Riley lived a solitary life. She had moved to Phillips, Arizona, from Baton Rouge, Louisiana two years ago, following a breakup with her high school boyfriend, who later joined the Marine Corps, and was now deployed. Perhaps she came here to get away from her past. Maybe it started as a vacation, and liking what she saw, she stayed. She had no close friends to speak of and seemed to like it that way. She worked at The Edgy Egg, five blocks from her place, as a waitress, and was well-liked by both her coworkers and her regulars. Riley was friendly but didn't get too close. She had kept everyone at arm's length. This seemed to be true of Brad as well. There was no indication that she knew he was coming for a visit, but despite their lack of closeness, he knew it was okay to show up unannounced.

So, is our guy a customer? Does she know him? More than likely, he didn't know Brad, so he would not have known whether they were close.

"What do you think? Where are you on this, Tuck?" Novetti asks.

"He posed them to mess with us."

"What? Are you sure?"

"Think about it," he says, then goes on to explain everything he's pieced together.

"Son of a bitch!" she exclaims when Tuck finishes. "He did it just to show us how good he is."

"Yep."

"We need to check into every unsolved murder in the last couple of years, where the killer has left little to no trace. Let's see if this guy has a pattern."

Roni looks at her watch, 5pm. Agitated, she blows out a deep breath, takes her jacket off, and hangs it over her chair.

"What's up?" Tuck inquires as she plops down behind her desk.

"Nothing."

"You sure? Cause it kinda seems like—"

"TUCK!" she says a little too harshly, just as the lieutenant comes out of his office, and gestures for Tucker to come. Tuck looks at his partner for a second before walking toward the office door.

"You too Novetti."

Once he was seated behind his desk, he asks, "Where are we with the Duncan case?"

Tuck and Roni tag team their boss the way seasoned partners do, not interrupting each other, but each picking up right where the other leaves off, at just the right time, to the point of almost sounding scripted.

Lieutenant Ames looks over his glasses from the report he was reading to follow along as they concluded. "Others?"

Tuck tightens his lips and nods, "Most likely."

"Serial?"

"Too soon to tell, but maybe."

"All right," Ames says, blowing out a deep breath. "I want you two on top of this. First thing in the morning. Get on the wire to every department in the state and see if anything matches up. If he's done it before, there will be a trail. He doesn't get to be that good without practice."

"In the morning?" Tuck asked.

"No OT," Ames says simply and picks up the report again.

"That's great," Tuck mutters as he pulls the office door closed.

14

Victor's eyes snap open. He's instantly awake. His heart is pounding in his chest as he goes through the motions of surveying the room. He knows it's the dream that woke him. They have been coming more frequently; almost nightly for the last week or so. Knowing that sleep has eluded him for the rest of the night, he looks to ensure Lindsay is undisturbed. She stirs softly, as a light snore escapes her. Shaken to his core by tonight's dream, he gets out of bed and wills himself to calm down. His breathing slows as he looks in on Shelby. Kona looks up and hops down from the bed, eager to be let outside. Shelby is the picture of innocence snuggled in her blankets. Taking a few more deep breaths, he trudges down the hall, opens the back door, and lets the dog out. By the time he reaches the kitchen to make coffee, his heartbeat is only slightly above normal.

Tonight's dream was not about the tan, angular girl with yellow toenail polish. He has dreamed of her often since seeing her in the grocery store, nor was it a dream about his mother, of whom the girl's resemblance is so uncanny. He cannot tell the difference between the two in his dreams. Tonight's dream was full of graphic details of the grisly death of the kid behind the counter at Circle K in Gilbert.

Victor wonders what it was about the kid that had grabbed his attention. He had stopped late in the morning to grab a cup of coffee; the kid's name, according to his name tag, was Ash. Victor handed Ash a dollar twenty-five for the coffee, said thank you, and told him to have a nice day.

Ash said, "Thanks, you as well," in response.

No big deal, but something in the way he'd said it had caught Victor's attention.

He's surprised that he dreamed about the kid, with Ash on his name tag. Victor is lost in thought, watching the morning news, when Lindsay walks into the room with her morning coffee. She leans down, kisses him, and says, "Good morning,"

He looks up, startled, looks at his phone and is shocked that he's been up for three hours. "Morning babe."

"Hey, how long have you been up?"

"Not long, maybe an hour," he lies.

She sees through it. "Babe, is everything okay? You haven't been sleeping well, if at all, lately."

"Yeah, just a lot on my mind, I guess."

"Anything you want to talk about?" she probes.

"No, just work stuff," he replies.

She has known, from early in their relationship, that he has a dark side. He confided in her one night, after getting a little too rough. He told her that memories from his childhood had haunted him at one time, but insisted that his "Demons," as he called them, were locked away in his past. He promised her it was a momentary lapse and that it would never happen again. She was so in love by that time that she saw no other choice but to accept him, flaws and all. She had brushed it off so, whenever he would act up, she told herself it was the booze or the drugs, or a combination of the two. She'd done her share as well, so she understood. She never associated his behavior with what he had confessed to her that night, but now, this seems different. Something is troubling him. Something is wrong. She knows this as she stands in the doorway watching him. She asks him again, "Babe, are you sure everything is all right?"

"It's nothing sweetie, it's just..." *He almost blurts it all out, the killings, both recent and from long ago. Would she still love him? Would she stay? Or would she grab Shelby from her bed and run? Probably the latter,* "between my new position and your new job, we are having to make some adjustments. I just wonder how all the changes in our lives are affecting Shelby. You know, just regular stuff."

"Uh-huh," she says, looking skeptical as she crosses the room and sits on the arm of the couch beside him.

Just then Shelby walks into the room. Rubbing the sleep from her eyes, she snuggles into her Daddy's lap.

"Good morning, baby," Victor says as he kisses the top of her head.

"Morning Daddy. Morning Mommy."

"How'd you sleep, sweetie?" Lindsay asks, leaning down to kiss her cheek.

"Good," Shelby says as she sticks her thumb in her mouth; a habit that she's almost but not quite broken.

Victor moves his body from beneath his daughter, kissing her one more time, and rises from the couch.

Lindsay gets up from the arm of the couch where she'd been sitting and wraps her arms around him, and says, "We're not done here, Victor. We need to talk and don't forget Angie is coming for dinner tonight."

He leans down to kiss her. "Just a few hours. I promise."

"All right," she says, releasing him from her arms. "As long as you are on time."

"I will be," he smiles. "What are we having?"

"Cordon bleu."

"Ooh, my favorite," he says and heads for the shower.

Three and a half hours later, after his paperwork is completed, reports signed, and emails read and sent, Victor pulls his company car into Circle K gas pumps, in Gilbert. Facing away from the main entrance, he fuels his car. Ash is leaning against the far side of the building, smoking a cigarette, presumably on his break. Ash does not indicate that he has seen him. Victor collects his receipt, quickly scans the parking lot, gets back in his car, and drives away. He circles the block and pulls into the Burger King across the street. He grabs a book from the glove box, goes inside, orders a meal, and sits at a window booth with a full view of the parking lot across the street. Two new cars have arrived. A black Mustang, and a late-model, tan Corolla. One car is gone. A blue Honda.

Forty-five minutes later, Ash walks out of the store and climbs into an older gray F-150. Without hurrying, Victor dumps his tray and heads to his car. He gets to the exit just in time to see the gray F-150 turn east on Center Street. He falls in two cars behind. The pickup turns left on Gallup Lane. Victor follows, staying about two-hundred feet behind.

It's an older neighborhood. At one time, it was upper-middle class. Now, however, it's almost ghetto, or as ghetto, as Gilbert gets, Victor thinks and laughs to himself. The pickup turns right on Lariat and pulls right into the driveway. Victor pulls over at the mailboxes along Gallop Lane and watches as Ash walks through the carport, unlocks the door to the house. The house is just a little over a mile from Circle K. That seems about right, he thinks; it makes sense that he would work close to the neighborhood in which he lives. He is young, though. *Does he live with his parents? Is it his first house? Does he have a roommate?* These are all the normal questions he asks himself while hunting. Time will tell. He will have his answers soon enough.

After Ash has been inside for about five minutes, Victor drives past the house looking for signs of another car in the carport. The concrete is old and cracked, so it's hard to tell. He doesn't see any other cars. That doesn't mean that there is no one else living there, or that there is no other car that parks there. *Time to go.* He follows Lariat Street, looking around the neighborhood, memorizing the layout, and setting up his escape route.

His phone rings. It's Lindsay. "Hey, babe."

"Would you stop and grab another bottle of wine on your way home? I didn't realize that we're about out."

"Sure, anything else?" he says as he watches the house where the kid with Ash on his nametag has parked his truck.

"No, I think that's it. I just thought we had more than we do."

The blue Honda that was in the parking lot at Circle K is now pulling in the driveway behind the pickup, and the kid with Ash on his nametag comes out of the house, walks to his truck, and pops the hood.

He will have to come back to survey the house more at length later, he thinks, as he puts his car in gear and pulls away from the curb.

"Careful!"
"I know, I know!"
"Where are you?" Lindsay asks.
"Almost home, babe, just stuck in traffic."
"Oh, okay," she says, not sure if she believes him or not. He has been a bit off lately.
"Ang will be here at six. When will you be here?"
"As soon as I pick up the wine," he says cheerfully. "Shouldn't be more than about twenty minutes, thirty tops."
"Okay, see you soon. Love you."
"Love you too, bye." He hangs up and drives toward his neighborhood.

There are rules.

Victor pulls into the driveway and hears Joe Jackson's music blasting from Alexa's speaker through the open garage door. He smiles to himself, knowing what he is going to see when he walks in: Lindsay in her groove. He walks through the garage as always, and he is not disappointed. She is dancing around the kitchen, putting together tonight's dinner, and singing into the wire whisk. She has a bowl of whisked eggs and a cutting board full of butterflied chicken breasts on the counter. Beside it are paper plates lined up in an assembly line fashion with the rest of the ingredients that she will need before putting dinner in the oven.

He leans against the doorjamb and just stares at her for a moment unnoticed. She is so amazing; he thinks. She is still the most beautiful woman he has ever seen in real life. At this moment, the rest of the world ceases to exist. Her natural beauty and charm enrapture him. It amazes him that she loves him the way she does.

"But she's not enough to keep the Demons away, is she?"

"How long have you been home?" Lindsay asks, blushing, her face still red at getting caught being goofy.

"Not long." His mouth breaks into an easy smile as he walks the rest of the way into the kitchen, places the wine on the table, wraps her in his arms, and kisses her. "ALEXA!" The music stops. "Turn the volume down to four." Joe Jackson resumes singing at about one-third the former level.

Lindsay returns his kiss, keeps her arms wrapped around him, and rests her head against his chest. "I hate it when you sneak up on me like that."

"I just walked in and enjoyed the show." He said playfully. "I love watching you when you're in your zone. Where's Shelby?"

"She's at Abby's tonight. I called Jen and they're having a sleepover."

"Oh, yeah?" his hands drop playfully down to her butt.

"Yeah," she says, her smile widening as she backs out of his grasp. "But not now. I've got to finish getting dinner ready."

"Bullshit." He laughs. He pulls her to him, then bends over and puts her over his shoulder. "We're taking full advantage of this!"

"VICTOR!" she screams, laughing as he carries her down the hall to their bedroom.

15

The doorbell rings just as Lindsay puts the chicken in the oven, and Victor is finishing the salad.

He looks at the clock; 5:58pm. "If nothing else, she's prompt," he says, wiping his hands on a towel, while Lindsay goes to answer the door.

"She always has been," Lindsay says.

Victor grabs two wine glasses from the rack, and then searches the drawer for a corkscrew, as Lindsay answers the door. He is not much of a wine drinker, except occasionally with dinner, so while the wine breathes, he goes to the garage fridge to grab two beers just in case Ang's boyfriend is a beer drinker as well. The female voices coming from the foyer get closer as he enters the garage. As he returns to the kitchen with the two bottles of beer, he's greeted by Lindsay, who walks toward him with eyebrows slightly raised.

"Honey, you remember Angie?" Angie turns at the sound of her name.

"Of course?" curiosity about his wife's strange question filled his voice. "Hi, Angie. It's always nice to see you. How are you?" he asks, hugging her.

"Hi, Victor. I'm good, thank you. I'd like you to meet my girlfriend, Roni. Roni Novetti, please meet my friend and Lindsay's husband, Victor Powers." They shake hands and exchange pleasantries. The look of surprise is gone in an instant, but it does not go unnoticed.

"Not quite what you were expecting, huh?" Roni asks.

"No, not at all," Victor almost snorts at the bluntness of the question. "Welcome to our home. What can I get you to drink? Please, have a seat."

"Wine please," Roni says as she takes a seat at the counter. "You have a beautiful home."

"Thanks, it's coming along," he says, reaching to the rack for another wineglass. "Ladies?"

"Absolutely!" Lindsay and Angie say in unison.

The conversation before dinner goes about, as expected: excitement that they are finally going to be working together, how different the job is from what was taught in college, Angie telling Lindsay what to expect at Channel 4, and how she will be the on-sight reporter in the mornings and on weekends to start, but not to get discouraged, because she will be in the studio soon enough.

Suddenly, feeling self-conscious, Lindsay looks across the coffee table at Roni, who is smiling politely, and apologizes. "Roni, I'm so sorry for being rude and leaving you out of the conversation. I'm just so excited about the new job. Please forgive me."

"Not at all." Her smile is genuine. "I understand completely."

"Tell us," Lindsay continues, "how did you two meet?"

Angie clears her throat. "Well, we met at work," she says, looking at Roni adoringly.

"Oh, do you work at the station as well?"

"Um, no, I... I don't."

Sensing the shift in the comfort level, Lindsay apologizes again. "I'm sorry. Did I say something wrong?"

Victor, watching curiously, reaches over to hold his wife's hand.

Roni looks from Lindsay to Victor and says, "About a year ago, Angie was doing a story, and my partner and I were the lead detectives."

"Really? You're a cop?" hoping he does not sound as interested as he suddenly is.

"Victor!" exclaims Lindsay.

Apparently, he does. "I'm sorry," he sputters. "You're just not exactly what I think of when I think of a police detective."

Roni smiles again over her glass of wine. "That's kinda the idea."

"Yeah, I suppose so," he smiles back. "Where? If you don't mind me asking."

"Not at all. Right here in Phillips."

Red flags are waving inside Victor's head. ***SHUT UP, YOU IDIOT!*** "Wow, which department? Vice? Robbery? Can I even ask?"

She takes another sip of her wine, but just a sip. "Of course, you can ask," she grins. "I'm homicide."

Oh, good, Christ! This is too close!

I know!

There's a homicide detective in your house!

I KNOW!! Back off!

"Homicide?" Lindsay says. "Wow! Good for you," she says. Her admiration is apparent. Angie is beaming. Victor's mind is racing.

Stay cool here.
BACK OFF!!

"Wow is right! I don't think I've ever met a homicide detective. How long have you been with the police dept?" Victor asks.

"In Phillips? Just about two years. I moved up from Tucson after seven years with Tucson PD."

Alexa's timer goes off just then. Lindsay hops up to check the oven. The smell of cordon bleu fills the kitchen as she opens the oven door, removes the dish, and places it on the counter to rest. She looks up to see Angie and Roni entering the kitchen.

"Smells delicious. How can I help?" Angie asks.

"Please, you two, relax," Lindsay smiles. "This just needs to rest a few minutes." She has already set the table. "I've just got to get the salad from the fridge." Looking past her guests, Lindsay asks, "Where's Victor?"

"I think he's in the bathroom," Angie says. "What do you need?"

Lindsay laughs and replies, "More wine."

⸸

"This might not be as bad as it seems," Victor says to the image staring at from the bathroom mirror.

There's a Homicide Detective in the kitchen...

"I know, I know, but hear me out... she's not here working, she's here for dinner, and we follow the rules."

Do we?

"Yes, we do. We kill no one we know, we leave no trace, we do not stick to a pattern, and we keep nothing, no trophies, or anything that we use. Everything is new. We are hunters. We are careful. Our victims are chosen randomly. It's not personal. We always follow the rules."

Except for the taxi driver, that was personal...

"We are adaptable. That was necessary."

Hmm, perhaps... but this, this is too close...

"I KNOW!"

She's dating Lindsay's friend...

"I KNOW! But we don't know if she's investigating anything we've done."

She's a homicide detective... we're murderers... she's in the kitchen...

"If we play this right, it may work to our advantage."

Too close. We're playing with fire here!

"We have no choice. We're in too deep now. We can do this."

He takes a deep breath, washes his hands, and looks hard at this reflection in the mirror.

The Demon's evil smile glares back at him. Victor takes a deep breath and thinks, *Game on.*

Reentering the living room, Victor picks up his empty beer bottle and follows the voices coming from the kitchen.

"Sorry about that, ladies," he says, walking into the kitchen and kissing Lindsay on the cheek. "Just a little heartburn from the wine, I guess."

Lindsay looks up from the salad she is tossing. "You okay?"

"Oh, yeah," he says and winks at her. "What'd I miss?"

During dinner, Victor tries a few times to steer the conversation back to Roni Novetti and her career, but to no avail. The topic has changed, and it is not the time to be too curious about a police detective he has just met. There will be other opportunities. The conversation is light and cheerful. The anticipation between Lindsay and Angie to be working together is obvious. After dinner, they move to the back patio, and Victor offers more wine all around. He's not surprised when Roni declines.

"Two is my limit when I'm driving."

"Are you sure?" he asks, holding the bottle up a little higher. His eyes scanning her face intently. "You can always take an Uber."

She smiles. "Next time. Can I just have some water, please?"

16

Stuck in traffic on the I-10 on the way to Phoenix to collaborate with a Phoenix PD detective about the recent murder of a taxi driver, Tuck looks over at Roni, who's deep in thought in the passenger seat, "So, how'd they take it?"

Still in thought, she answers, "How did who take what?"

He debates for another second and sighs. "Your girlfriend coming out to her friends. How'd they take it?"

If she's surprised, it doesn't show. She looks at him with a blank stare, debating just how deep he is going to dig this hole and if she's ready to open up about her personal life to him. Searching his face for anything malicious and seeing nothing but a smile, she chuckles, looking at him, but doesn't say a word.

"Come on, I AM a detective."

Roni snorts in a fit of laughter then covers her mouth and nose with her hands, "Yes, yes you are, aren't you? Well, it wasn't too bad. They weren't expecting it, but they recovered quickly. I was just thinking about him."

"Why did he say something inappropriate?"

She looks at her partner for a moment. "No, nothing like that, and nothing I can put my finger on. He's just a little odd."

"Odd how?"

"Like I said, nothing I can put my finger on. It's just something about him."

"Example?"

"Well, he was in the bathroom, and Lindsay, his wife, asked me to grab a dish towel from the linen closet, and when I walked past the bathroom, I heard him talking to himself."

"So, lots of people talk to themselves."

"Yeah, I couldn't make it out. I was trying not to eavesdrop, but this sounded more like a conversation. He was in there a while, and when he came back, he said the wine had given him heartburn, but he was drinking beer, not wine and he just seemed different when he returned."

"Different how?"

"I don't know. That's what I'm trying to figure out. Like I said, he just seemed odd."

"Eh, it takes all kinds, Roni."

"Yeah, I guess."

She is silent the rest of the way to Phoenix.

"Why are you so interested in Jonas Jackson, Tuck?" asks Phoenix Police Detective Logan Spears.

"I'm not sure if I am, but he may be tied to a case we're working over in Phillips."

"The waitress?" inquires Spears.

Tucker nodded, then asks, "What do you have on him so far?"

"Not too much." Flipping through his notes, he rambles, "0430, a homeless guy that goes by Bingo, was pushing his cart in the alley behind the liquor store on Thirty-Second Street and McDowell when he sees a taxi idling and notices the driver hunched over the steering wheel. He opens the door to check on him and sees an icepick sticking out the back of his head. He'd been dead maybe three hours before we got there."

"Believe him?"

"Sure, no reason not to," Logan says. "Bingo's been around this area for years. We've had no trouble with him before."

"What about Jackson?"

"He's a lowlife, wannabe tough guy with a short temper and no balls. Blames the world for his problems. Looks like he may have pissed off the wrong person."

"Whaddaya mean?"

"M.E. says he was stabbed several times: twice in the heart, and five times in the face, plus the back of his head with an icepick."

"And he left the pick in the guy's head?" Roni asks.

"Again, must have pissed someone off," is Spears's only reply.

"Prints?"

"Nothing on the icepick. If that's what you mean? It looks brand new."

"New?" Roni's interest is now dialed in and hyper-focused. "Anything special otherwise?"

"No, other than it was cleaned with bleach before he used it. It's run-of-the-mill. Can get it anywhere."

Roni and Tuck share a look.

"What?" Spears asks.

"How do you think it went down?"

"Come on, Tuck! I've answered yours, now answer mine."

"In a minute. How'd it go down?"

"You'd better not fuck me on this, Tuck."

Tucker just looks at him.

Spears sighs, "The driver's last dispatch was to the airport at 9pm. He made the drop and checked in. The dispatcher had nothing for him, so we think he headed downtown and got flagged from someone at a bar."

Roni asks, "What about GPS?"

"Of course not. Your turn."

"Well," Tuck replies, "There seem to be some similarities between your case and ours. Everything he uses seems to be brand new; never used before. He left nothing at the scene but a clean weapon, a common tool that anyone could buy anywhere."

"What?"

"A claw hammer to the forehead."

"Jesus."

"Yeah, except that he picked her," Tuck said.

"Hunted her really," Roni added.

17

Life for Victor Powers and his family has changed drastically over the last two weeks since Lindsay started at the station. She is at the bottom of the totem pole, and hence, is on call twenty-four seven, and she is indeed the onsite weekend reporter covering everything from the animal shelter being overcrowded; 'Reporting Live from Maricopa Animal Shelter, I'm Lindsay Powers. Back to you in the Studio Ted,' at four-thirty in the morning, to 'History of the Corn dog' type stories. She even did the annual 'Reporting LIVE from the Crosswalk' story this year because school has started and reminding people how to drive in a school zone is of utmost importance. She is in bed by 7:30pm and at the studio, before 3:00am The camera loves her face, and she is well liked by the NEWS personalities, the behind-the-scenes people, as well as the viewers.

So now, Victor has taken on all the responsibility for Shelby Wednesday through Sunday. He gets her up, feeds her breakfast, hair's combed, teeth brushed, dog fed, and they're out the door by seven-ten so they can make it to school by seven twenty-five. Saturday and Sunday aren't too bad. Shelby sleeps in a bit but is one of those children who needs a set schedule, so sleeping in on the weekend for Shelby is normally no later than seven-thirty. Although, getting her to bed is sometimes a chore. Lindsay picks her up from school, and they have the afternoon for mommy and daughter time. Victor tries to be home between four-thirty and five. They make dinner together as much as possible and always eat as a family. Lindsay puts Shelby in the tub and goes to bed, leaving Victor to clean up after dinner, get Shelby into her PJs, and be tucked into bed by eight.

Victor's sleep is dark and haunted as of late. The Demons are more active than ever. He tries to get over to Gilbert to surveil Ash's house, and learn more about the blue Honda, but fiscal year audits are coming up, and he needs to have them ready, so Ash and the blue Honda have been put on the back burner. This delay causes immense anxiety. His Demons are impatient.

He parks his car four blocks away, and is walking Kona around the neighborhood, in a random pattern, but always within sight of Ash's house. He strolls with leisure. Kona still has his summer shoes on to protect his feet from the Phoenix sun on the hot sidewalk. He's just a guy walking his dog. They stop under the tree by the mailboxes, and he gives Kona a drink of water from his bottle. Kona lies down in the grass for a rest. *This couldn't be any more perfect,* "Good boy, Kona." Ash's pickup is in the driveway, but the blue Honda is not.

Questions come to mind. Who drives the Honda? Girlfriend? Roommate? Both are possible. Just a friend? Would a friend be welcome to park in the driveway? Family member? Victor is confident that, in time, he will have all the information he needs. Like all experienced hunters, he knows that patience is key. Now that the hunt has begun, the Demons will ease up on him.

Kona gets up and sniffs around, as Victor searches in his pack for a plastic bag. As Kona squats to do his business, the blue Honda pulls into the driveway. Ash is driving. There is a girl with brown hair in the passenger seat. He checks Kona, who is still in his poop stance, his tail working up and down like a jack handle. He looks back toward the Honda as the trunk lid pops. Both doors open. Ash gets out of the driver's side and drops his keys in his pocket as a pair of long, skinny, tanned legs swing out of the passenger side. Victor catches his breath as she exits the car. His heart rate intensifies, racing into overdrive. "It's her!" he says out loud. "Oh, good Christ, it's her." Same bony hips, Same mousy brown hair pulled back in a ponytail.

He's not sure if it's in his mind's eye or if he can see her angular face and thin lips, but he knows it's her. He imagines her piercing, green eyes; she's the girl with the yellow toenail polish, the girl that looks so much like his dead mother. She goes to unlock the carport door with keys from her oversized purse and returns to the car. They both are loading up their arms with plastic bags from the grocery store. **Stay calm. She's not your mother!** Booms in his head. His heart is pounding, and his breathing is labored. He bends over and puts his hands on his knees, takes some deep breaths, and wills himself to calm down.

I know it's not my mother. It can't be.
We need to go!
No, I can't. I want to kill them now. I need to —
CONTROL YOURSELF. WE DON'T ACT ON IMPULSE.
In his mind's eye, Victor sees himself bitch slapped. **We've learned enough today. Let's go...**
What? What have we learned?
She lives here...
What? How...?
She has her own key.

Victor smiles in relief and thinks *of course she does* and walks towards his car.

Don't worry. I'll show you what to do.

Victor is quite relaxed by the time he reaches the car. He is even smiling as he opens the back door for Kona.

18

It's Saturday. Victor and Shelby begin their latest daddy-daughter-day by watching Lindsay's report with 'Bill the Garden Guy,' who's talking about trees that pollinate in the fall, and the allergens that will soon be in the air around the Phoenix area. She is radiant on camera, and her beaming smile makes it clear that she has found her calling and loves her new job.

In a while, he, and Shelby, following their tradition, will go to The Waffle House just off US-60 in Mesa to have breakfast. They have been enjoying their daddy-daughter-days at least once every couple of months for the past two years since Shelby's been old enough to enjoy hanging with just dad. Victor asked her once if she wanted Abby to go with them on their outings. To his surprise and delight, she said, 'No, those are our days.' His heart swelled.

After breakfast, they play it by ear. Sometimes they go to museums or the park to swing on the swing set. Sometimes they go to Bass Pro Shop and play hide and seek in the upstairs campground.

Today, Victor is planning a surprise for her. After Lindsay's last segment, they get ready for their day. Victor is in the garage getting fishing poles and tackle boxes together when Shelby comes out to announce she's ready. Her eyes get wide, and her mouth drops open, giving Victor the exact reaction he was hoping for.

"We're going fishing!?" Shelby shrieks with excitement.

"Yes, ma'am, we sure are." Victor smiles at his daughter as he puts the fishing gear in the trunk.

There are several man-made lakes in the Phoenix area that are regularly stocked with fish. Victor chooses the closest one in Tempe. They spend the day fishing until they run out of worms, then they buy some food for the ducks and feed them. Later, Victor pushes his daughter on the swing set. Yet another thing that Shelby never tires of. She laughs and constantly screams, "Higher Daddy, Higher!" Victor laughs back and jumps to comply.

Most of the time, they finish their day at Shelby's favorite frozen yogurt place, and today is no exception. They walk in the door and Marci, the early twenty-something girl behind the counter, who happens to be the owner's daughter, greets them with a smile. "Hey, guys. Busy day?" Marci is behind the counter most days when they come in. She has dark hair, hazel eyes, and olive skin. She has a slightly crooked smile that appears without effort and the type of body that keeps young men awake at night. Shelby adores her.

"Daddy took me fishing today!" Shelby exclaims.

"Oh, what fun," Marci replies with enthusiasm. "Did you catch anything?" Her glance shifted to Victor.

"A few," he says. "Catch and release though, so I guess we're not having trout for dinner."

"That's too bad," she says. "Want your regular?" she asks as she hands them medium-sized cups.

"Yes, please!" Victor and Shelby say in unison, taking the cups.

As Shelby turns and heads toward the yogurt machines, Marci reaches out and touches Victor's forearm. "I think it's great that you spend so much time with Shelby. You're making lots of memories with her."

Victor looks into Marci's ever-changing eyes, then slowly lowers his, pausing when they reach her fingers still lingering and gently tugging at the hair on his arm, then looks back into her face, and says, "Marci?"

She smiles with what he is sure she thinks is her most bewitching twenty-something smile.

"Yes?" she answers, smacking her gum a little too loudly.

Victor's eyes go deadpan; his face grows slack, and he gives the innocent flirting girl across the counter a glimpse of the Demons lurking just beneath the surface. Her face grows from flirtatious to just this side of terrified in an instant.

He leans in and nearly growls, "I'm not the man you want, giving too much attention to you."

She pulls her hand away as if she had touched something hot and quickly hurries to the restroom.

That was a little harsh!

Maybe...

Victor, she's a kid.

Exactly. Hopefully, she learned a lesson and won't try picking up on men like me in the future. Especially at her age.

There aren't many men like you.

Let's hope...

Victor forces a believable smile on his face and catches up with Shelby at the cake batter yogurt dispenser. They get their usual toppings and go to the counter to pay. Marci never makes another appearance while they are there. Victor places twenty-five dollars, what he normally pays for two frozen yogurt cups, plus a tip on the counter when they leave.

They pull into the driveway, and Lindsay's car is already there. They can hear music blasting through Alexa's speaker as they exit the car.

"Mom must have had a good day," Shelby says.

"Sounds like it," Victor replies.

They come into the kitchen through the garage, as Lindsay is pouring what appears to be her second glass of wine. She looks up, beams at her family, and without hesitation turns and grabs another wineglass from the rack, fills it, and hands it to Victor.

"Wow!" he exclaims. "What are we celebrating?"

"I GOT MY FIRST BIG STORY!" she screams up to the ceiling with her head back and her arms shaking in the air.

"Wow! That's great, babe. What is it?" Victor inquires.

"Let's just say we need to take Angie and Roni out to dinner because I owe Angie HUGE!"

"Slow down," he says. "What are you talking about?"

"Remember the pretty waitress that got murdered at the beginning of the summer?"

The bottom of Victor's stomach drops like he's just reached the top of the world's biggest roller coaster and is spiraling down the other side.

"Yeeeaahhh, what does that have to do with you?" he asks, now feeling anxious.

"Well…." she says in an almost trembling voice, "Roni and her partner are investigating it, and it's turning out to be bigger than just her and her brother. Angie hinted to me that Roni needs a news source, but they don't want to make their relationship too obvious yet, so Angie suggested me! Isn't that GREAT?" she squeals, wrapping her arms around his neck, jumping up, and wrapping her legs around his waist.

Victor wobbles a bit but holds her. "That is wonderful news. I'm thrilled for you," he says as he lets out a deep breath into her shoulder.

The three of them go to dinner to celebrate. Red Robin is their traditional celebration spot. A family recognizes Lindsay as soon as they walk in the door. She relishes the attention without being pompous. She is polite, and thanks each of them for watching, including the teenage boy who turns three shades of red when she flashes her TV smile at him.

Victor can barely choke down his burger as the Demons scream at him.

Good Christ Victor, this IS too close!
I know! Back off and give me a minute.
The cop that was in your house is investigating us!
I KNOW!
Your wife will be putting what we did on TV.
I KNOW GOD DAMMIT BACK OFF!

But the Demons don't back off. They continue through the evening. Victor ends up getting a to-go box for most of his meal. Lindsay misplaces his obvious discomfort by thinking he is just shying away from the spotlight as four more people disrupt their dinner and approach their table. Shelby doesn't notice Victor's mood shift at all because her mother's sudden celebrity enraptures her.

On the way home, Victor, lost in thought, feels Lindsay's hand touch his arm. "Victor, are you okay? I wasn't expecting all of that. They told me at the studio that this was going to happen at some point. I didn't think it would be so soon."

He snaps out of his inner conversation. "Wha...? Yeah, I guess it's something we'll have to get used to."

"Wait until I tell Abby that you had people asking for your autograph!" Shelby shrieks from her booster seat.

19

Shelby finally settles down and goes to sleep about ten minutes after they tuck her in.

Lindsay goes into the bathroom to take her makeup off and puts on one of Victor's old tee shirts for bed. Victor pulls on a pair of sweatpants and picks up his laptop.

"You're working?" Her disappointment is obvious.

"Yeah, I've just got to check a few emails and make sure the Prescott thing is going like it's supposed to. I won't be long."

"You'd better not be. I've got plans for you tonight, mister." She flashes her best Victor-only smile.

"Fifteen to twenty minutes, tops," he promises, winks at her, and walks out of the room.

Once on the couch, Victor opens his laptop, logs into his email, and thinks *Holy fuck! What am I going to do?*

You know what you have to do.

No, absolutely not.

Victor... In for a penny...
No!
Well, if you're not willing to do what needs to be done...
I said NO!
Then let's give her something to report. She's waiting... go to her... we'll talk tonight.

Victor has the most vivid dream he can ever remember that night. He wakes with a start, wondering if the scream caught in his throat was out loud. He looks over at Lindsay. She is up on her elbow, looking back at him. She reaches over and caresses his cheek with concern.

"You okay?"

He is sweating profusely, takes a deep ragged breath, and lets it out slowly as he tries, in vain, to forget the images still fresh in his mind. "Yeah," he says as he tries to swallow the taste of bile that has crept up his throat. "Just a dream," he adds. "Did I say anything?"

"No, sweetie, just a lot of moaning and thrashing about. Do you want to talk about it?"

"No," he says, rolling over as if to go back to sleep. "I just want to forget it."

Just then Lindsay's alarm goes off. She turns it off, and when she turns back to her husband, he is sleeping peacefully, as if nothing had happened.

"How does he do that?" she asks the otherwise empty room.

Victor lets out a soft snore in response. She gets out of bed and heads to the kitchen to make coffee. Kona hops out of Shelby's bed and follows to the back door. She lets the dog out as she notices the aroma of freshly brewed coffee. Victor had pre-programmed the pot for her.

She pours herself a cup and thinks, *God I love that man.*

20

Lauren likes rough sex. She always has. If she doesn't wake with at least handprints on her ass, bruises on the inside of her thighs, bite marks on her tits, or any combination of the three, she considers it a wasted night. Tonight, she is hoping he will give her all of it and then some. Ash called her from work earlier today and told her to be naked and ready for him when he got home. He's not always as aggressive as she would like, but when he is, he curls her toes and wears her to exhaustion.

He's been holding out on her for almost two weeks. It's a game he likes to play sometimes. He'll tease her throughout the week, sometimes with an inappropriate touch or pinch, or he will send her texts telling her what he wants to do to her at that moment. Later, when she's worked up from just thinking about it all day, he will tell her that the moment has passed.

Yesterday morning was the worst. She was in the kitchen getting a cup down for tea when he came up behind her and grabbed both of her breasts and started nuzzling her neck. Her nipples went hard under his touch. When he started pinching and pulling on them, they got even harder. Each pinch and pull sends shivers straight to her womanhood. It always surprises her how he can get her so wet, so fast. She responded by standing up on her tiptoes, arching her back, and grinding her ass into his groin. His hands moved from her nipples to the top of her shoulders, and in one fluid move, he bent her over the counter. His hands slid down to the waistband of her panties and pulled them down. Dropping to his knees, he took them off. She thought she knew what was coming, so she pushed her ass out a bit more to give him better access. He inhaled her heady aroma and stuck his tongue as far into her as he could, just missing her clit. She braced herself on the counter, arched her back a bit more, and pushed her ass even further into his face. He dragged his tongue across her pussy and up the crack of her ass. His tongue moved further up, passing the small of her back along her spine to the middle of her shoulder blades. Then he grabbed her by both hips and plunged his cock deep inside of her, hard, held it there for a second, maybe two, and plunged again, deeper, and harder this time. Her hips banged against the countertop hard enough to leave her beloved bruises. Groaning, she knew one more thrust, and she was going to cum. She braced herself, wanting to meet his thrust with her own.

Then, without a word of explanation, the son of a bitch pulled out of her, buttoned up his pants, walked out of the house, got in his truck, and went to work, leaving her there to finish the job. To make it worse, yesterday was her long day. She had a full day of classes at MCC, followed by the dinner shift at Dos Gringos, where she works as a hostess. By the time she had gotten home, Ash was already asleep because he had worked the early shift at Circle K this morning. Now the level of frustration is beyond belief. It's all in fun, and she knows she will get her payback at some point. She debates not giving him the satisfaction. She could go to the bedroom, take care of herself, then call Tanya and Jessica for a girl's night out, but she decides against it. She enjoys his games. He loves her, she knows and being honest with herself, she admits that she loves him, too. The realization of it makes her smile.

Ash will be home at seven. With five hours to prepare, she walks into the bathroom, turns the hot water on in the tub, squeezes a couple of drops of lavender and eucalyptus from her essential oils, and then adds a few more drops of baby oil to the water before adding her bubble bath. She wants to soak in a hot bath before getting ready for tonight. As is her habit, she goes through the house and checks the doors before getting in the tub. She makes a mental note to have Ash talk to the landlord about fixing the carport door again, as she slams it shut and checks the lock before turning towards the bedroom. Lost in the thought of being in love with her boyfriend, she strips down and gives herself a once-over in the full-length mirror hanging on the door.

She has always accepted her body for what it is. She is tall and skinny. Her features are angular. She sees herself as pretty, but nothing spectacular. She feels good in her skin and likes the person looking back at her in the mirror. Walking naked across the hall to the linen closet, she grabs her favorite towel. It's purple, made from Egyptian cotton, and was a housewarming gift from her mother when she and Ash moved in together. The bathroom is steamy and smells of the oils in her bath as she closes the door, drops the towel on the counter, turns off the water, and steps in. *One day we'll have a Jacuzzi tub,* she thinks to herself as she leans back and lets the hot water embrace her. She grabs a washcloth, wets it in the hot water, spreads it over her face, and closes her eyes. As the water cools, she sits up and grabs her razor and body wash, and then shaves her legs and armpits. When she's done, she stands up, turns on the shower, and rinses off. Emerging from the bathroom with her hair wrapped in the towel, and her favorite nail polish in her hand, she walks down the hall from the bathroom, intending to do her nails in the living room while she watches Dr. Phil.

Passing the kitchen, she sees the open carport door. "Goddamn door," she swears under her breath as she steps out with one naked leg, grabs the doorknob, pulls it closed, and locks the deadbolt. She picks up her phone to call the landlord herself when it rings in her hand.

It's Stacey from work. *I bet she wants me to work for her tonight,* she thinks, as she answers.

"Hi, Stac!"

"Hey Lauren, I was wondering if you'd cover my shift tonight? Please, please, please?"

"Not a chance," Lauren says. "Ash and I are going to turn off our phones and lock the doors tonight." She sits on the couch and picks up the remote.

"That sounds nice. I'm jealous," Stacey pouts into the phone.

"You should be," Lauren teases as she apologizes to Stacey, adding, "I would any other time, but not tonight."

"Okay, thanks anyway."

They hang up as the new girl on Channel 4 fills the television screen, ending her segment with, 'Live for Channel 4, I'm Lindsay Powers. Back to you Angie.' Angie Keller closes the show with, 'Thanks Lindsay,' then turns to the next camera, looks straight at

Lauren, and says, 'Thank you for watching Channel 4 NEWS. Dr. Phil is up next. We hope you'll stay tuned.'

"That's why I'm here, Angie," Lauren says to the television.

21

Victor walks back to his car, careful to be nonchalant. There are rules, after all.

What about what you just did do you consider following the rules?

"Shut up! I was doing reconnaissance."

Oh, that's what that was?

"Would you leave me alone, please?"

She is not your mother.

"I know."

You killed your mother.

"I know!"

You chopped her head off!

"I KNOW!"

With a machete!

"I KNOW!"

You were in the house while she was there—

"I needed to see if I could get in."

You're getting sloppy.

"We both know I had to get in there."

Sloppy!

"Sloppy how? I got in. I learned what I needed and got out without being seen."

You left the door open.

"I couldn't slam it."

It was sloppy, and sloppy will put you on the news.

"Cute. I've got to get Shelby. We're going to have a busy night."

On the way home, he drives past the Circle K, where Ash works and as luck would have it, the parking spot next to Ash's pickup, on the passenger side, is vacant. Victor sees it as a sign. He pulls into the spot, puts his car in park, gets out, and drops his keys and an empty Coke bottle on the ground. The bottle rolls toward the back of the pickup. He takes a deep breath and scans the area. Confident it's safe, he reaches down and pulls the knife from his boot as he bends to retrieve the items. Victor quickly slashes both passenger-side tires and grabs the empty soda bottle and keys. He drops his keys in his pocket and throws the bottle in the trash as he walks in the door. He pays cash for a bottle of water and goes home satisfied that he's bought himself enough time.

After dinner, Shelby takes her bath while Victor and Lindsay clean up the kitchen. He tries to portray a calmness he doesn't feel. He's impatient and on edge. His nerves are apparent each time he looks down to check the time; his illusion of calm is cracking. Timing will be crucial. It's imperative Lindsay and Shelby follow their routine and are asleep before eight o'clock. Ash gets off work at seven, which puts him home between seven-fifteen and seven-twenty. Slashing the tires should buy him enough time to get in and situated, but not a lot. He knows what she is planning when Ash gets home, and he wants to watch for a while. This is something he hasn't done since his mother was alive; flashing back to the look on his mother's face, the last time he saw her, makes him shudder.

He hears Lindsay telling Shelby to dry herself off, brush her teeth, get into her PJs, and she'll be in to do her hair before bed. She then goes to their bedroom and changes out of her clothes and emerges wearing one of his tee shirts that barely covers her underwear, then leans against the wall, watching as her husband finishes cleaning up.

Something is going on. He's jumpy, and he's in a hurry.

Her bare feet pad the floor as she walks up from behind and wraps her arms around him as he puts the last glass in the dishwasher. He jumps from the unexpected embrace but manages to not drop the glass. Lindsay giggles as she presses the side of her face into his back and squeezes her arms tighter around him. She can hear his heart pounding in his chest as he tries to relax in her arms.

"Thank you." She says holding him, his back still towards her, as he rinses his hands in the sink.

"For what?" he asks, puzzled.

"You've stepped up so much since I started my job at the station. I appreciate it more than you know. I love you. Thank you!"

"Aw baby," he says. Turning to face her, he raises his arms, returns her embrace, and kisses the top of her head. "Of course."

"No, not of course. You don't deal with change well, and my new job has brought more change to our lives than even Shelby did." Victor checks the clock on the microwave. Six-fifty.

It's time.

Shut up! I'm with my wife.

Trying to hide his apprehension, he says, "It's just life, sweetie. We all have to adapt."

Just then, Shelby comes in from the hallway and announces that she's ready for bed. Lindsay looks up into Victor's face, stands on her tiptoes, kisses him with semi-parted lips, and says, "I just want you to know that I appreciate your efforts. I've got to go to bed, too. 3:00am comes early, plus I'm meeting with Roni and her partner for coffee." And with that, she takes Shelby's hand and leads her down the hall.

22

Thirty minutes later, after making sure that both his wife and daughter are fast asleep, Victor changes his clothes, walks into the garage, grabs his gym bag from its hiding spot, and opens it to make sure that he has forgotten nothing.

You are obsessing.

"I'm double-checking."

When did you pack the bag?

"Two weeks ago."

Did you check and double-check everything then?

"Yes."

Was everything there?

"Yes."

Then it still is. You are obsessing, let's go!

He pops the trunk, puts the bag in, and starts the car.

We need to figure a few things out.

"Right now, I need to focus on the task at hand."

Lindsay is interviewing the homicide team that is investigating the murders that we committed tomorrow over coffee.

"Not now."

When?

"It may not be as bad as it seems. We might get some inside information about where the investigation is heading and if there are any suspects."

Perhaps.

"Right now, I need to focus."

Just then, Victor drives past the Circle K. His truck is there and parked next to it is the blue Honda. Lauren is in the driver's seat, waiting for Ash. She doesn't look happy.

Victor checks the rearview mirror. The Demon smiles back at him.

Lauren is ready for tonight; more ready than she ever has been. She has spent the last two and a half hours preparing her body. Two sessions of naked yoga followed by massaging her limbs with oils and lotions rich in vitamin E have limbered her up and left her smelling amazing. She likes rough sex, but she needs to be able to walk tomorrow. She's been teasing herself off and on, staying in a constant state of arousal; edging herself, keeping ready, but not allowing release.

A half-hour before Ash is due home, she inserts her favorite butt plug to loosen her rectum, *just in case,* she thinks to herself, smiling. She sets out the studded collar with a leash and a blindfold. She plans to be kneeling in the foyer with her mouth open when he walks in the door. She is anticipating having a sore throat for the next couple of days. Thinking about it gets her excited as she resumes twisting and rubbing her nipples with one hand while playing with her clit with the other. A mindless re-run of Big Bang Theory is playing in the background when her phone rings. It's Ash.

"You're late. Are you almost home?"

"You will not believe this, but someone slashed my tires. I need you to come and get me."

"Are you fucking kidding me?"

"No, I'm not. Just come get me, please?"

"Who the hell would do that? Did you piss someone off?"

"Listen, I don't know, but I don't want this to ruin our night, so just come get me, and I'll deal with my truck in the morning."

Lauren sighs into the phone. "Okay, but I'll be a bit. I've got to get dressed."

"Why?" he asks.

She can almost hear the smile on his face as he tries to salvage the evening. "Ash, I know what you're thinking, and no! I can't come to get you naked."

"So, you are naked. Have you put the collar on yet?"

"Maybe." Dammit! She hates that he knows her so well. Not really, but right now it's irritating.

"Just throw on a robe and come get me."

"No, I have to get dressed," she repeats, though she hears the loss of conviction in her voice.

"Okay," he says, his disappointment is obvious. "Just get here as fast as you can, please."

"See you soon, baby." She presses the end button on her phone and grabs her keys from the hook in the kitchen. She is in the carport buck naked when she second-guesses herself. Though she likes the thought of it, she can't go get him with no clothes on at all.

Anything could happen. *I could get pulled over, get in an accident, or my car could break down.* She goes back inside, slips on her sandals, and pulls a hoodie from her closet. "This is as close as you're going to get, babe," she says under her breath. As an afterthought, she grabs the collar and buckles it around her neck. Hurrying across the living room, she realizes the plug is still in her anus. She almost turns back to remove it but smiles at the thought of Ash's face when he realizes it's there. *What the hell,* she thinks as she pulls on the hoodie, shortens her stride, and gets in the car.

The disappointment on Ash's face is clear as Lauren pulls up, and he sees the hoodie. On closer observation, he realizes the hoodie is unzipped and there is a collar around her neck. The leash is between her tiny bare breasts and trails down her taunt torso; the look of disappointment disappears.

She cracks the driver's side window and tells him to get in.

Ash smiles the devilish smile that always excites her. "Wait here, I'll be right back."

"Are you fucking kidding me? Get your ass in this car right now!" she yells as he rushes back inside the store.

Three minutes later, Ash runs out of the store with a bottle of wine in one hand, and a dozen roses in the other, which he tosses in the back seat.

"Would you like me to drive, milady?" he asks, reaching in the open window and caressing her thigh, high enough that his fingers stroke the trimmed hair just hidden by the hoodie.

"I'll drive, get in."

Lauren has not quite pulled away when Ash grabs the leash in his right hand and begins pinching and twisting her nipples with his left.

They pull into the driveway, and the carport door is open.

"I've got to call the landlord again about that damned door," Ash says, more to himself than to Lauren.

23

Ash has outdone himself tonight, Lauren thinks as he nuzzles her from behind. They are spooning after their third session when he bites the back of her neck and tweaks her already sore nipple. She can feel his erection growing, pressing against her tender opening.

"Again?"

"Oh, yeah," he says, pushing his way into her from behind, not pounding this time more of a slow, hard circular grind he knows she likes. Not this time. This time, she wants to feel his body against hers. She pulls away from him and turns over to her back. Opening her arms and legs, she pulls him on top of her, wraps her long legs around him, and hooks her feet behind his knees so that she can meet his thrusts with her own. Her fingernails drag across his back as his thrusts get faster and his breathing becomes more ragged. She reaches down, digs her nails into his ass, and pulls him into her harder and deeper. Aching to cum with him, she lets herself go. Her orgasm is building as he pumps faster. She's meeting his thrusts, and moans louder, as she rakes his back with her nails. Ash groans into her neck. Getting close, she feels him striving to control himself. Overcome with need, he thrust once more, hard, and deep, and unloads inside of her, triggering her own release. Her legs lock around his hips, her arms hook around his shoulders. He can't move, but he feels her pulsing and exploding around him. Enveloping his body, she holds on and rides the wave of her orgasm.

A movement next to the bed forces her eyes open just as the blade of a machete comes down on the back of Ash's neck. Blood covers her face as his head loosens from his body and rolls to the side of the bed. Before she can scream in surprise or fear, the man grabs her hair, snatches her from beneath Ash's twitching body, pulls her from the bed, and slams her face-first into the wall, causing the world to go black.

When Lauren comes to, she is groaning in pain, trying to process why her face hurts so much. It feels swollen, and she can only open one eye. There's a coppery taste of blood in her mouth, and she soon realizes she is missing at least one tooth. She can feel her arms and legs, but they will not move. She lifts her head as far as she can and sees that she's naked and tied spread eagle to the bed. As she turns her head, she sees a man sitting in one of the patio chairs from their backyard watching her.

Behind him, under a bloody smear on the wall, lies Ash's headless body. Lauren whimpers as the memory of what happened comes flashing back to her.

"There's no point crying over him," the man says in an almost conversational tone. "You'll be joining him soon enough."

At that, Lauren screams in terror. The man looks at her, furrows his brow, and tilts his head as if curious. He leans forward from the chair until his face is mere inches from hers and screams back in her face, shocking her to silence.

He stands and looks down at her on the bed.

Her eyes follow his, and she becomes even more aware of her naked helplessness. Their eyes meet, hers filling with tears. "Please, No-No. Please don't," she says through swollen quivering lips; her nose running as she begs. With the terror of him reflecting on her face, Victor looks at her in disgust and fights the urge to laugh.

"You pompous bitch. Do you think I want to fuck you? After all this time? Are you still that conceited, you cunt?" Rage fills his face as he spits the words at her.

"Mister, I don't know you; I've never seen you before. I don't know what we did to you, but I'm sorry! Please believe me!" she sobs through her swollen mouth.

He glares at her. "Shut up," he growls. "If you had stayed dead, neither of us would be here now, but I know my mistake now, and I won't make it again," he says as Lauren screams.

Victor turns and leaves the room. He grabs the five-gallon bucket just outside the back door and fills it from the spigot. He returns to the bedroom and dumps the bucket over the screaming girl's swollen face. She coughs, sputters, and gags as Victor takes the bucket out of the room again. When he returns, he sets it down by the chair with a thud and sits in the chair while she catches her breath.

"You need to listen to me," he says. "I need you to not scream anymore. If you do, I promise you a very slow and painful death. Do you understand?"

Lauren looks at him. Her one good eye is open as wide as it will open, and her other eye, though swollen shut, is leaking tears. She is silent.

In a fit of rage, Victor is on her. His face right up to hers she can feel their noses almost touching, "DO YOU UNDERSTAND? he shrieks.

Terrified, she stammers, "Y... Y... Yes, I understand." Tears are flowing nonstop now.

"Good." He says and sits back in the chair.

"Please don't hurt me anymore. Please let me go."

Victor rises from the chair, leaves the room, and returns with a bag of ice from the freezer. He drops the bag on the floor to break it up, rips it open, dumps it in the bucket of water, and sits back down. Crossing his legs, and folding his hands over his knee, he looks at her as if she were a dim-witted child, and says, "I think we both know that we're past that, now, don't we? I'm doing the speaking. Do you understand?"

Listening to her captor and hearing the ice crack and shift in the bucket frightened her more than she'd thought possible. Complete fear rushes over her. Victor grabs the bucket and dumps the icy water on her face. She shrieks in shock and pain as the cold grips her, taking the breath from her lungs. He walks out of the room again. She hears him rummaging in the kitchen and the faucet turning on. The ice surrounding her is hurting her skin, but the cold feels good on her face.

Victor returns to the room, sets the full bucket on the floor, and sits back down. "You should know, this is the last of the ice, but I've put some water on the stove to boil. The choice is yours," he says. "Let's try this again, shall we?"

What about this is following the rules? We need to go! Finish her!

Quiet! "Do not speak unless I ask you a question. Do you understand?"

Wide-eyed, Lauren nods.

He slams his foot on the floor and reaches for the bucket.

"Ye... Yes, I understand," she stammers.

"Excellent," he says. "Do you know why I killed you?"

"Mister, I don't know how else to tell you. I don't know you. I've never seen you before," she sobs.

"NO!" he screams. "I killed you because you were always fucking every man you met. That's the reason daddy left! You couldn't keep your legs closed! You even tried to fuck me. Your son!"

His rage is building. Lauren cries, knowing that her fate is coming.

"I watched you that last night. He says calmly again. Did you know that?"

"No, no, no." whimpering.

"But I did. I watched you ride him like a whore," he spits his anger surging. "I watched you suck his cock like a greedy pig and watched as he grunted and sweated over you, then when he came, ON YOUR FACE, YOU TOLD HIM YOU LOVED HIM!"

"It wasn't me." she cries. "Please know that whoever she is, she's not me!"

"AND YOU HAVEN'T CHANGED! YOU'RE STILL A FILTHY WHORE!"

His breath is coming in ragged bursts. Somewhere in his mind, Victor knows that he's been here too long, that he has broken too many rules, and it's going to take more time to ensure he leaves no trace of himself in the house. He needs to regain control of himself.

Time to wrap this up.

"I'm not done."

Yes, you are. It's almost eleven-thirty. We need to clean up and get home before Lindsay gets up. Kill her and let's go!

Trying to regain control of himself, Victor looks down at the terrified girl tied to the bed and takes a deep breath. "You're right Lauren. You aren't the woman I killed. I'm sorry that you reminded me so much of her when I saw you in the grocery store that day. I'm sorry that Ash caught my attention at Circle K."

A look of recognition registers on her face. "You're that guy from Fry's, the one in the ice cream aisle. Oh my God!"

Victor gives a sinister smile. "Guilty as charged, and you.... you are not my mother, but you have seen and heard too much." He digs through the gym bag at his feet, stands up with the machete in hand, takes a step toward the bed, then pauses... *I'm not done with her.*

No, you are not keeping her!

Quiet!

You know better.

Realizing that the Demons are right, Victor steps to the bed, raises the machete over the terrified girl and plunges the blade into her as he drops to his knees. Lauren's screams are silenced when the blade pierces her heart, pushes through the mattress, and pins her to the floor beneath the bed. Victor looks into her eyes as her body twitches beneath him and the throes of death embrace her. She coughs, her final breath spraying his face with blood. Her eyes glaze over, and her face goes slack as her body relaxes for the last time. "Stay dead this time, bitch. Next time, I'll eat your fucking heart," Victor growls.

You're losing it. Clean up and get out!
"Leave me alone! I know what I'm doing!"
Do you?

24

"Where have you been?" Lindsay asks as Victor comes through the door.

"I went for a run," trying to keep a calm composure.

She gets up from the table and pops the lid on the Keurig, drops in a pod, and waits for her coffee. *Oh Boy, she's pissed.*

"I woke up at eleven-thirty and you weren't here. I waited up, thinking maybe you went to the store for something, but then I kept asking myself, what the hell could you need that couldn't wait till morning? I waited for half an hour before calling your phone, then realized it was on the counter. It scared the shit out of me when it rang. Now you come strolling in at one o'clock in the morning saying that you went for a run. Do you think I'm that stupid? Who is she, Victor?"

"Who is who...? What are you talking about?"

"I saw you tonight, Victor."

He's now concerned. Very concerned. "Whoa, slow down. You saw... what? What did you see?"

"I saw how antsy you were after dinner. You couldn't wait until Shelby and I went to bed. What the hell would you think? You have been so edgy lately. You're not sleeping, and when you do, half of the time it's on the couch. Then tonight, I woke up to find you weren't home, and you don't have your phone with you? Now, all you can say is that you went for a run. Why did you take the car if you went for a run? Why wouldn't you just run along the canal? I want to know who she is."

Victor sighs a true sigh of relief and chuckles to himself.

"What's so funny?" Lindsay demands. "I don't think it's funny at all." She is fuming now.

"Babe, there's no one else. I promise. You are the only woman in my life. You're right, I haven't been sleeping well. I know, so I went to Dr. Google to find out what I could do about it. One study said to get more exercise, and another suggests not going to bed unless you're tired. I wasn't tired. Yes, I admit, I've had a lot on my mind with work and all the changes around here, but I didn't want to burden you with it because I know you. I didn't want you to feel bad or guilty about accepting your dream job, so I went for a run. I went to Kiwanis Park because it's well lit, and the canal isn't in a lot of places. The police patrol Kiwanis more than the canal. I didn't take my phone because I have no pockets in my running shorts, and I don't like carrying it in my hand when I run. I've been falling asleep on the couch because you go to bed at seven-thirty or eight, and I'm nowhere near tired at that time, so I stay up and watch TV. When I sleep, I have weird dreams, so I thought I was doing you a favor by not disturbing you since you get up so early."

Seeing the sincerity in her husband's face, mixed with the fact that as far as she knows, he's never lied to her, she believes him. "Well," she says. "Am I supposed to believe that load of crap?" she asks, smiling as she walks toward him.

"Absolutely not," he says, accepting her apologetic embrace by wrapping his arms around her and taking in a deep breath of relief.

Lindsay holds him close, lays her head against his chest, listens to his heartbeat, and says, "I'm sorry."

"No worries," he says. "I have been a bit off lately, haven't I?"

"Yeah, a bit." She says, holding him tighter.

"How could you think I would want anyone else?"

"I don't know. I am pretty great," she purrs, looking up for a kiss.

"Yes, you are," he agrees, kissing her upturned lips.

"Honey?" she reaches behind her to unlock his hands.

"Yeah?"

"Take a shower before you come to bed. You stink," she says, her nose wrinkling.

With that, she turns on her heel and pads down the hall to their bedroom.

Victor quit smoking a couple of years ago, and only smokes now when he's stressed or after a few beers. Tonight, he is the prior. He rummages through the coat closet to the jacket that holds his secret stash of cigarettes, pulls the pack and lighter from the pocket, walks out to the back patio, and closes the door. *You were going to keep her...* He digs out a cigarette, lights it, and inhales deeply. Enjoying the kick to his lungs, he holds it a few seconds longer before blowing it out. He chuckles at the thought of Lindsay thinking he would ever cheat on her. She had saved him. Saved him from himself, granted, but saved him just the same. He would never cheat on her. After his smoke, he goes to take a shower. After turning the water on as hot as it will get, he steps in. The scalding water embraces him as he washes away the night's events.

You're losing it.

I'm fine.

You wanted to keep her.

Yes, I did, but I didn't.

She's not your mother.

I know.

Do you?

Yes!

Not her.

I know!

He gets out of the shower, dries off, and pulls on a pair of basketball shorts. The clock says 2am Lindsay is already asleep and snoring as he walks through the bedroom and goes to check the house. He knows what the world is like. He opens Shelby's door, and Kona lifts his head from her pillow, ever alert. "Good boy, Kona." Shelby is sound asleep beside him and doesn't stir. Victor closes her door and resumes his walk-thru, making sure the garage is closed, and the doors and windows are locked. Halloween is a couple of days away. The chill in the fall air often convinces people in the valley to open the windows in the evening. This, he well knows, is a bad idea. He makes coffee for Lindsay and programs it to brew fifteen minutes before her alarm goes off and goes to bed. He sleeps, a sound sleep, for the first time in months.

Victor startles awake not from a dream, but from his alarm blaring at his bedside. Not something he's used to. Lindsay is already gone, and he needs to get Shelby up for school. He turns on the TV in time to hear his wife say, "I'm Lindsay Powers, back to you, Angie." There is a note taped to the refrigerator written in her delicate script.

'Sorry about last night. Hope you slept well. Thanks for the coffee, Love you!' Victor puts a coffee pod in the Keurig and waits for his cup to fill. He drinks his coffee and finishes watching the NEWS before waking Shelby and getting her ready for school.

25

Lindsay is in the coffee shop waiting when Tuck and Roni arrive. "She's early," Tuck says, holding the door for his partner.

"Not surprised. It's her first story," Roni replies, walking into the diner.

Lindsay and Roni greet each other with a hug, and she shakes Tucker's proffered hand. They sit and the waitress is there right away to get their drink order. Tuck and Roni both order the breakfast special with coffee. Lindsay orders a cup of coffee and an English muffin.

When the waitress leaves their table, Lindsay jumps right in. "Okay, I've gone through all the station's tapes about the killings of Riley Duncan and her brother. Do you have anything new?"

Tucker looks at her, somewhat surprised by her directness, and says, "First, until we say so, we are an unidentified police source."

Disappointment flashed across Lindsay's face for just a second, and then it was gone. "Okay, no problem."

Tucker looks over at his partner, who shrugs as if to say, let her have it. They don't pull any punches or sugarcoat anything as they tag team her with the details of the murders for two reasons: first, they want to see how she is going to react to it. Tuck has long believed that if a reporter could handle the brutality of a murder, yet still show compassion for the victim, they were someone he could trust to not only do a good job on the story but also get his message out when he needed to leak something to the press. Second, if she can't handle it, it's better to find out sooner than later. So far, she is on track to be a news reporter. She calls the victims by name. A good thing in Tuck's eyes. She flinched when he told her she couldn't use their names, but she recovered and moved on. Tuck watches her reactions to what they tell her. If it shocks her, it doesn't show. Not only does she have the look, but she asks smart and inquisitive questions as well. She's on point, professional, and likable. She is, in Tuck's opinion, the perfect cub reporter. He decides to hold off final judgment until this story is reported, but so far...

"So, what else?" Lindsay asks, reading back through her notes. "He's more than likely a white male, thirty to forty years old, five-ten to six feet tall, two-hundred to two-hundred-twenty pounds. He doesn't seem to have a rhyme or reason to kill that you've found yet. You don't know what triggers his need to kill, but once it takes hold, it's all but over for his victim. He's smart, never uses the same weapon or means of killing more than once, and except for the weapon, he leaves little to no evidence behind. He doesn't have a pattern to speak of, and as far as you can tell, it's not personal."

"Right, it's not personal..." Roni trails off.

This gets Lindsay's attention. "What?" she asks.

"Not sure yet, let me work it over."

"He could be married with a family," Tucker says, picking up where Roni left off, leaving her to her thoughts.

"Married?" Lindsay asks with eyebrows raised.

"Yeah," Tuck says, looking at Lindsay and gauging her reaction. He decides not to disclose that he and Roni think their guy may be linked to past murders. They had already tossed around ideas about his lapse in time. He could have been in prison on another charge, or maybe he moved out of the area, and now he's back, but they didn't think so. Having a wife, and maybe even a family, could explain it.

"Why would you think he's married?" she asks.

"This guy blends into the masses too well. He's not a raving lunatic all the time, or we would have him by now. No, he's cold and calculated. He's a hunter. Being married would allow him to blend in with society. I imagine he comes off as warm and engaging to the outside world; the 'nicest guy ever sort,' but, based on his profile, I think it's safe to say, he has very few friends, and he's hard to get close to. I would bet that he keeps a small inner circle."

"So, if there is a wife, do you think she knows what he is and that she is sleeping next to a monster?"

"We don't believe so," Roni says, returning to the conversation. "That would blow his cover. No, I bet she is clueless about these murders and any others that may have happened in the past."

"Others?" Lindsay looks to Roni as Tuck gives his partner a tight-lipped stare.

"Oh yeah," she says. "Almost definitely. This guy is too good for this to be his first time. He's had a lot of practice." Noticing Tuck's reaction, she asks, "What's up?" He shakes his head instead of answering.

Lindsay, feeling the tension between them, pushes forward. "And you think the wife is clueless?"

Detectives Novetti and Tucker share a knowing look and say in unison. "If she's still alive she is."

Seeing that she is back from her thoughts, Lindsay returns her attention to Roni. "Hey, did you figure out whatever it was you were thinking about earlier?"

Surprised at Lindsay's ability to read her, Roni answers, "Yeah, I think so. Jonas Jackson was personal. He was stabbed several times in his face and twice in the heart. It was a frenzied attack rather than calculated like the Duncan's."

Tuck chimes in, "The only reason his murder hit our radar is because the icepick was brand new, and it had been cleaned with bleach just like the hammer in the Duncan's case."

Lindsay flips back a few pages in her notebook. "Jonas Jackson is the cab driver?"

"Yes, in the words of the investigating officer..." Roni's eyes roll towards the ceiling as she tries to remember how Logan Spears had put it. "He pissed someone off," she says, taking the final bite of her toast as she lowers her eyes to Lindsay's and chews thoughtfully.

"So, you think the guy that killed Jackson is the same guy who killed the Duncan's, but in that case, it was personal?"

"Yes, I do, but Tuck isn't so sure."

"Why not?" Lindsay inquires, focusing on Tucker now.

"For that exact reason," he says. "Our guy is a planner, a hunter. It's never personal to him. It's almost like a job. He's cold and methodical. We're going to look at some other unsolved cases that the Cold Case department has pulled that may be linked as well. The way we understand it, there are several that seem to fit our guy's MO, and none of them indicate it was personal."

"But Tuck, whoever did the cab driver fits every other way," Roni exclaims.

Lindsay watches the exchange between the partners, somehow knowing that this is a conversation they've had before.

"We'll see," Tuck says.

Lindsay picks this as her moment and asks, "So, how far back are you looking?"

"Well," Tuck says, wiping his mouth with his napkin, "we started going back five years and came up with nothing. Then we jumped back eight years, and we landed on Pedro Flores, a twenty-year-old college kid here on a student visa, who was killed with a tire iron in a parking garage."

Lindsay looks up from her notes. "What about him caught your interest?"

Tuck takes a deep breath and answers her, "According to the report, it was a bloody scene. The killer most likely ambushed him from behind, spun him around, and hit him in the face with it, knocking out his front teeth and shattering his jaw."

"Jesus," Lindsay says, covering her mouth with her hand.

Tucker continues as if she had said nothing. "Then our guy runs the pointed end of the tire iron through Pedro's heart, pinning him to the hood of a car, and disappears into the night without leaving a trace. He's in, does his thing, and is out. There were no prints on the weapon, no tracks on the floor, and no cameras, of course; the man just disappeared."

Lindsay has regained her composure by now and is once again in "journalist mode". "And the tire iron?"

"Could've been bought at any parts house, and no one would have raised an eyebrow, or it could have been stolen, and the owner wouldn't even know until he needed it. Oh, and it had been washed with bleach. There are similarities with other cases, but we'll leave it there for now."

He watches Lindsay to see her reaction and is not disappointed when she furrows her brow and flips back to the last page of her notes. "So, there's an eight-year gap, she asks, looking up, and that's why you think he's married, but how could he just stop like that?"

Roni takes over, effectively tagging Tucker out. "We believe he thought he had it under control for a while and conned himself into believing that he could control it, but the yearning got too strong when he came across Rylie Duncan and BOOM."

26

Detectives Novetti and Tucker drive back to the station in silence, contemplating the conversation that just took place. "What was the look about?" she asks as they ride the elevator down to the Cold Case vault.

"Nothing," he replies. "I wasn't going to tell her about anyone but the Duncan's, and Jackson until we knew how she'd handle it, but I didn't let you know, so no biggie."

"She did well. I think she's going to be fine."

As the elevator doors slide open, Tuck says, "She knows she didn't have to pick up the tab, I hope."

Roni bursts out laughing. "I'm sure she meant it as a gesture of good faith. Jesus Tuck, haven't you ever talked to a pretty reporter?"

"Not without trying to get her into bed," he replies.

Roni punches him on the shoulder and laughs again. "You pig."

They are strolling through the aisles filled with evidence boxes and files for all the cold cases in Phillips, Arizona from the last fifty years, when Roni asks, "Seriously, Tuck, what do you think?"

Tucker smiles at his partner and says, "I think that she's got a lot of potential. Her questions are on track considering she's a new reporter, but she may be somewhat naïve. Did you see the look on her face when we told her that our guy could be married with a family?"

"Yeah, I caught that too, but she recovered pretty well."

"She has good instincts, but she's still green. We'll have to see."

They come to the end of the aisle and find a desk along the back wall manned by Janice McKinny's intern.

"Hey Court, Janice around?"

Courtney Scott looks up from her computer screen and grins a big, toothy grin. "Oh, hey Tuck! Yeah, she's in her office. Want me to get her for you?"

"Naw, we'll go on back."

"Hey Roni."

"Hi Courtney. How's school going?"

"Study, study, study. You know how it is."

"I do," says Roni. How's the second job?"

"I quit three days ago. Louie, the bouncer, was creeping on me."

"Want me to have a word with him?"

"No thanks. It wasn't my gig, anyway."

"Good call. You're too sweet to work there," Roni says, walking past the desk.

"Bouncer?" Tuck asks with raised eyebrows.

"She's been stripping down at Kelly's Thursday through Saturday."

"Ah," Tuck grunts, "you're right. She is too sweet to work there."

Just then Janice McKinny comes out of her office, reading a report, and almost runs right into them. "Well, good morning, Janice."

"Tuck! How are you, sweetie?" she asks, throwing her arms around him in her usual greeting for him.

"I'm good Janice. How are you?"

"I couldn't be better," she says, winking at Roni and poking Tucker in the ribs. "Since you won't take me out on a real date, I've gotten myself a boy toy to play with. How are you, Roni?"

"I'm good, Janice, thanks," Roni says, holding back a smile as the slightly older woman flirts with her partner.

"Oh, you're killing me," Tuck says, clutching his heart.

"Three nights with me and that heart attack would be real," she says with another wink.

"Three?" Tuck looks surprised.

"Eh, I'm slowing down in my old age."

"I somehow doubt that." Roni laughs.

"Me too," agrees Tuck with a wink.

Coming to Tucker's rescue, Roni asks Janice if she had found anything more in her archives.

"Well, of course, I did," she says, walking back into her office, and with more than a touch of arrogance adds, "As per your request," she smiles, placing her hand on top of a stack of thirty-plus files. "This here is every unsolved murder in The Valley, where the killer left no trace, going back fifteen years."

"You don't think all of those are by the same guy?" Roni asks, incredulously.

"That I can't say, but these are the cases that meet the criteria that you asked for where the killer left little to no trace other than a dead body, a weapon washed in bleach, no pattern, or suspects over the last fifteen years..." Janice trails off for a second then focuses her attention fiercely on the detectives. "My God, Tuck! You think there's a serial killer loose in Phillips, don't you?"

"We're not sure Janice, but maybe," Tuck says grimly.

Roni quickly grabs the files from the desk and turns for the door as Janice recovers and shifts back to business mode by saying, "I'm going to expand your search another five years and go statewide."

"Thank you, Janice," Roni says, as she walks toward the door with her arms loaded with the case files. Roni looks over her shoulder to her partner and says, "You coming, Tuck?"

"Go ahead. I'll catch up."

Roni gives him a curious look but says nothing else.

"Where are you, Tuck?" Janice asks her old friend.

"With the investigation? This guy is good, Janice, and he's been around a long time."

"How long do you think?"

"That's why we're here."

"Tuck... we've known each other for too long. Don't bullshit me."

"Seriously, sweetie, I'm not sure. He's too good to have just started."

"Maybe he's new to town," she proffers.

"It doesn't feel like it. I think this guy has been around, hiding in plain sight. He's a hunter. He's careful, but now he wants to mess with us."

"What do you mean?"

"He posed the Duncan's for no other reason than to throw us off track."

Janice furrowed her brow. "Are you sure?"

"About ninety percent," Tuck replies and goes through the Reader's Digest version of everything he and Roni have discovered in their investigation.

"Son of a bitch!" she says, walking to the corner of her desk and turning back to him. "Jesus!"

"Yeah," Tuck says, "again, that's why we're here."

"Okay, I'll have Courtney get right on expanding another five years."

"Uh Janice, I'd consider it a favor if you'd handle this one personally."

"Tuck, Courtney is a fantastic researcher. I trained her my—"

"Please Janice," Tuck says, looking her square in the face. "Please?"

Seeing how sincere her old friend is about his request, she answers, "Sure, no problem. You okay Pete?"

Tuck smiles at her use of his first name. "Yeah, I'm fine. No need to worry, I just want to catch this guy. He's been out there too long. I know that I have a few unsolved cases. It makes me wonder if I've been on his trail before."

Walking Tuck to her door, she says, "I'll call you by the end of the week."

"Thanks, Janice," he says, as he leans in and kisses her on her cheek. "I owe you one."

"More than one," she laughs and holds the door for him.

"Yeah," Tuck says, winking at her as he walks out the door and past the front desk. "See ya Court," he says.

Courtney looks up from her screen and smiles. "Bye Tuck."

Roni glances up from the case file she's reading as Tuck walks to his desk with raised eyebrows.

He shakes his head at her. "Later." he says.

Roni purses her lips and sits back in her chair a bit. "Okayyy."

"It's not what you think."

She winks at him. "Sure, it's not," she says, leaning back over her desk.

"She was my first partner, okay?"

Roni just looks at him and says, "Oh."

Tuck takes a deep breath and blows it out. "She took a bullet in the hip that was meant for me about twelve years ago."

"That's why she has a slight limp," Roni says.

"Yeah, she was a good cop but couldn't work the street with her injury, so our Captain pulled a few strings to keep her on the force. She's been in The Vault ever since. She wasn't crazy about it at first. She's a street cop at heart, but she adapted and made the most of it."

27

After dinner, the Powers family cleans up together. Victor loads the dishwasher with dishes handed to him, freshly rinsed, by Lindsay, who received them from Shelby, who has cleared the table and scraped the plates. Even Kona is doing his part, hovering next to the trash can for anything that hits the floor.

With the dishwasher loaded and the delay start set for after 9pm Lindsay looks at Shelby and says, "All right kiddo, ten minutes till bath-time," as she wipes down the counter.

Shelby looks from one parent to the other thoughtfully, as if she is choosing what she is about to say with great care. "I've been thinking," she says, suddenly serious. This gets both of her parent's undivided attention. Victor finishes drying his hands on a dishtowel, and Lindsay stops wiping. Both look on as their daughter declares, "I'm a big girl now, right? I mean, I'm almost seven," she says with all the confidence she can muster.

Lindsay looks from Shelby to Victor then back. "You are sweetie, what's up?"

"Well, big girls take showers, right?" Shelby says looking at her mother.

Lindsay smiles and looks beyond Shelby to her husband, who is also grinning ear to ear.

"Yes, I suppose they do."

"I think I should start taking showers... all by myself," she says with added emphasis.

"Okay, are you sure you can wash your hair and get all the shampoo out by yourself?"

"I'm pretty sure, but you can still check it, right?"

"Of course, baby," Lindsay says, walking over and kissing the top of her head. "Go hop in the shower and let me know when you're done."

"Okay Mommy," she says, leaping off the barstool and rushing to the bathroom.

Lindsay turns to Victor with tears in her eyes and walks into his open arms. "I love giving Shelby her bath," she says with a sniff. "It's our time together."

"I know, baby," Victor says, wrapping his arms around her as she lays her head against his chest. "We'll both have to adapt to this whole growing-up thing she seems intent on doing."

Lindsay gives him a light slap on the butt and holds him slightly tighter. "Stop it."

Find out about her meeting with the cops.
Back off I'm with my wife.
We need to know what they know...
NOT NOW!

"How about you go change your clothes, and I'll open a bottle of wine. You can tell me about your day," he says, gently turning her and rubbing her shoulders.

"Hmmm, that sounds nice," Lindsay murmurs, leaning back against him.

He drops his arms down and clasps her just below her breasts. "What did you think about Roni's partner?"

"Tuck? He's great. The quintessential old school homicide detective," she says a little too enthusiastically for his liking.

"Tuck?" Victor asks, trying not to sound objectionable.

Lindsay turns in his arms and scans his face, looking for sarcasm, and apparently finds what she is looking for because she lays her head against his chest and continues, "Yes, Tuck, Detective Pete Tucker, reminds me of Lennie Briscoe, but not as old."

"Lennie Briscoe? On Law and Order?"

She laughs against his chest. "Yeah, on Law and Order. He's a nice guy. Roni idolizes him, and he respects her."

"Oh?"

"Yeah, they work very well together." She leans away from him and looks and leans into his face with sudden seriousness. "They think there's a serial killer loose in Phillips."

"What?" he asks incredulously just as Shelby screams from the bathroom, "MOOOMMMYYY!"

Lindsay smiles more to herself than her husband and says, "Someone got shampoo in her eyes and still needs her mommy." She pulls out of his grasp and starts for the bathroom. "I can't wait to tell you about it. Pour the wine. COMING BABY!" she calls as she hurries to the bathroom.

This is too close, Victor!

Ya think? She won't tell me everything.
Yes, she will...
They will have told her not to mention any of it to anyone, including me.
You're her husband, she'll tell...
It's her first big story. She doesn't want to fuck it up.
Pour the wine...

Lindsay is in the bathroom longer than expected because Shelby did get soap in her eyes, and she had to help rewash her hair and comb it after the shower. Victor comes down the hall and watches his wife and daughter enjoying their time together, knowing that Lindsay is saddened by the knowledge that this is ending sooner than later. Running a comb through her daughter's wet hair, Lindsay looks over at Victor and smiles as if to say, *I'm going to enjoy it while it lasts.* Shelby is telling her about, "Clifford the Big Red Dog" the story that they are reading in her class this week. He puts her wine on the bathroom counter and ducks out, letting them have "their time."

Victor's phone rings. He looks at the screen before answering. Eddie, the crew foreman in Maricopa, is calling. *Fuck, this can't be good.* "Hey, Eddie, What's up?"

"Sorry to bother you at home, boss, but the number four magnet is down again."

The shredder chews up used tires, and the recycled rubber is then used in playgrounds at schools and parks around the state. It's also used to make the rubberized asphalt that the state is placing on all the highways for noise reduction. After the tires go through the shredder, they go into the grinder to be chopped into the appropriate size of rubber chunks for whatever order is being filled. Before going in the grinder, the shredded tires pass under a giant electromagnet that pulls all the steel cords and bands from the shredded rubber. If the magnet is down, and the steel makes it into the grinder, it will bind up and the entire process will be down for at least two weeks.

"God Damnit! What happened?"

"I got it shut down in time, boss. Don't worry about that."

"All right, good! I'm going to call Todd over at System Tech and have him get out there first thing. Shut down Number four mill, clean off the belt, and make sure that no fucking steel got into that goddamn grinder. I'll be there in an hour."

"You don't need to come out here, boss. I've got it covered."

"I know you do, Eddie, but number four has been down three times this quarter, and I've got to have answers when I get called to the carpet. We're going to strip it down and find out why this keeps happening. If I can get Todd out there tonight, I will have him run diagnostic checks on every fucking resistor, wire, and gauge on that system."

Lindsay is coming out of the bathroom as Victor hangs up his phone. She watches him in the kitchen. He seems edgy tonight. She knows that their new life has been stressful for him. He has never liked big changes. They had joked about how he was addicted to routine when they first got together. Overall, he seems to be coping okay, but he's not sleeping well. That is an enormous concern. He tries to laugh it off and uses an old movie line, saying that he'll get enough sleep when he dies, but it concerns her. She talked to him about getting a sleep study done a couple of days ago, and he seemed receptive, but she knows if she doesn't mention it again that he won't do it.

"Trouble at the plant?" she asks, disappointment evident in her face and tone.

"Yeah, give me just a second babe," Victor replies while scrolling through his phone, finding the contact he's looking for, and pushing the send button. He paces even before the call is answered. *He's in full-on business mode*, she thinks to herself as she turns back to help Shelby finish getting ready for bed, still half-listening to her husband's voice.

"Todd, it's Victor. The number four magnet on the shredder is down again."... "Well, I don't know Todd, but we're going to find out together. Can you meet me out there in an hour?"... "Yea, Eddie is cleaning it up as we speak."... "Right, see you within the hour," he says as he hangs up the phone.

Victor sticks his head in the bedroom door. "I've got to go out to Maricopa."

"I gathered that," Lindsay says with a smile. "Any idea how long you're going to be?"

"Not really, a couple of hours at the least. Could end up taking all night though, plus I'll have to call Jared tomorrow with a full report depending on what the problem is this time."

"Ooh, your favorite person," she teases.

"He'll be touched that you remember, I'm sure," Victor replies with a smirk. "I'm sorry, sweetie," he says as he kisses her cheek.

"It's okay, babe. I'm off tomorrow, and little miss here has an eye appointment at ten, so maybe I won't take her to school until after lunch and we can have a girl's night." Shelby looks at her mother's reflection in the mirror, wide-eyed and shocked at the suggestion that she was going to play hooky with her mother. "What?" Lindsay asks, looking at Shelby's reflection. "Don't you want to stay up and make cookies and pop popcorn and read stories to each other, or we could snuggle up in mom and dad's bed and watch a movie?"

"Yeah, I DO!" Shelby shrieks, her pitch increasing with each word.

Victor leans further in and kisses his daughter on her forehead. "See you tomorrow, pumpkin."

"Bye Daddy."

Lindsay is right behind him as he grabs his keys from the hook. He turns and hugs her. "I'm sorry about this. I can't tell you how interested I am in your interview with Roni and Tuck." The emphasis on Tuck is so evident that she sees it for the sarcasm it is.

She pokes him in the ribs, anyway. "It's okay," she says, squeezing him tightly. "I need a night alone with her almost as much as I need some alone time with you."

"Me too," Victor says and kisses her on the mouth. "See you soon, I hope." With that, he grabs his keys from the hook and walks out of the garage to his car in the driveway.

28

Knowing that it's going to be a long night, but hoping that he's wrong, Victor stops at the Circle K closest to his house to get gas, a pack of cigarettes for Eddie, and a Coke for himself. Eddie, a chronic smoker who always seems to be out of cigarettes, will appreciate it and repay the small act of kindness with his loyalty. Victor sees it as a self-serving time-saver by not having to watch him look for his cigarettes all night long, and maybe some actual work would get done.

As he pulls up to the gas pump, Victor notices an older Dodge work van with no windows and a sliding door pulling in alongside the red BMW that pulled in right before him.

Pay attention!

"I see it. Probably nothing," he says to himself as he inserts his company card into the pump. Minutes later, the pretty oriental teenage girl who was driving the BMW comes out of the store having purchased whatever it was she had gone in for. She's looking at her phone and not paying attention to her surroundings as she walks back to her car. Victor watches the brake lights in the van shine just before the reverse lights come on. The girl crosses in front of the van, still staring at her phone as the sliding door slides open just a crack.

This is about to go down...

"I see it!" Victor says, hurrying to his door.

She steps down from the curb next to the driver-side door of her car, keys in hand, just as the door to the van slides all the way open. A man steps out, grabs the young girl from behind, then pulls her into the van, and closes the door as the driver calmly backs out of the parking place.

Victor quickly starts his car, drops it into gear, floors the accelerator, and crashes into the side of the van effectively, T-Boning and pinning it between his car and the parked cars behind it.

The airbag in his car deploys and knocks him unconscious. When he comes to, he's not sure how long he's been out. Long enough, he summarizes for the paramedics and the police to get here because he's strapped to a gurney and an EMT is shining a light in his eyes.

"DETECTIVE! He's coming around!"

Victor is blinking hard against the light being shone in his eyes and asks, "What's happening?"

"Take it easy, buddy. You're going to be fine. You've got a bloody nose, but I don't think it's broken, a black eye, some bruising on your chest, some scrapes and lacerations on both arms, and a possible concussion. Airbags do that. It'd have been a helluva lot worse if you hadn't put on your seatbelt."

"What happened?" Victor asks again.

"Seriously? YOU'RE A GODDAMNED HERO MAN..."

Just then, a man's voice comes from the other direction. "We'll take it from here, Kenny."

Kenny excuses himself with a reassuring pat on Victor's shoulder, and says, "We're going to take you to the hospital when the Detectives are done."

Detectives? Victor wonders as a classic old-school-looking police detective walks into view. *She's right* Victor thinks as the detective approaches.

"Mister Powers, I'm Detective Pete Tucker. You've been in an accident."

It all comes crashing back at once. "AN ACCIDENT? OH, GOOD CHRIST YOU'VE GOT TO CALL MY WIFE!"

Suddenly, Roni is beside him and takes his hand. "Victor, calm down. You're going to be fine, but you're going into shock. I called Lindsay, and she's going to meet us at Phillips Regional."

"Hospital? How's my car? It's a company car."

Detective Pete Tucker chuckles, "Your car is toast, man, but on the upside, you stopped a kidnapping in progress. The Company will probably understand."

Victor's breathing is erratic, and his heartbeat is racing. "I crashed a company car on purpose. I am so getting fired over this."

Roni nods at Kenny, who shines his light back into Victor's eyes, which Victor immediately closes, then shakes his head. "Victor, I can't give you anything right now," Kenny says, "because I think you've got a concussion. I know it hurts, but I need you to take some deep breaths and listen."

Victor suddenly remembers why he crashed his car into the van. "The girl, how is she?" Victor asks, looking at Roni.

"Kim Su? She has some bumps and bruises from the crash, but she's going to be fine, thanks to you. We'll meet you at the hospital," she says as the paramedics put his gurney in the ambulance.

Victor lays his head back as the world fades. Kenny waves some smelling salts under his nose, and he startles awake. "God, that stinks!"

Kenny laughs, "Buddy, I need you to stay with me, okay? We're on the way to the hospital, and you've got to stay awake until we know what's going on with your head, okay?"

Victor scoffs, "I promise you; you do not want to know what's going on in my head. Just let me go to sleep."

"Can't do that, buddy. I'm not a doctor, but I took the same oath they do. I can't let you do something that may cause your harm."

"Maybe dying wouldn't be so bad if I could just get some sleep," Victor tries to joke.

Kenny looks him square in the face. "My friend, when it comes to brain damage, there are some things that are worse than death. Now, I need you to do everything you can to stay awake. I'm going to help you, but it lies on your shoulders. I need you to stay awake and answer my questions, okay?"

Listen, this is important. You need to be in control of your answers...

Are you sure? He asks inwardly and smiles.

Stop fucking around Victor!

"Victor, are you with me?" Kenny asks again.

Victor shakes his head and blinks his eyes a few times. "Yeah, I'm good. What do you need from me? My face hurts. Can you give me an aspirin or something?"

"Have you eaten anything tonight?"

"Yeah, we had just gotten up from dinner when my phone rang... Fuck, I've got to go to Maricopa."

"Not tonight, you're not. How about a Tylenol?"

Victor lays back against the gurney. "Sure, that'll be fine. They're going to keep me, you think?"

"You? Yep, absolutely. You're a Goddamned hero man! God only knows what those derelicts were going to do to that girl."

"Yeah..."

"Are you married? Have you got a family?"

Victor smiles at the thought of his family. "Yeah, I'm married."

"Oh, that's right. I heard Detective Novetti tell you she called Lindsay."

Victor watches the ball hit the hole as Kenny's face lights up.

"Wait a minute... Victor Powers. You're married to Lindsay Powers from Channel 4?"

"Yep."

"Wow, man! I'm a huge fan."

"Yeah, well, I'm sure she appreciates it," he says with a sudden darkness. Kenny notices the abrupt change in Victor's tone. "Hey, no offense meant. I mean, I am a big fan and all, but nothing creepy. She's just a fresh face and you can tell she loves her job is all."

Victor just looks at Kenny sideways and wonders if he will be in his dreams anytime in the future.

"Seriously, Victor, I meant no offense. It's part of my job," Kenny says as the ambulance comes to a stop and the back doors swing open. "I've got to keep you talking, man."

"What do we got, Kenny?" asks the burly Mexican who opens the ambulance doors.

"Hey, Nacho! We've got a white male thirty-five years old, about two-hundred pounds, a car accident, multiple bruises on his face, chest, and arms, and a possible concussion. He has been conscious for about twenty continuous minutes. He has eaten and is cognitive. He's a little sketchy on the details but remembers the accident. I gave him 200mlg of Tylenol approximately," he glances at his watch, "ten minutes ago."

"So, you're our hero for the evening, huh, Mr. Powers?"

"Victor, please."

"Victor it is. You can call me Nacho. All right, Victor, we're going to bring you into Emergency Trauma so we can run some tests on you, okay? Nothing too serious, mostly x-rays, some bloodwork, and a few others just to make sure everything looks good. Then we're going to get you into a room where your wife, and the nice police detectives, can come see you, okay? Until we get you into your room, I'm going to be right here beside you."

"Okay. Thanks, Nacho." Victor looks at him quizzically. "Why Nacho? Isn't that... politically incorrect?"

"Oh yeah," he chuckles. "White people's problems, man. White people are the only ones that worry about hurting someone's feelings after devastating race after race, generation by generation." Just when Victor thought he was going to get a whole political point of view about the evils of the white man, Nacho laughs. "I'm sorry, man, I can't do that to you. My name is Fernando, and I went by Nando for the longest time. When I married my wife, Kenny's sister, by the way, his son was three. He couldn't pronounce Nando, so he called me Nacho, and I've been Nacho ever since." Nacho wheels the gurney through yet another set of doors and into an open elevator. "Dr. McGraw we're on our way to x-ray, but since you'll be his doctor during his stay, let me introduce you to Victor Powers."

Victor looks up to greet a tall bald man with a mustache. "Doctor, it's a pleasure."

"Mr. Powers, your reputation precedes you. The pleasure is indeed all mine. We're going to take excellent care of you during your stay." The doctor says with what some would call a very pronounced country accent.

Victor has a puzzled look on his face as the doctor exits on the next floor. He looks over at Nacho and asks, "Why am I getting this kind of treatment?"

Nacho laughs out loud. "You don't know what you did, do you?"

Victor shrugs. "I saw a girl that was in trouble and helped her the only way I could."

"Uh Huh. You could have called the police."

"And told them what? That I saw two men in a van grab a girl from the Circle K parking lot on Dobson and Elliot, and they're headed north on Dobson Road?"

"Yeah, that's what most people would do had they seen it."

"I'll be completely honest with you, Nacho. It never occurred to me. I saw those men grab a girl out of a parking lot, and I had to do something."

"Well, Victor, based on what I know and have seen, most people like to think they are action-oriented, that they would do exactly what you did, but the truth is, most wouldn't even have noticed. Those who do often second-guess what they saw and probably wouldn't have even called the police. They would have waited to see if it was on the NEWS, and then maybe. But you didn't, man! You acted! You saved that girl from God knows what."

29

Tuck and Roni are waiting outside Victor's room as Lindsay hurries from the elevator. The sign on the wall has arrows that point toward room numbers 300-315 to the left and 316-330 to the right. She turns right.

"Lindsay! Are you okay?" Roni asks as Lindsay approaches.

"I'm fine. Where is he?" she asks as she hugs Roni and then Tuck.

Tuck is taken aback by her comfort level with him and his for her.

"He's still downstairs," Roni says, sensing her partner's discomfort.

"When he gets up here, I'm going to fucking kill him! I mean, what in the hell was he thinking?"

Tuck stifles a laugh. "Excuse me, ladies," he says and walks toward the men's room.

"Lindsay, do you know who the girl he saved is?"

"No, why? Who is she?"

"Her name is Kim Su Li. Her grandfather was the founder of one of the three biggest triads in Taiwan."

"Triad...? Do you mean the Chinese Mob? Here In Phoenix?"

"Yeah, believe it or not, they've been here since the mid-seventies. There are almost a dozen tongs or gangs in the Phoenix area under their protection, but they were pretty competitive with each other at one time. Her father, Li Chen or Jimmy Li, as he's better known, moved here about four years ago to organize and unify the tongs. He moved his family here eighteen months ago."

"So, my husband thwarted the kidnapping of the daughter of a Chinese Mob Boss?"

"Yeah."

"Was it organized? Are we in any danger of retaliation?"

"The truth is, we don't know yet," Tuck injects, returning from the men's room. "We'll know more tomorrow after we talk to Mutt and Jeff."

Lindsay looks from Tuck to Roni, puzzled. "The yahoos in the van," Roni says.

Tuck continues, "Tonight, there will be an officer outside of his room, and a car will be outside of your house."

Lindsay is utterly speechless as the elevator doors open and Victor's gurney is wheeled out.

"Check it out Victor, your wife AND the nice police detectives are here, just like I told you."

"So, you did," Victor replies, his speech slightly slurred. "Hi babe, do you know Nacho?"

Lindsay's mind is still reeling from the information she's just been given as she stares blankly at her husband.

"Mrs. Powers, it's a pleasure," Nacho says, wheeling past her into the room snapping her out of her trance.

"I'm sorry, Nacho, is it? The pleasure is mine. Thank you for taking care of my husband."

Nacho smiles. "Of course, ma'am. Victor, you take care, and I'll check back in with you in half-hour, or so."

"Thanks, Nacho."

Tuck catches Nacho as he leaves the room. "Can he talk?"

"Yeah, he's a little groggy, but he should be okay for a little while. I gave him a painkiller about ten minutes ago. He's pretty banged up. He'll want to go to sleep, but you've got about fifteen minutes before he conks out."

"Thanks, pal," Tuck says, patting Nacho on the back, as he walks back into Victor's room where Roni is already asking questions, and Victor is answering to the best of his ability.

"... I had to get gas before I went to Maricopa, so I stopped at Circle K. I noticed a newer red BMW pull into a spot towards the front of the store. I got out of the car and put my card in the pump. As I did, I saw the van pull into the spot next to the BMW. Something told me to pay attention. Nobody got out of the van, but when the girl walked out of the store, I saw the brake lights come on for a second before the reverse lights came on. The girl was on her phone and not paying attention. I saw the sliding door open, and thought, holy fuck, this is going to happen, so I ran to the door of my car. I started it and hit the gas."

"Victor, what were you thinking?" Lindsay asks.

"I don't know. I saw a girl in trouble, and I just did the first thing that came to mind."

"You could have called the police," Tuck suggests from the foot of the bed.

Looking Lindsay in the face, Victor says, "If it had been Shelby, I'd want someone to do something, wouldn't you?"

Lindsay leans over the bed and kisses Victor on the forehead and says, "My hero... the dumbass."

Victor chuckles as Dr. McGraw enters the room. "Evening folks. How's everyone doing tonight?" he asks, checking Victor's chart before logging in to the bedside computer.

"I'm as good as can be," Victor answers. "A little sore, but I guess I should expect that."

"Indeed you should," the doctor says, looking at Tuck and Roni. "Detectives?"

Tuck answers, "Yeah Doc, we're about done here." He reaches across the bed and grips Victor's forearm and gives him a simple nod of his head.

Roni playfully rolls her eyes at Lindsay and asks, "Can you believe these two? Victor, we're going to need to talk to you a bit more when you get out of here," Roni says, walking toward the door. "Lindsay has my number. Call me in a day or two, okay?"

"Not a problem," Victor says, turning his attention back to Dr. McGraw.

Lindsay stays after Tuck and Roni leave and listens to the doctor as Victor nods off.

"Mrs. Powers, he's going to be fine. He's a little banged up, and he's going to be pretty sore for a few days, but that will pass. The concussion seems to have subsided. We're going to keep him tonight for observation, and unless he vomits or starts running a fever, we will release him in the morning. I'm going to write him a script for 800mg of Motrin for both pain and as an anti-inflammatory." Looking Lindsay squarely in the face, he adds, "He's going to be fine. Do you have any questions for me?" Lindsay shakes her head and moves closer to Victor's side and takes his hand. "Okay, I'll give you a few minutes, but then you're going to have to let him rest."

"Thank you, doctor," Lindsay says as he leaves the room.

Once she is alone with her husband, Lindsay sits in the bedside chair, still holding his hand, and begins to sob as Victor mumbles in his sleep.

30

Victor is brushing his teeth when he hears the morning headline on the TV from his hospital room. "A suspected kidnapping attempt was interrupted last night in Phillips when someone very close to our Channel 4 family rammed his car into the alleged kidnappers' car. Angie?"

"That's right Ted. We have learned that the two accused men had been following the victim for some time before seizing their opportunity at a Phillips Circle K and pulling the victim into their van." As Angie turns to face the new camera, she smiles slightly. "Lucky for her, our own Lindsay Power's husband was getting gas at the same time and took action by ramming his vehicle into the getaway car. The suspects are in custody, and the victim and her benefactor were taken to the hospital for observation. We'll be following this story closely and keeping you informed as the investigation continues."

Victor is staring at the TV in disbelief, still holding the toothbrush in his mouth as Lindsay walks in. "Did you know about this?" he asks matter of fact.

"No, I didn't. I mean, I knew the story would be reported. It is news, after all, but I had no idea that they'd throw in the whole 'Channel 4 Family' thing."

Victor is infuriated for about half a second until he looks at his wife and sees the look of genuine sorrow on her face and empathetic tears filling her eyes.

He takes a deep breath to calm down. "Well, at least they didn't give out our address," he says as he gingerly accepts her embrace and grimaces.

"I'm sorry. Did I hurt you?"

"Nah, don't you know I'm bulletproof?" he says with a smile, squeezing her tighter.

"Apparently," she says, laying her head against him. "Please never do anything that stupid again. Shelby and I need you. Promise?"

Victor smiles and grimaces again as he kisses the top of her head. "Promise."

Just then, Nacho knocks on the door. "Good morning, Victor, Mrs. Powers."

"Hey Nacho," Victor replies.

"Are you ready to get out of here?"

"Good Lord YES!"

Nacho chuckles. "Looks like all your tests came back in the norm. Dr. McGraw has already signed you out. I'm going to run down to the pharmacy to get your scripts. Give me twenty minutes and you'll be out of here."

"Sounds good."

Thirty minutes later, Lindsay is driving Victor home, with little conversation. Both were lost in their thoughts. "Whatcha thinking?" Lindsay asks.

"Oh, just all the stuff I need to do today," he says to the window.

"Victor, the doctor told you to take it easy for the next few days."

"I know, but I've got to report to Unicall that I wrecked my company car. Then I'll have to call Jarod and kiss his ass for a while and hope he doesn't fire me."

"He's not going to fire you, for Christ's sake."

"Lindsay, I crashed a company car on purpose. At the very least, I'll get a warning of dismissal."

"Sweetie, it's not like you got a DUI and crashed your car. You saved that girl from being kidnapped and God knows what else."

"Yeah, well, I've still got to call him."

"Okay," she says. "I'm going to the station for a while to find out what they were thinking, opening the story like that."

"If I've still got a job, I've got to call Eddie and Todd and find out what in the hell is going on with that flipping magnet."

"Victor, you're not going to Maricopa today, not only because of the doctor's orders, but tomorrow is Halloween and you're expected to be here, and you're not going anywhere tonight."

"Halloween?" he says, more than a little surprised. "Of course, how could I have forgotten?"

Pulling into the driveway, Lindsay says, "I'll pick you up at ten forty-five."

Victor looks at her for a second and it dawns on him that the costume parade at Shelby's school starts at eleven. "Okay babe, he says, kissing her goodbye. See you soon."

31

Once inside, Victor makes a pot of coffee and then looks for his company phone as the coffee brews. "Fuck, I bet it's still in the car." He goes into the bedroom and retrieves his personal phone from his nightstand to make the calls that he needs to make.

The first call goes predictably well, as the operator for Unicall is someone who answers the phone in a call center and starts the claim. After asking if he is all right and giving Victor the claim number, the rep asks if he'd like a follow-up call from a company-provided nurse. Victor refuses, stating that he is already under a doctor's care and should be fine. Victor debates on the next call as he pours himself a cup of coffee. On the one hand, he knows he needs to call Jarod in Boston to let him know what all has transpired in the last eighteen hours, but he'd like to first be able to first tell him what's going on with the number four magnet on the shredder. He doesn't have Eddie's number on his phone, so he calls the office. "Hey Julia, it's Victor. Is Eddie in yet, by chance?"

"Oh! Hi Victor! I'm so glad that you're okay. You're quite the topic of conversation around here today."

"Thank you, I appreciate it. I'm sorry, but I'm in a bit of a rush. Is Eddie around?"

"I'm sorry Victor, he's not, but he was still here when I got in this morning and said he was going home to get some sleep."

"Of course he did," Victor says, irritated.

"He and Todd from System Tech were here all night troubleshooting the number four magnet."

Victor breathes a sigh of relief. "Oh good, did they tell you what was wrong by chance?"

"Not really, but they asked for a PO for a circuit board as soon as I got here. Todd had to go to Phoenix to pick it up, and then he said he was going home to sleep. Both plan on coming in at two to put in and said it should be up and running again by eight this evening."

Good job Eddie, Victor thinks to himself. "Okay, great. Would you ask Eddie to call me at this number as soon as he gets in, please?"

"Yes, sir."

"Also, Julia, I need you to do a couple of things for me as I am under doctor's orders to take a couple of days off."

"Sure boss. What's up?"

"I need a letter of appreciation on company letterhead for both Eddie and Todd for the work they did last night and are continuing to do. You know, going above and beyond, blah, blah, blah."

"You got it, Victor. It'll sound like they've saved the world when I'm done and the other thing?"

"Take the company credit card and buy two one-hundred-dollar gift cards to Black Angus."

"Consider it done. Anything else?"

"That should do it. If anything comes up, call me on this number since my company phone is still in my car."

"You got it, boss. Rest up and take care."

"Thanks, Julia," he says and hangs up the phone.

Now for the call that he doesn't want to make, not because he's afraid of telling him, but because Victor thinks his boss is a pretentious asshole. He pours himself another cup of coffee and dials the phone. Jarod answers on the third ring, seemingly unaware of last night's events. Victor explains everything that had taken place from when Eddie first called right up to the present call.

Jarod listens in silence until he's done and says, "Okay, Vic. The important thing is that you're all right. Hell, it sounds like you're quite the hero all the way around. The shredder will be back up around eight?"

"That's what I'm told." Victor can hear this morning's news story in the background. Jarod must have Googled the broadcast as they were talking.

"You know that we'll do our investigation, but if it went down, as you say, I doubt you'll have anything to worry about. I'll requisition a new car for you, and it should be approved by next week. The investigation should be over in a couple of days. Until then, you're on paid leave. Take a couple of days and relax."

"Wow, thanks, Jarod."

"Don't mention it. Enjoy your time off."

"Okay, I'll talk to you again in a few days."

"Oh, and Vic?"

"Yeah, Jarod?"

"Good job."

"Thanks, I guess," he says and hangs up the phone, more bewildered than anything else. Victor walks toward the bathroom to take a shower when the doorbell rings. Kona barks once and lets out a low growl as he stares at the door. Victor debates not answering but does, anyway. When he opens the door, he's surprised to see Roni and her partner standing in the doorway. He hopes the alarms going off in his head are hidden.

"Hey Victor, got a minute?" Roni takes the lead.

"Of course," he says. "Come on in. Can I get you a cup of coffee?"

"Please," replies Tuck. "We haven't formally met yet. I'm Detective Pete Tucker," he says, extending his hand.

"Victor Powers," he says, shaking the proffered hand. "How do you take your coffee, detective?" Victor asks, leading them to the kitchen.

"Black is fine."

"Roni?"

"Black as well, please."

"Please, have a seat," Victor gestures toward the barstools that line the double-wide countertop and turns to the cabinet to retrieve coffee cups. "What can I do for you?" he asks as he serves the coffee.

Roni starts. "Victor, we need to let you know a few things about the investigation so far."

"Okay, shoot," he says, pulling up a stool across the countertop from them.

"First off, not many people would have done what you did. You should be proud of yourself."

"So, I'm told," Victor replies humbly, looking down at his cup.

Roni continues, "Do you know who Kim Su Li is?"

"The girl? No, why? Should I?"

"No, in fact, we'd be more surprised if you did. Kim Li is the daughter of Li Chen."

Victor looks at them both with no recognition and shrugs.

"Better known as Jimmy Li?"

Victor shakes his head and says, "Okay, so?"

"Victor, he's a Chinese Mob Boss."

"A WHAT?" Victor asks, stunned. "Chinese Mob? In Phoenix?"

"Yeah," Roni says point-blank.

Beside her, Tuck says nothing but watches Victor for his reactions. "Let me get this straight. I interrupted the kidnapping of the daughter of a Chinese Mob Boss?" Now, concerned, he asks, "Are we in danger of any retaliation?"

Victor watches as both Roni and Detective Tucker smile. "Chances are no. We don't believe it was sanctioned. The boneheads that we arrested last night were just two yahoos that saw a pretty girl and decided to grab her. They had no idea who she was. Don't get us wrong, they were going to have their own brand of fun with her and probably would have killed her when they were done, but they're clueless," Tuck says.

"They're in protective custody now, and if they live to see the inside of a courtroom, they will be going to jail for a long, long time," Roni adds.

"Or the rest of their lives, whichever comes first," Tuck says.

At that, Roni laughs out loud, and Victor just looks at the two of them. "Sorry," she says. "Cop humor."

"What about Kim Su? Is she hurt?" Victor inquires.

"No, she has a bump on her head from the crash, but she's fine. The guy that grabbed her paid hell for it. He's got fingernail scratches around his eyes, and she almost bit off his left nipple."

"What a little wildcat," Victor says, impressed. "What about... is it, Jimmy Li?"

"You saved his daughter from what was probably certain death. He has no reason to come after you except in gratitude, Tuck answers, and by the way, if he does, we'd like to know about it."

"What are the actual chances of that?" Victor asks.

"A possible maybe is the best we can say right now," Roni explains. "I mean, no offense, but you're a nobody. You're not a player in that game. You're just a guy who did the right thing."

"None taken. More coffee?"

"No thanks," the partners say in unison. They get up from their stools, and Roni takes their cups to the sink. Just then, her phone rings. "Novetti," she answers. "In Gilbert? Yes, sir, we're on our way. Tuck, we've got to go."

"What's up?"

"Double in Gilbert, that the lieutenant thinks we may have an interest in."

Tuck turns to Victor. "We just wanted you to be aware of the situation, and up to date with where we are, Mr. Powers."

"Well, I certainly appreciate it," Victor says, seeing them to the door and hoping that his sudden apprehension isn't showing.

32

"Nina, how have you been?" Tuck asks, slipping paper covers over his shoes before entering the crime scene.

"I'm good Tuck. How about you? Roni, good to see you," she says tersely.

"Nina, always a pleasure," Roni replies, flashing a one-sided smirk.

Tuck interrupts the tension between the two women. "What have you got, Nina?" Putting her personal feelings for Roni aside, Nina Lasko turns professional in the blink of an eye. "My lieutenant told me to give you full cooperation," she says with hesitation. "Tuck, why are you here?"

"Hey," he says, holding up both hands. "We got a call from our lieutenant to come and see if this might be related to a case we're working on in Phillips, that's all. If it's not, we're out of your hair in an hour, hour-and-a-half tops. So, what have you got here?" he asks, stepping inside.

"Ashlin Murray and Lauren Jacobs. They've been together for about two years and have been living here for the last six months. The landlord was pretty sure they were going to resign their lease. Double homicide. Beware, it's gruesome inside."

"Yeah?"

"Yeah, looks like he walked in on them either having sex or just after. Both are naked. He's beheaded and piled up in a corner. She's tied to the bed and pinned to the floor with a machete."

"Rape?"

"Hard to tell. She's got some bruising on her thighs, vaginal area, and anus, and she has semen in both cavities, but we won't know any more on that until the rape kit comes back."

"Prints?"

"Not one. The whole house has been wiped down and cleaned. Except for the bedroom and the bodies, it's the cleanest crime scene I've ever been to."

"Who called it in?"

"Landlord. They had complained about the carport door not staying shut, so he came over to fix it. He puked when he saw the master. Be careful."

"How long ago?"

"At least four days."

"Okay, give us a few minutes, all right?"

"Go," Nina huffs and stalks out of the carport.

Tuck and Roni stand in the foyer inside the carport door for a few minutes, taking in what they can see. To their immediate right is a small dinette under a hanging lamp. Beyond that is the kitchen with inexpensive, white appliances, Formica countertops that are out of date, and a typical stainless-steel sink. Beside the sink, on the counter, a large stockpot rests on a drying towel. The cupboards have been painted more than once. The walls are painted white, and the floor is linoleum.

To their left is the living room. The walls here are also white with light-colored laminate flooring that leads down the hall to the bathroom and bedrooms. A couch, which has seen better days, sits under the picture window. The blinds are closed. Beside the couch, an end table holds a lamp. The TV sits on a cheap entertainment center on the wall that separates the kitchen. Pictures of two young, smiling faces adorn the walls. The front door is closed, the deadbolt thrown, and it appears to be rarely if ever used. The faint smell of bleach hangs in the air.

Down the short hallway, the bathroom is the first door on the left. Tuck stands in the doorway and turns on the light. Basic is the best word to describe it. Tub, toilet, sink, with a rectangle-shaped mirror above it and an updated light fixture above that. A medicine cabinet hangs next to the sink on the adjoining wall. A towel rack is on the wall next to the tub and across from the toilet, and a framed picture of a dog with a bandana around its neck hangs above it. The smell of bleach is more prevalent here.

Directly across the hall from the bathroom is a bedroom that, from the looks of it, is used as a library. The carpet was probably changed right before they moved in. The walls are white in here as well, and the only furnishings are a large beanbag next to a small bookshelf that is jammed with books and has a reading lamp sitting on top next to an ashtray with what's left of a roach, laying in the rest. A water bong sits on the floor between the beanbag and the bookshelf. The blinds on the window are closed. The closet is empty.

Further down the hall, purposely staying away from the master bedroom, they open the next door on the right and find the room empty save for three hangers on the floor in front of the closet and an ironing board with an iron sitting on it. Opening the closet confirms what they both suspect: that Lauren used this closet for her clothes that wouldn't fit in the closet they shared.

They both take a deep breath and start across the hall to the master bedroom, with Tuck taking the lead. He steps in far enough to let his partner in and stops. The first thing they see is Lauren tied spread eagle to the bed. She is naked and has the hilt of a machete sticking out of her chest. Her face is swollen and covered in dried blood. The sheets are pink with what Tuck guesses to be diluted blood. Surveying further, they see a patio chair set facing the bed with an empty five-gallon bucket on the floor beside it. The smell of vomit is strong. Tuck turns to his right and looks down at the glistening puddle of fresh puke on the floor and shakes his head. Looking further along the wall, they see Ash's headless naked body piled in the corner. His head lies beside him, looking up at the ceiling. Blood spatter is on the wall across from the bed, and there is an indent in the wall that vaguely resembles a face. The door to the closet is open.

"Okay," he says, "What do we know?"

"You mean other than the landlord had hotdogs for lunch?" Roni says with a light snort.

"Yeah," Tuck says, unamused. "Did Ash tie her up or was it the killer?" he says, giving her the lead.

Stepping around her partner, Roni crouches next to the bed and studies Lauren. "It was the killer. Do you see how there is no blood on her forearms or hands, but it's everywhere under her arms on the bed? She was tied after he killed him." She turns toward the closet, then rises, and crosses the room. Just inside the door are two boot prints on the carpet. Being careful to step behind the boot prints, she turns to get another perspective. "The son of a bitch stood right here and watched them having sex." She walks over to the bed, raises both hands over her head, brings them down together, then turns and looks at the wall behind her. She looks at the chair and bucket, turns back to the bed, reaches out and touches it, and rubs her fingers together.

She turns back to Tuck and says, "Want to know what I think?"

After watching her work it over, both in her head and physically, he is excited to hear her theory. She is brilliant when it comes to working out crime scenes. "Let me have it."

"He stood in the closet and watched them having sex until the time was right," she begins.

"Which was when?"

"Who knows?" she says. "They're twenty years old, and probably fuck like rabbits. She has semen in all her cavities, so unless some of it is the killer, he must have waited until they were finished. Who knows? The point is, I think he watched them for a while. Okay, for the sake of argument, let's say our guy watches until he's satisfied, then waits for the perfect opportunity. Ashlin is on top, and they are caught up in the throes of passion, so neither would be paying attention. Our guy picks his moment, crosses the room, raises the machete, and brings it down, severing Ashlin's head, but Ashlin isn't the target. He is just in the way. Lauren is the target."

Tuck stays quiet, letting her roll with it, knowing that she has it all worked out in her head, and his questions will be answered if he gives her the time to finish. "So," she continues, "our guy pulls him off her and tosses him aside. Lauren must realize what has happened by now and starts screaming, but our guy doesn't want to kill her. Not yet, so he snatches her up and throws her face-first into that wall, knocking her unconscious." She points across the room to the wall with the face-shaped blood spatter. Following her in his mind's eye, Tuck can see it happening as she continues. "While she's out, he ties her to the bed, grabs a patio chair from the backyard, and waits. He has time, so does he wait for her to come out of it, or since he doesn't want to be seen, does he fill this bucket from the tap out back, and dump it on her to bring her out of it? How she wakes up is not the point. The point is that she wakes up, and he wants to spend some time with her before he kills her. Maybe he wants to torture her, and then, when he's done, he runs the machete through her heart with enough force to pin her through the bed and to the floor. He then scrubs every room that he's been in and gets out. He's angry, no, not angry, he's enraged with her. Why? Why is he so enraged with her?" Roni raises her eyebrows and tilts her head slightly before she says, "If we figure that out, we'll have our killer."

"Okay, let's say it goes down just as you say. Is he, OUR guy?"

"Check this out, she says, crossing back to the closet and pointing to the boot prints still visible on the carpet. "They look like a size thirteen and a half to me, and I'll bet you dollars to doughnuts that there are traces of Aqua Net hairspray in this closet."

"Let's take a look at the backyard," Tuck says.

The patio is dusty, and right in the middle is a clear trail of boot prints made by brand-new Caterpillar work boots. "Good Lord," Roni says, more to herself than to Tuck. "He made at least five trips out here and back."

"Yeah, let's go tell Nina the good news. What's your beef with her, anyway?"

Roni scoffs, "It's not my beef, it's hers." Tuck just looks at her blankly, waiting for a better explanation. "She doesn't approve of my lifestyle," she says with the same smirk that she gave Nina forty-five minutes ago.

"Ah, that," Tuck says and shakes his head. "When do you think people will stop with that nonsense?"

"I don't know, but I hope it's sometime soon. I get tired of it. Thank you, by the way."

"Thanks for what?" he asks, confused.

"For not making a big deal out of it when you found out."

Tuck looks at his partner with sincerity and says, "Roni, you're my partner, and I'm going to tell you the same thing I told my son when he came out a few years ago." The surprise on her face is clear as he continues. "It's not up to me to tell you whom you can love. I can advise you, and I'm here to support you, but whom you choose to sleep with, and love is none of mine or anybody else's business. If the person you choose is good to you, and you're happy with them, who am I to disagree? I didn't make a big deal about it because it's not a big deal."

A single tear slips down Roni's cheek as she looks at her partner with admiration. "You're the best, Tuck."

Tuck just winks at her. "Shhh, don't tell anyone. I've got a reputation to think about. Now, do you want to tell Nina that we're taking her case, or do you want me to?"

A smile broadens across Roni's face. "I got it."

33

"Good morning, I'm detective Pete Tucker, and this is my partner Detective Veronica Novetti. with Phillips PD. We've got an appointment with Sarah Perkins. Is she here?" Tuck asks the clerk at the Circle K where Ash worked the following day.

"Yeah, she's in the back. Are you investigating Ash's murder?"

"We are. Were you working the night he was killed?" Tuck asks.

"Yeah, I was," the young man says, as he wiped a sudden tear from his eye.

"I'm sorry for your loss. Were you close?" Roni asks.

"Yeah, we were. He was my roommate before he and Lauren moved in together.

"Have you given a statement yet?" Roni asks.

"No, today is my first day back. My girlfriend and I went camping up by The Grand Canyon the morning after it happened. I just found out about it."

Tuck glances at his notebook. "So, that would make you Jasper Flynn, correct?"

"Jazz, please. The only one who calls me Jasper is my grandmother." He says with a lighthearted smile.

"All right," Tuck says his voice full of empathy. "We'll need to talk to you after we've talked with Ms. Perkins."

"Sure, no problem." Jazz says wiping another tear away. "I'll get her. Excuse me."

The office in the back of the store is no bigger than a cubicle but much more cramped. Video monitors showing the door, cashier, and various angles of the store line the shelves above the desk. Immediately eyeing the video bank Tuck introduces them both to the store manager, a pretty, but slightly plump woman in her mid-thirties. "Ms. Perkins, first let me offer my condolences. I understand Ashlin was well-liked around here."

"Thank you, Detective. He was, and please call me Sarah, and he went by Ash."

"All right, Sarah. What do you know about that night?"

"Well, not much to be honest. I've gone over the tapes again and again, and I don't see anything out of the norm. Nothing that stands out. I talked to Jazz when he got in this morning, and he said that someone slashed Ash's tires at some point that night, but other than—"

"Someone slashed his tires?" Roni inquires.

"Yeah, according to Jazz, he didn't realize it till he got off work, and he had to call Lauren to come to get him. His truck was here the following morning, and I noticed it, but I didn't see that the tires were slashed until the next day. He had the next couple of days off, so I thought they'd gone out of town or something and figured he'd take care of it when they got back."

"Where is his truck now?"

"It's still in the lot. It's the gray F150 over in the second spot from the corner."

"All right, we're going to have to impound it. I don't suppose any of these covers the parking lot?" Tuck asks indicating the monitors.

"We're a small store Detective," she explains. "Inside is all we have as of this second. We were due to get outside cameras around the beginning of the year, but that's been moved up to next week now... ya know, considering... Sorry."

Tuck nods while tightening his mouth and pulls a flash drive out of his pocket. "Okay, can you pull up the video from that night for me, please? I'll need to put it on this flash drive and have it analyzed."

"I've already taken the liberty," she says opening the desk drawer and retrieving a drive of her own, "here you go." She says placing it in tuck's hand. "If he's on here, I hope you catch the son of a bitch and fry his ass," she says as a tear rolls down her face.

"We're going to need a few minutes with Jazz if you don't mind." Sarah wipes her nose with a tissue before saying "I'll get him."

Roni begins the questioning of Jazz. They have found during their partnership that young men seem to respond better to a pretty female detective's questions than someone who reminds them of their father, while girls on the other hand are the opposite. "Okay Jazz, talk to me. What can you tell me about that night?"

"They were planning a big night. Ash was very excited about it."

"Excited how?"

"Oh God, he wouldn't shut up about it. It was almost like they were going on their first date. It was like he was walking on air all night just watching the clock. He wanted to ask her to marry him."

"Was that his plan that night?"

"Naw, Ash was old-fashioned. He wanted to do it right. He didn't have a ring yet and hadn't talked to her father. That night was just about fun. That's all."

"Sarah said you told her that someone slashed his tires?"

"Yeah, that sucked. He was pissed when he realized what had happened."

"Did Ash have any problems with anyone that night or any other time that you can recall?"

"Not at all. Ash was one of the most likable guys you've ever met. I mean it. You know how everyone has a bad day once in a while?" Roni nods and gives him an encouraging smile to get him to continue. "Well, Ash didn't. He was always in a good mood. He kinda laughed it off saying 'At least it didn't happen two hours before.' That was the only time I ever saw him even slightly miffed."

"Why, what happened two hours before?"

"He took his last break and ran to the liquor store and flower shop to get flowers and a bottle of wine."

"And what time would that have been?"

"About four-thirty or five I think, we're not supposed to take our last break with the last two hours of our shift, and he got off at seven that night, so... yeah right about then I guess."

"So, you're saying that his tires got slashed somewhere between four-thirty and seven?"

"Yeah, I guess so," he says thinking back.

Tuck makes notes in his notebook to watch for those specific times on the video. Putting his notebook away he pulls a business card from his breast pocket and hands it to Jazz. "If you think of anything else, anything at all, please don't hesitate to give us a call."

34

Halloween comes and goes without further incident for the Powers. Shelby was the cutest Pirate Princess ever in Halloween history according to her grandmother's response to the pictures that Lindsay sent. Victor agrees with his mother-in-law on this point.

After the kidnapping attempt, the Demons have been relatively quiet, and since the killings of Ash and Lauren, Victor is sleeping better. On his third day back at work, his new car arrives at his office. It's a typical company car: a no-frills four-door Ford sedan with the company logo on the driver's side and passenger doors. An envelope sits in the driver's seat. Figuring it contained the keys and a gas card, Victor opens the envelope and was surprised to find a handwritten note from Jarod.

Hey Vic,

Here's your new car. Try not to crash this one. Ha Ha.

By the way, the company wants to formally recognize you for your actions that night at the Christmas party. Look for an email later this year.

Congratulations again!

Regards,

Jarod

"You're still a prick, Jarod," Victor says to himself. Following a walk-around inspection, Victor starts the car and notices that it needs gas. *Of course, it does,* he thinks as he returns to his office to grab his jacket and laptop before leaving for the day. Exiting the building, Victor sees a black Yukon with tinted windows blocking his new car. All his senses are instantly hyper-alert as the doors open and two well-dressed, very capable-looking Chinese gentlemen approach him.

"Mr. Powers," the driver says, with a very slight accent, as the gentleman from the passenger side opens and holds the rear driver's side door. "Our employer requests your company immediately."

Victor is awestruck by their all-business approach and politeness. "I don't suppose I have a choice, do I?"

The driver, with his hands crossed in front of him, smiles a smile that Victor imagines a snake would smile just before it strikes and gestures to the Yukon, simply saying, "Mr. Powers, please."

Seeing no other choice, Victor nervously climbs in and buckles up. The passenger closes his door, crosses around the rear of the vehicle, and climbs in beside Victor. The driver returns to the driver's seat and neither says another word. The SUV makes its way to SR 101, turns north for two miles, then turns west on

Warner Road, following it to the Ahwatukee Foothills. They pull up to a gated mansion. The gate opens, the SUV pulls through, and comes to a stop in front of the house. As the driver gets out and opens Victor's door, he sees an older, equally well-dressed, Chinese man and a beautiful Chinese girl in a traditional dress, whom he recognizes instantly, awaiting his arrival.

"Mr. Powers, I am Li Chen, and this is my daughter Kim Su. It is a pleasure to make your acquaintance."

Kim Su places her hands together and bows her head. "Mr. Powers, I would like to thank you for your vigilance and for saving me. I am grateful. Thank you."

"Kim Su, I think I was just in the right place at the right time. I'm glad it worked out as it did." Kim Su bows once again, and politely leaves them alone.

"Mr. Powers, I thank you for agreeing to meet with me."

"I don't know that I had a choice... Mr. Chen?"

Li Chen smiles at the American in front of him. "It's Li actually, but if it would be more comfortable, you may call me Jimmy. Please, come in. I apologize for my associates' abruptness." He shows Victor inside. "Perhaps we will be more comfortable in my study. Please, come with me." Jimmy Li turns and gestures with his arm to a door across the foyer.

Victor enters the study in front of Jimmy Li. The showpiece of the room is a massive mahogany desk in front of a window adorned with heavy velvet drapes. Behind the desk sits a large, high-backed leather chair. Shelves filled with oriental sculptures tastefully line the walls, and an air purifier is hidden behind a Ficus plant in the corner. There is a faint smell of cigar smoke lingering in the air. Two blue velvet chairs, separated by a small table, sit in front of the desk, one of which Jimmy Li points to and says, "Please, Mr. Powers, have a seat." He takes the chair behind the desk. "May I offer you anything? A drink perhaps? Coffee?"

"No, thank you," Victor says, shifting in his chair.

"Mr. Powers, I find myself in the very unusual position of being indebted to you for saving my daughter's life."

"Mr. Li, honestly, you don't owe me anything. Anyone else would have done the same."

"It's funny you should say that Mr. Powers. You say that anyone would do the same, yet in a parking lot with twenty-five people, you are the one who acted."

"I... I can't speak for anyone else, Mr. Li, but I'm a father of a daughter, myself. I just did what I hope anyone else would if they saw something like that happening to her."

"Let's talk about you for just a moment."

Victor looks across the desk into Li Chen's eyes, returning an intense stare.

Take it easy here...

"Mr. Li..."

Picking up a piece of paper from the desk, "You have been employed by Little General Recycling for ten years. You have been married for just under seven years. Your wife, Lindsay, has recently been hired at Channel 4, and you have a six-year-old daughter, Shelby, who attends Phillips Elementary."

"It's clear that you've done your homework, Mr. Li," Victor says with annoyance, sitting forward in his chair, "but I don't see how—"

Li interrupts. "How would you like to retire in three years?"

Taken aback, Victor stammers, "Excuse me?"

"I believe you heard me, Mr. Powers. I did, as you say, do my homework, and by outward appearances, you are an honorable man," he says, looking up from the paper and matching Victor's stare.

The hair on the back of Victor's neck stands on end. "I have seen the video surveillance from the store's camera. You didn't do what you did to benefit yourself in any way. You didn't think; you acted."

"Again Mr. Li... I didn't—"

"Mr. Powers," Li interrupts again. "I know what you must be thinking. Surely you have been told who I am, and you're not only overwhelmed by how we have come to know each other, but you are probably a bit nervous as well, yes?"

"Well, to be completely honest with you, yes, I am."

A genuine smile broadens across Li's face, as he opens his arms, rises from his chair, and comes around the desk to sit next to Victor. "Mr. Powers," he says as he places his hand on Victor's forearm. "I make this offer not as who you have been told I am, but as a father whose daughter has been saved from a horrible, and almost certain, death. I am indebted to you for that, and I am a man that pays his debts. I assure you that you are in no danger. Like I told you before, this is an unusual position for me to be in, so if I come across as abrupt, or if I have given you the impression that you don't have a choice in this matter, please accept my most humble apologies."

At this, Victor relaxes. Li's smile grows wider with approval.

Victor takes a deep breath and blows it out. "How would I be able to explain it?" Victor asks, contemplating the offer.

"I have very good accountants, Mr. Powers. There will be no trouble with the law; however, I must insist that you never speak of this meeting to anyone, including your wife." Victor looks at him with hesitation. "Surely, Detectives Tucker and Novetti told you I may contact you and asked you to let them know if I did."

More surprised now than he's ever been, Victor asks, "How did y—"

"Mr. Powers," Li states as his face takes on a reptilian air, "I know your wife went to school with Detective Novetti's girlfriend and that Ms. Keller helped her get hired at Channel 4. Your wife is an investigative television reporter whose very good friend, also a television reporter, is in a relationship with a homicide detective. It is in my best interest to know things about people, Mr. Powers. I will go one step further to show you I am sincere in our relationship. Most of what they must have told you about me is true, and if you believe nothing else in your life, believe me when I tell you, that you would much rather know me as a grateful father than the man who will deal with the men that the police have in protective custody, as we speak. I never act on impulse, and I always make informed decisions."

Think before you respond.
Quiet
You need to think about this...
A plan begins to formulate in the back of Victor's mind.
In for a penny...
In for a pound.
"Mr. Li," Victor smiles blankly, meeting and holding Li's eye with a hard glare, "please believe me when I tell you I can appreciate everything that you have just told me. I too believe in educating myself about a task at hand and not acting impulsively, and I do not doubt your sincerity, or the truth in your words, but knowing what you must know about me, you know I cannot accept your offer as it would require me to be dishonest with my wife. There are a few things that she doesn't know about me, and if she were to find out about them, though it would cost me dearly, I still would not lie to her. I will, however, honor your request

that I never mention this meeting to anyone, ever, but please Sir, with respect, please understand that I can't accept your offer."

Disappointment flashed across Li's face and was instantly replaced by a look of admiration. "Mr. Powers, may I call you Victor?"

"Of course."

"Victor, I am once again put in an unusual position. I am not used to being told no, but in this instance, I will accept your denial," Li says thoughtfully, "but I am still indebted to you, so I must ask, what is it I can do to repay you?"

"Believe it or not, Mr. Li, I have given this some thought during our meeting today."

"Have you?" Li replies with more of a statement than a question. "What was your thought?"

"To be honest, Mr. Li," Victor says with a laugh, "I wished you had offered just about anything else, but I believe I have come up with something if you are going to insist."

Li takes a deep breath, and says, "Victor, the price is yours to ask."

"First, I'd like to take you up on your offer of a drink if you will join me."

"Of course, Victor. What would you like?" he says, standing up and going to the bar. "Crown Royal on the rocks?"

Hiding his surprise behind the deadpan stare that in his youth caused grown men to wilt, Victor replies, "Make it a double, please." Followed by, "My compliments to your investigators, Mr. Li."

Li hands Victor the glass of whiskey with a smile and asks, "Anything else?"

"If I may be so bold," Victor states simply. "I'd like a cigar if you have one."

Impressed by Victor's nerve, Li smiles again. "Ah Victor, you have a refined sense of smell. Would you prefer Cuban or Nicaraguan?"

"Nicaraguan, please."

Li nods his approval as he opens the humidor, retrieves two cigars, and clips the ends. He hands Victor a cigar and a box of wood matches as he returns to his seat next to him. Victor lights his cigar and takes a long pull from the glass, relishing the burn sliding down his throat and warming his insides.

"Now, Victor," Li says, sipping from his glass, "what is it that I can do for you?"

Setting his glass on the end table between them, Victor turns in his chair to face the man next to him and puffs his cigar. "Mr. Li, I would like to take out a life insurance policy from the Li Brokerage House for an unspecified amount, so that in the event of my death, my family will be taken care of financially, and will fall under your protection, for the rest of their lives, without their knowledge of course."

Li looks at Victor without emotion, contemplating the depth of the request for a long while.

"Just to be clear, you do not want this while you're alive, but in the event of your death, I am to take care of your family financially, as well as protect them as if they were my own?"

"Correct."

"They can never know anything other than you purchased a life insurance policy, and they must never know that they are under my protection."

"That sums it up," Victor says, sipping from his glass again and puffing his cigar. "I can provide for and protect them as long as

I'm alive, but if anything were to happen to me, I'd like them to be well taken care of."

"Victor, you understand that there will be nothing on paper until after your demise, and only then there will be just enough to justify annuity payments to your wife, and after her death, to your daughter?"

"I do, and in all honesty, I was hoping that you'd see it that way."

"Victor, you have piqued my interest, and I'd like to know more about you."

"Mr. Li, I don't think you would. Earlier, you alluded to your dark side. I assure you I have my demons as well."

Li laughs loudly with genuine respect. "Yes, I suppose you do, and I will not ask about them," he says, looking Victor in the face, intrigued. "I'm saddened that we will never see each other again. I think that in time, we would grow to be good friends, but also, I think we know that would compromise us both. I will honor your request and trust that after today, we will never speak again."

"Mr. Li, I believe we have a deal," he says as he reaches his hand out.

Li takes his hand and shakes it firmly. "Let's finish our drinks and enjoy our cigars like the friends we will never be, and I will have Min Cho take you back to your office."

35

"Angie and Roni invited us to their house for Thanksgiving," Lindsay says, turning off the water and stepping out of the shower as Victor shaves in the mirror. "Think you'll be up to it?"

Victor rolls his eyes playfully at his naked wife as she towels off. "Thanksgiving is what… three weeks away? Yeah, I'll probably be fine. What do we need to bring?"

"Not sure yet," Lindsay says, brushing past him and wrapping a towel around herself. "She said she'd let me know when she has a better idea of the menu."

"Menu? For Thanksgiving? What's there to think about? Turkey and or prime rib, mashed sweet potatoes, stuffing, gravy, green bean casserole, cranberry fluff, and pies. What else is there?"

"For us maybe," Lindsay says, stepping into her underwear, "but Angie never was much of a cook, and apparently, neither is Roni. I think they are going to have it catered."

Victor leans back and looks out of the bathroom door at her. "Catered?" he asks, confused.

Lindsay laughs. "I think so, but I'll check to be sure. Does it matter? We're going even if they serve peanut butter sandwiches."

"I know, but if that's the road they're going to go down, let's volunteer to help them cook."

"Victor!? We can't insult them like that," Lindsay says, miffed at the thought of insulting her friend.

"I know babe, I was just thinking out loud... mostly, but let's make a turkey here at least."

"What are you talking about? You don't even like turkey," she says, walking across the room to the closet for an outfit.

"Yeah, but I like sandwiches after dinner," he says with a smile, watching her.

"Okay, but don't say anything about it tonight. I'll find out more tomorrow," she says, reaching for a hanger. "How's this look?" she asks, holding a black and purple cocktail dress in front of her as he exits the bathroom with a towel over his shoulder.

Victor stops, frozen in place, enraptured by her beauty and grace. His mouth drops open as he looks at his wife in awe. "Good Lord! You're beautiful!"

Gushing from her husband's spontaneous compliment. "It's good to know you think so."

"Lindsay, I am just enamored by you. Sometimes I look at you and try to figure out what it is I did to deserve you. I believe with my whole heart," he says not moving but looking deeply into his wife's face from across the room, "that you saved my life. Thank you!"

The sincerity in Victor's voice and his expression brings tears to Lindsay's eyes as she drops the dress on the bed and crosses the room to embrace him. Holding him tightly, with her face pressed against his bare chest, she sniffs. "I think that's the sweetest thing you've ever said to me."

"It's true though. I hate to think of where or what I would be if you hadn't come into my life," he says, holding her just as tight and kissing her damp hair.

They're standing, embracing, in the middle of their bedroom when the doorbell rings. "Shit, that will be Jen," Lindsay says, pulling away reluctantly. "Can you get the door?"

"Yep," he says, pulling on a pair of pajama bottoms and a tee shirt. "To be continued?"

"You know it," she says with a wink and a smile.

"Shelby! Jen and Abby are here," he calls, walking down the hall and to the front door.

"I'm almost ready, Daddy!" she calls from her bedroom.

Victor opens the door to Abby's smiling and almost toothless face. "Girl, if you lose any more teeth, you're going to starve to death. Hi Jen, come on in."

"Hey, Victor, thanks," Jen says, shifting Joey, Abby's two-year-old little brother, from one hip to the other. "Is she ready?"

"Just about. She's in her room." Abby brushes past him and runs down the hall to Shelby's room. "Thanks for letting her spend the night tonight," Victor says.

"Not a problem. She's always welcome. Besides, what's one more?" she says, tilting her head to the side as Joey grabs her earring. "Plus, it's pizza night. Easy peasy. Where are you guys going?"

"We're meeting Angie and Roni at Fleming's."

"Ooh, nice."

"Yeah, we haven't been out in a while. We're due."

"Be careful, though. There's something in the cheesecake."

"Oh?"

"Oh yeah," she says. "The last time Bill and I had dinner there I had the cheesecake and BAM! Nine months later, Joey showed up." Unable to keep a straight face, she bursts out laughing.

Victor laughs and hooks his cheek with his finger. "Oh, good Lord," he says, rolling his eyes. "If you'll excuse me, I need to get dressed."

Still laughing at her joke, Jen waves as Lindsay comes down the hall. "WOW! You look great, Lady!"

"You, see? I'm not the only one," Victor says, brushing past his wife and knocking on Shelby's door. "Come on girls, it's time."

"Okay Daddy," Shelby says, opening the door and pulling her suitcase behind her. "A suitcase? Good Lord, girl! How long do you think you're going to stay?"

"Daddy..." she says as Abby giggles behind her.

"See you tomorrow, kiddo," he says, bending to kiss her goodbye. "Have fun and behave yourself."

"I will Daddy."

Victor closes the bedroom door to finish dressing. He has just finished tying his shoes when Lindsay comes in. "Well, they're off... Wow! Don't you look handsome!" she says, straightening his tie. "What's the occasion?"

"I've got a hot date."

"Yeah? Think you'll get lucky?"

"Anything is possible," he says, leaning down to kiss her lips and dropping his hands past her hips to her butt.

"No, no, no, we can't be late," she says, pulling out of his grasp and turning towards the bathroom. "I need twenty minutes and we're out."

36

Angie and Roni are walking to the door of the restaurant hand in hand as they pull into the parking lot. Victor toots the horn of Lindsay's SUV, and they wave. After parking the car, Victor walks around, opens the door for Lindsay, and offers his hand to help her out. Together, they meet their friends at the door.

The maître d' greets them. "Good evening, folks. Do you have a reservation?"

Angie smiles at him and says, "Keller, seven-thirty."

Checking the reservation list, "Yes, Ms. Keller's party of four?" he says, looking up. "Of course, one moment, please. Daniel?"

Daniel introduces himself as their waiter and asks them to follow him to their table. At the table, Daniel holds Angie's chair, then Roni's, and Victor holds Lindsay's. Once seated, Daniel pours water from a chilled decanter and asks if they would like a glass of wine while they look over the menu.

"I think we'll start with a bottle of pinot Blanco, please," Angie says, taking the lead.

"Very good, Ma'am," he says and is gone. He soon returns with four chilled wine glasses and an unopened bottle of house wine. After the wine is poured and their salads are ordered, Daniel disappears but is somehow always available to refill an empty glass or replace a dropped fork, without hovering.

"So Victor," Angie begins, "Lindsay tells me you're going to get a commendation at work for your actions the other night."

"Well, I guess they didn't have much choice after your story aired," he says. Lindsay squeezes his thigh under the table, indicating that his answer is slightly snippy.

Oblivious, Angie replies, "Well, I suppose so. Any chance that we can cover it when it happens?"

"I don't think so," Victor says, his discomfort evident.

"Angie, we talked about this." Lindsay interrupts.

"Oh, I know Lindsay, and I'm sorry Victor. I know that you're not crazy about being in the spotlight, but it would be a great wrap-up for the story."

"I'd rather not if it's all the same."

"Speaking of that," Roni chimes in, looking at Victor with intent. "Have you heard from anyone that may have an interest in your actions?"

Here we go... At that moment, Daniel arrives at the table with their salads, and Victor lets out a small sigh of relief.

"Have you had a chance to select your entrees?" The ladies all order petite filet mignons with roasted vegetables and scalloped potatoes, while Victor goes with the sixteen-ounce ribeye, roasted vegetables, and steak fries.

Dinner is served on sizzling plates, about twenty minutes later, and everyone agrees it is the best steak they've ever had. The conversation is light, and the earlier tension has been forgotten, though Roni keeps looking thoughtfully across the table at Victor. Daniel, who seems to appear and disappear out of thin air, has appeared after clearing the dinner service and is asking if there is room for dessert.

"Ladies, I have it on good authority not to order the cheesecake. There is something drastically wrong with it," Victor suddenly blurts out, instantly capturing everyone's attention, including Daniel, who is ever so politely quiet but looks on with interest. Victor tells the story that Jen told him earlier and everyone laughs, even Daniel, who visibly relaxes.

"Well, I guess that settles it," Lindsay states with an ever-so-slight slur. "Cheesecake all around!" More laughter erupts as Daniel once again pulls his disappearing act.

Angie and Roni share a look and nod. "Angie and I have something that we'd like to tell you," Roni says as they join hands on top of the table. Victor and Lindsay look from one another to the couple across from them and listen. "I don't know how to say this, so I'm just going to put it out there... We've decided to get married," Roni says point-blank. Victor looks from one to the other. Angie is glowing with tears welling in her emerald-green eyes and tightens her grasp on Roni's hand. Roni is looking into Angie's eyes with a single tear running down her cheek as she turns her head to face their friends and says, "I love Angie more than I ever thought possible, and we feel that it's time that we take our relationship to the next level."

Lindsay lowers her hands from her mouth, tears of happiness running freely down her cheeks, and says, "Oh Angie, I am so happy for you," and stands up to hug her friend.

Angie and Roni rise together and the three of them embrace. "Congratulations to you both. I am so happy for the two of you."

As the ladies retake their chairs, Victor stands with glass in hand and toasts them. "Congratulations to you both. May your love be strong, and may your marriage be as happy as ours," he says, looking lovingly at his wife.

With perfect timing, Daniel reappears with their desserts on a silver tray. "Would anyone like coffee with their dessert?"

Victor answers for the table. "No thank you, Daniel, but we will have another bottle of wine."

Lindsay looks at Victor with raised eyebrows. Victor smiles and says, "We're celebrating. We'll take an Uber."

With that, the women say in unison "MORE WINE!!!" and raise their glasses. Over dessert, Lindsay asks, "Have you set a date yet?"

"We're thinking sometime in January, but well after New Year's," Angie says.

"So soon?" Lindsay asks, surprised.

"Yeah, we don't want it during the holidays, and Roni's father isn't in the best of health, so it needs to be soon."

"We'd like to ask something of both of you," Roni interjects.

"Oh?" Lindsay says, intrigued.

Angie reaches over and takes Lindsay's hand and says, "Lindsay, would you please stand up with us and witness our wedding?"

Lindsay looks from Angie to Roni, who is smiling with tears in her eyes, again, nodding in agreement.

"Of course, I will. I'd be honored."

"Victor, we have something to ask of you as well," Angie beams.

Victor smiles and waits to hear what will be asked of him. "Name it."

"If I remember correctly, you are ordained, yes?"

Caught by surprise, Victor stammers, "Uh yeah, but that was years ago."

"We'd like you to officiate our wedding," Angie says with the same smile that she uses on camera.

"Um, I don't know if my credentials are still valid."

"Well, how hard can it be to find out?"

Victor looks around the table at the three women looking at him expectantly. "I'll check tomorrow," he smiles. "Of course, I'd be happy too. If I'm not currently, I will be ordained by your wedding day."

You have lost your fucking mind!

"Thank you so much," Roni says. "You two have been so warm and friendly to me since we met, and I just want you to know how much I appreciate it."

"It's not a problem, and I'm happy to do it. I understand that we're having Thanksgiving at your house. We can talk more about it then."

"That sounds perfect. I'm glad that you'll be there. Tuck was a bit concerned about being the only guy not connected to the station, who will be there," she says, laughing.

"Does Tuck know?" Lindsay asks.

"We're taking him to dinner on Wednesday."

Daniel brings the check, discreetly places it on the table, and disappears. Victor and Angie both reach for it, but he is just a bit closer than she is. "Victor, please, we invited you. It's our treat."

"Um no," he says with a grin, checking the bill and placing his credit card at the top of the folder, then holding it out to Daniel, who magically appears to take it.

37

"That was very sweet of you," Lindsay says, snuggling against her husband in the back of their Uber.

Victor is having a silent argument in his head and the sound of her voice momentarily pulls him away. "Yeah, well, I'm a sweet guy."

No, you're not, and we're not done...

Would you please just go away? In his mind's eye, Victor sees the Demon smile at him.

It's a little late for that, don't you think?

Maybe, but I've enjoyed the quiet lately.

"Victor?" "Are you listening to me?"

"Wha...? Oh, I'm sorry, babe. I guess I just got lost in thought. What did you say?"

Lindsay pulls away from him and looks at him through wine-glazed eyes that are suddenly filled with hurt. "What is going on with you?" she demands.

Realizing that this has been building up in her for a while now, Victor focuses on her and does his best to shut the demons out. "What do you mean?" he asks, hoping it doesn't sound rhetorical.

"Victor, you have been zoning out more and more for the last couple of months, and when I try to talk to you about it, you play it off like it's nothing."

"Babe..."

"No, you listen to me. Shelby came into the living room the other day to get you to play with her, and she couldn't even get your attention. She came to me crying. I tried to tell you about my day after I interviewed Roni and Tuck when you got out of the hospital, and you sat on the couch and muttered to yourself. You only snapped out of it when I brought you a sandwich. Victor, you don't sleep, and when you do, you thrash around. You have dreams that even scare me. You look like you've been on a week-long bender most of the time, and I know you haven't but—"

"What dreams?"

"Please don't interrupt me, Victor. I probably wouldn't be talking about it now if we hadn't ordered that last bottle of wine, but here we are, and I don't want to stop now." Victor simply shrugs and waits for her to continue. "You're not sleeping well, if at all, and your dreams," Lindsay continues, "most of the time you thrash about, but sometimes you talk or cry in your sleep. Two weeks ago, you were crying, 'Mommy NO!' and covering your head with your arms. I know it's affecting you because your dreams have been terrible over the last few months. That's about the time you started running at Kiwanis Park. You do realize that, right?"

Looking at her blankly, he concedes he does. Thinking that he needs to get out of this conversation he blurts quickly, "Sweetie,

I just got out of the hospital a couple of weeks ago, and I have been on painkillers because I took a pretty good blow to the head, remember?"

"Bullshit, I've seen you high, and this started before the accident," she says, calling him out. "This isn't like that at all. You are completely zoned out lately, and I'm worried about you. I listen to you scream about your mother in your sleep and realize that I don't even know what happened to her. The only thing you've ever told me is that she died when you were a kid, but I don't know more than that. Don't you think it's odd that a wife doesn't know what happened to her husband's mother? And you won't tell me about it, which I guess I understand, but sweetie, you're going to have to talk about it to someone. It's affecting our family. Don't you see... it's affecting us?"

She reaches up and gingerly brushes his face as the driver pulls in front of their house and turns down the radio. "Okay folks, here you go, all safe and sound."

They continue looking into each other's eyes a moment longer. She is expressing concern for her husband, and he is terrified that he's about to spill everything to his wife.

Get out of the car before you say something stupid.

Victor looks away first, climbs out of the car, and holds the door for her. They thank the driver, who in turn wishes them a good night. Victor pulls the key fob from his pocket and opens the garage door with the button.

As they walk through the garage, she takes his hand and stops. Turning him to face her she says, "I don't know why you won't, and I will try to understand if you don't want to talk to me about it, but I need you to promise me you'll go to a counselor. Please?"

"I will find a counselor. I'll start looking tomorrow." He looks into her eyes and says, "I promise. I didn't realize that it was affecting you like this."

"Not just me," she says, tears welling in her eyes, "us. I don't know why it's surfacing after all this time, but it is. We need you to figure out why, and then I need you to tell me about it."

"No!" he shouts, "I told you at the beginning that I would never talk about my mother or my childhood, and I won't. There are things about me that, believe me when I say, you don't want to know! Please," he begs. "I will never lie to you, but don't ask me about it."

"Victor, I'm not just a girl you've taken to dinner a few times. I'm your wi—"

"I know who you are!"

"There is nothing I don't want to know about you."

Victor looks down over the top of his glasses, and glowering at her, growls, "You need to trust me, Lindsay. Do not push me on this. I promised you I'll find a counselor and I will, but I will never talk to you about my childhood or my whore of a mother."

Lindsay is shocked to silence as Victor turns from her and stalks into the house. For the first time in her married life, she realizes she is afraid. She sits down on a cooler and hears him rummaging in the coat closet for the cigarettes that he doesn't know that she knows about. Never has she ever thought that he could frighten her until tonight.

She had seen him look at men that way when they started dating, and she almost broke up with him because at the time she thought he was being possessive, which was something that she hated. She remembers that she and her girlfriends were being flirted with by a couple of guys at the next table when one of them noticed Victor staring them down. They overheard him telling his friends, 'This guy isn't playing around,' and then talked his buddies into leaving.

Lindsay had looked over and saw Victor as he tried to recover and smile at her. "What in the Hell was that?" she had asked.

"What? I didn't say anything. I just looked at them."

At that point, she had gotten up from the table and was walking out of the bar determined to walk home alone when she stormed into Billy, Victor's friend, who was heading back to their table from the bathroom.

"Whoa Lindsay," he'd said. "Where are you going?"

"I'm leaving," she said and continued to tell him what happened.

Billy laughed and said, "Oh hell. He just peed on you a little bit. They left, didn't they? That's all he wanted. Calm down, come back to the table, have another drink, and if you still want to go, I'll get you a taxi myself."

When they went back to the table, everyone was laughing, and the tension from ten minutes ago seemed to have been forgotten.

"Where have you been, babe?" Victor asked, putting his arm around her.

"Oh, she got lost on the way to the bathroom," Billy said.

A look of concern crossed Victor's face as he asked her if she was okay. His eyes were so intense, making her feel as if she were the only person in the world. "I'm fine," she'd said, forgiving his indiscretion. She gave a nod of thanks across the table to Billy, who winked at her. That was the last time she had seen him look at anyone like that. And now she understood why the guys at the next table had left that night.

She knows Victor would never hurt her, and he would be devastated if he knew he had frightened her, but the point remains that he had frightened her, and at this moment, she doesn't know what she is going to do. She takes a deep breath and walks into the house as Victor comes in through the back door.

"Finish your smoke?" she asks with contempt.

He looks at her humbly and apologizes. "Baby, I'm sorry. I didn't mean to be that harsh with you."

"Do I hear a but coming?" she asks, still unsure of her feelings, but willing to accept his apology.

"No, no buts. I love you, and I'm sorry. As I said, I'll start looking for a counselor tomorrow. I know I've got to come to terms with my demons, but I'm going to ask that you let me do it on my own. This is not something that you can help me with. I told you I would do it, and I will, but I've got to do it alone."

"Sweetie," she says, crossing the room to him and taking both of his hands in hers. "You're my husband, and I will respect your wishes regarding your mother, and I'll let you do this the way you think you need to for now, but if you think that it only affects you, you're delusional. We are in this together for better or worse, in sickness and in health and all that shit, remember?" she says, smiling at him.

"You sound so sure."

"I am sure. You are my husband, and I love you. I will go to the ends of the earth for us just as I know, beyond any shadow of a doubt, that you would. We are the team, sweetie. Remember?"

"How is it that you love me the way you do?"

She raises his hands to her mouth and kisses the right hand gently, then bites the middle knuckle of his left. "Take me to bed, Cowboy, and I'll show you how I love you."

38

Lindsay sits in her cubicle and spends the better half of the next morning looking blankly at the computer screen on her desk, stewing over the events of last night. On one hand, she'd given Victor her word that she would let him go to counseling on his own, but she worries that he will drag his feet on it. Ultimately, she thinks he will keep his word to her, and she wants to be a good wife and partner and honor her word to him. On the other hand, she is more than irritated by a couple of things, like why he refuses to talk about his childhood. All she knows is he is from a small suburb outside of Santa Fe, New Mexico, and that his father left a couple of years before his mother died. *Hell, I don't even know what she died from.* After she died, he went into foster care until he turned eighteen and joined Job Corps, where he learned to be an electrician. The way he tells it, he threw a dart at a map, and it landed on Phillips, Arizona, and he's been here ever since.

He had gotten on with Little General Recycling shortly after taking scrap from his construction job to the recycling plant. He had gotten along well with Brad, the guy behind the counter, and they soon became drinking buddies. Brad had taken an opening in sales, and as soon as another position became available, he called Victor.

As his wife, she feels she deserves to know more. "We've got a kid together for Christ's sake," she says to the screensaver; it's her favorite picture of them as a family. They were on a camping trip in the Forest Lakes area.

She can't stop thinking about how frightened she was last night. She's not sure if she is more irritated at him for the way he had looked at her or with herself for being frightened in the first place. She knows he is sorry, and that there is no way in heaven that he would ever hurt her or Shelby, but last night, for those few seconds, she wasn't sure that he was in complete control.

Her mind keeps going back to when she first met him. She had liked him a lot, but her parents had advised her to be smart when dating anyone while she was away at college, so she Googled his name and was surprised when she found nothing about him. He didn't even have a Facebook profile. Later, she remembers feeling relieved. He's only in his late twenties, she'd thought; maybe it's a good thing that there's nothing in his background. He was handsome and charming in a "country boy lost in the city kind of way." He had a crooked smile that made her melt every time he flashed it. He drank too much, and occasionally would do a line or two of coke, but that was as far as his dark side went, she'd thought. He held a steady job and could support himself. Later, she learned that his "occasional line or two" was more than she'd been led to believe, much more, but by then, she was more than okay with it because she was riding the rails right along with him.

She was a week from graduating from the Walter Cronkite School of Journalism at ASU and had a job lined up at a Phoenix TV station when she found out that she was pregnant. The two of them were having dinner at her and Angie's apartment when she told him. His reaction had flabbergasted her. At first, she thought that he'd almost smiled, but then he got an odd look on his face, and then, in the middle of dinner, he put down his fork, got up from the table, and turned toward the door.

"Victor!" she remembers crying out in disbelief.

He had turned at the door, flashed his crooked smile at her, and said, "I'm sorry. It's not what you think, but I'm going to need a day or two." Then he walked out the door.

When she tried calling, he didn't answer, nor did he return her calls. He didn't respond to her texts. He didn't answer the door at his apartment, and his car was gone.

She called Brad, and he said that Victor had taken some vacation time. He seemed surprised that she wasn't with him.

Her parents had driven in from San Diego, where they had been visiting friends the day before her graduation with a dual purpose. First, of course, was to see their baby girl graduate from college, and the other was to meet the fellow she'd been dating and spoke so highly of. She didn't have it in her heart to tell them she was pregnant and had been abandoned by her boyfriend the same week she was supposed to graduate from college, so when they asked about him, she told them a partial truth. She told them she hadn't seen him for almost a week and that she and Victor had broken up. Her mother hugged her while she cried, telling her it was okay, and that sometimes these things work themselves out. Her Dad offered his condolences and jokingly offered to find him and break his knees.

Lindsay laughed through her tears and said, "Maybe."

They all laughed at that, and then her father suggested she get cleaned up and he and her mother would take her and Angie to dinner. When they arrive at the restaurant, the waiter immediately escorted them to a table adorned with two dozen red roses and white rose petals spilling off onto the floor.

Victor was standing behind the chair at the head of the table and came around with his hand extended to her father. "Mr. Flack, it's a pleasure to finally meet you. I am Victor Powers."

Lindsay remembers watching in shock as her father and Victor shook hands. "Please son, call me Rod."

Victor then turned to her mother, took her hand, and snapped his heels together as he kissed it. "Mrs. Flack, it is indeed a privilege," he said before bowing his head to her.

Her mother had blushed before saying, "Cheryl, please."

"Cheryl, it is then, and now Rod, and Cheryl, if I may?"

While her mother was still gushing, her father had said, "By all means. Please do."

With that, Victor turned his full attention to Lindsay, who was standing, astonished, between her mother and Angie.

"Lindsay," he began, "I am so sorry for what you must have gone through this past week, but" he said, pulling his hand out of his suit pocket, "I wanted to do this right." Opening the ring box, dropping to one knee, and gazing into her face in one fluid motion, he said, "Lindsay, I have loved you since our first date. This past week, I have been talking with your parents to get their permission. I bought this ring over a month ago, and I have been waiting for the right time. I put a deposit on a rental house for us, and I've already started moving in. It's small, but the rent is fair, so if we play our money right, we should be able to come up with the down payment for our first house by the time the lease is up." Tears welled in her eyes and streamed down her cheeks as he spoke. "Will you please marry me?" he asked as he presented the ring.

At that moment, time, for her, stood still. There was no one else on the entire planet except for her and the man she would spend the rest of her life with. Tears were streaming harder as she choked out, "YES!" and gave him her hand to place the ring on. Applause erupted throughout the restaurant as Victor rose to embrace her.

Breaking their embrace, Lindsay reached back and slapped him across the face, then immediately hugged him again. "You asshole," she said, crying into his shoulder. "I love you so much."

She remembers her father laughing in the background, saying, "I told him she would do that," which led to an eruption of laughter from the onlookers in the restaurant.

Victor whispered to her that he'd needed a week to sever his ties from his lifestyle. When she looked up at him, he continued. "That part of my life is over. No more drugs, no more booze, just you and me, I promise, we are the team," he said and kissed her cheek.

She is relishing in the memory when her phone rings, snapping her back to reality. Roni's name and number flash across the screen on her phone. She answers on the second ring.

"Hey, Roni, what's up?"

"Are you ready for a leak from an unidentified source?"

"Absolutely," she says, grabbing a pen and notepad. "Hit me."

The call lasts a little over ten minutes, with Lindsay writing as fast as Roni is talking. "Did you get all of that?"

"I did. Thanks, Roni. Anything else?"

"Nope, that's it for now. I'll talk to you later."

Lindsay is about to hang up when a thought crosses her mind. "Hey, Roni?"

"Yeah, what's up?"

She hesitates for a moment. "I need a favor..."

39

Victor turns on the morning news in time to hear Angie's co-host, Ted Payne, the forty-something news anchor with a made-for-TV face, say, "In other breaking news, the two men accused of attempting to kidnap Kim Su Li last month at a Phillips Circle K were found beaten and stabbed to death in their cells this morning."

Turning his head to face another camera, he continues. "Lloyd Henderson and Tommy Poole were moved from protective custody last night to the Fourth Avenue jail where they were awaiting trial. Isabel Cruz is on the scene now. Isabel, what can you tell us about what has happened so far?"

Victor smiles to himself as he exits his office to get a bottle of Coke from the machine. He has met Isabel before and likes her. She's a Mexican National whose mother came to the US. when Isabel was a child. Her mother had gotten her Green Card after marrying her long-time American boyfriend, and they raised Isabel together.

Isabel had graduated high school locally, but soon after, joined the Navy. She got on with Channel 4 around the same time as Lindsay and is a hit with the Latino audience. Victor knows there will be nothing for her to report this early, if ever. Li Chen didn't get to his position by being sloppy.

He returns to his desk and opens his computer, intending to finish the quarterly reports when Lindsay's voice captures his full attention. It's not her voice that redirects his attention to the TV, so much, but what she says. He looks up and sees his wife, not in the studio, but in the Newsroom, following what he presumes to be a rolling camera.

"Is there a serial killer on the loose in Phillips? An unnamed source in the Phillips Police Department seems to think so. According to the source, several recent murders in the Valley of the Sun appear to be connected and could date back several years. The source tells me that the killer seems to have no pattern and leaves little to no evidence at the scenes of his grisly crimes. I will report more on this story as it progresses, Angie."

Lindsay is instantly replaced by Angie, who is now on the screen. "Thank you, Lindsay. We certainly look forward to hearing more on that interesting report," she says with too much enthusiasm in Victor's opinion, but he figures she is trying to help her friend out.

He knows that this is directed at him. It's the police's way of letting him know they are on his trail. He also knows that they know more than they told Lindsay.

If only they knew how close they are...

"Yeah, if only." Victor smiles.

Just then, his phone rings. He looks down to see Lindsay's face and name appear as he picks up. "Hey, babe! You were great!"

"You saw it then?" she asks, excitement filling her voice.

"I sure did."

"I was so nervous. Roni just called me about an hour ago, letting me know they wanted me to break the story."

"If you were, no one could tell. Seriously, babe, you did great! In fact, how about a family celebration night?"

"That sounds great, but do you mind if Ang comes with us? Roni is working late, and her car is back in the shop for another recall."

"Heh, genuine GM parts," Victor chuckles under his breath. "Of course, then we'll take her home after. Do you think Red Robin will be okay with her?"

40

Tuck is sitting at his kitchen table at six on Sunday morning going through the current case files and comparing them with the cold case files that Janice delivered late last week, trying to see if there are any similarities linking any of them. Having already been up for over an hour, he takes a sip from his coffee cup and grimaces... *cold.* "Jesus Christ," he mutters. As he gets up to refill his cup, his phone rings. "Hey, Roni, what's up?"

"Tuck, I need you to come over here right now!"

Hearing the distress in his partner's voice, he replies, "Whoa, calm down, what's going on? Are you okay?"

"No, I'm not fine! The mother fucker knows where I live, Tuck! I need you here right now!"

"Ten minutes," he says as he runs full tilt out the door of his apartment, down the stairs, and through the parking lot to his car. He does the ten-mile drive in eight minutes. Roni is outside taking pictures of the dew-covered grass with her phone as he parks his car in front of the house and comes up the walk. He sees a measuring tape lying on the dirt in the flower bed next to two prints made by what appear brand new Caterpillar boots size thirteen and a half. He crouches down for a better look.

"Look familiar?" she asks over his shoulder.

"What happened?" he inquires, standing up and turning to face her.

"What happened? The mother fucker knows where I live. That's what happened!" she shrieks at him.

"Where's Angie?"

"She's inside. She's a little shaken, but she's okay. Tuck, the fucker knows where we live. He was here!"

"Roni, I need you to calm down. We're going to go through it all and figure this out. Trust me, we will catch this son of a bitch, but to do that, I need you to be a cop and not a victim right now. Let's go inside and get a cup of coffee while you and Angie tell me everything that happened this morning. Then you and I are going to come back out here and read the scene. Do you understand?"

"He was at my house, Tuck," she sobs as she wraps her arms around him.

Tuck holds her and strokes her hair as she cries a moment longer. "I know hon, I know."

Inside, seated around the breakfast table, Tucker begins. "Okay, start from when you opened your eyes this morning and finish when I pulled up to your house."

Angie begins, "I... got up, used the bathroom, and came downstairs to make a pot of coffee. Roni was still asleep, but I knew she would be up soon, so I turned on the TV to have background noise while the coffee brewed. I was strolling through my Facebook when

I heard Roni moving around upstairs, so I poured her a cup, and we had our morning coffee together like we do every weekend morning."

"At this point, you hadn't been outside yet?"

"No, then we made breakfast and ate. We were just enjoying our morning together. We went to a nursery yesterday and were planning on planting some flowers in the flowerbed after breakfast."

"Okay, then what did you do?" he continues, prodding gently.

"I went to get the flowers from the garage, and Roni went out back to grab the shovel from the shed, and then we met at the front of the house. Roni was there when I got there, and she was just staring at the ground. When I asked her what she was looking at, she just told me not to move and ran back into the house. When she came back, she had her gun with her and began checking the perimeter of the house. Then she called you and started taking pictures of the ground. She kept saying 'The fucker knows where we live' over and over. I asked her whom she was talking about, and she told me the guy you are investigating."

"Okay, good. Roni, you got anything to add?"

"That's pretty close," she says, having shifted into work mode. "I ran inside, grabbed my weapon, and cleared the house. Once I swept the exterior, I called you. Then I noticed the footprints in the dew on the grass. I knew they wouldn't last, so I got pictures of them."

"Good thinking. Let's go read the scene."

Standing outside by the boot prints, Tuck turns and surveils the front of the house and yard. Something isn't clicking, but he's not able to put his finger on it yet. Nodding towards the front door, he says, "It'll be a good idea to get a doorbell camera and a few security cameras around the house."

"Way ahead of you," Roni replies, looking at her phone. "Amazon will deliver it by one this afternoon. It'll have four cameras, including one for the doorbell. I'll have it installed before dark."

A breeze picks up, adding to the chill in the late November morning, causing Tuck to wish he'd grabbed his jacket when he left his house. "Good. Okay, what do we know?"

"Based on the prints, he came from the east corner of the property, but why not come down the walk and leave no trace? We have an alarm, so we know he didn't try to break in, and this... this doesn't make sense, Tuck," she says, pointing at the boot prints.

He turns and looks at them, then up at the windowless side of the garage, back to the prints, and then to Roni when it suddenly clicks in his mind. "There's no way to break into the side of the garage, as you said, so why didn't he just come down the walk, so you'd never know he was here? Thinking out loud, he goes on. "It's because he's already done that. He knows you don't have cameras or a dog. Tuck looks at her solemnly and says, Roni, the son of a bitch wants you to know he was here."

For a half-second Roni's eyes widen, and her jaw goes slack in fear, but she quickly recovers. "I'm going to kill this cocksucker," is all she says as she turns and stalks to the front steps.

"Roni..."

"No, fuck this Tuck," she says, turning on the top step to face him. "The son of a bitch comes to MY HOUSE AND WANTS TO SCARE ME? FUCK THAT! HE'LL BE LUCKY IF I ONLY SHOOT HIM!"

"Roni," he says, approaching her on the step. We are doing this by the book. The first thing we're going to do is go inside, make a fresh pot of coffee, and calm down. Then we're going to call the lieutenant and get a forensics team over here and some black and whites to go door to door to check if any of your neighbors saw anything or have cameras that may have caught this guy." The look on Roni's face says she doesn't agree with him, but she nods in approval.

Once inside, Tuck gets on his phone and calls Lieutenant Ames as Angie hands him a fresh cup of coffee. As he paces around the great room. Roni fills Angie in on the details of what is going on. Visibly shaken by the turn of events she asks, "Are we in danger?"

"Probably not. Tuck and I both think he's just trying to scare us."

"Well, it fucking worked," she says un-nerved. "Wait until I get on the air tomorrow! I'm going to tell this bastard exactly what I think of him and his scare tactics."

"No, sweetie, no, you're not," Roni says, reaching across the corner of the table and taking her hand.

"Roni, if you think that we're just going to lie down and take this…"

Squeezing her hand tighter, to get her attention, Roni says, "Angie, this is a police investigation, and you will not go on the air and say anything that may jeopardize this investigation or your life. This guy is scary. He's a killer who shows no mercy and no compassion. He is not the kind of person you want to taunt."

"But he was here, at our home."

"I know," she says, looking into her lover's face, "and if my lieutenant doesn't pull me from the case, Tuck and I are going to find him and stop him."

"Wait, WHAT? Why would you be pulled from this case?" Angie's fear is being replaced by anger.

"Protocol," she says simply. "Not only am I one of the investigating detectives, but now I'm personally involved."

"Ames is on his way, and forensics will be right behind him," Tuck says, reentering the room.

"The lieutenant is coming?" Roni asks, somewhat surprised. "It's eight-thirty on a Sunday morning."

"Yep, and you're one of his. You couldn't keep him away from here with a shotgun."

Lieutenant Jonathon Ames parks his car behind Tucker's and, as though on a mission, walks up the walk. He glances down at the boot prints as he strides past them then looks up to the eaves for cameras. He takes the steps two at a time and rings the doorbell.

Angie answers. "You must be Lieutenant Ames," she says, holding the door for him. "I'm pleased to meet you. I'm Angie Keller," she says, extending her hand. "Please come in. Can I get you a cup of coffee?"

"The pleasure is mine, and yes, black, please."

She leads him to the breakfast table where Roni and Tuck are waiting. "Please have a seat while I get your coffee."

Ames sits down, eyes the two of them with concern, and immediately gets to work. "Novetti, you, okay?"

"I'm good Lieutenant. I was a little shaken up at first, but I'm okay now."

"We'll see," he says as Angie sets a mug of coffee in front of him and takes the fourth seat at the table. "Ms. Keller, how are you?"

"Angie please, and I'm doing all right all things considered," she says with a nervous laugh.

"Tucker," he says, still looking at Roni. "Am I up to date on your investigation?"

"Yeah Boss. You know everything we do."

"Don't bullshit me, Tucker," he says, turning and giving his full attention to Tuck. "We've got a lot to go over before forensics gets here, and we don't have a lot of time. I'm going to be in front of the Chief tomorrow morning, and I need to know if I'm up to date."

"I put the report in your door when we left Friday night."

"Is the part about how a cub reporter with less than six months of experience already has an 'Unidentified Police Source' in it?"

"Yes sir, it is," Tuck says, holding his gaze.

Ames looks at Tuck a moment longer and says, "Okay, you took a Hell of a chance Tuck, but it may pay off. I think we must be getting close." Turning his attention back to Roni, he says, "Okay, Novetti, take me through this morning." He watches her intently as she tells him what happened. Reading her face, and listening to her voice, he silently debates whether to pull her from the case. If he follows protocol and pulls her, he knows it will set the investigation back by at least a month. If he keeps her on, he needs to know she can still be at one hundred percent from here on out.

She's a target now, and though he knows she knows it, he also knows that she can't get personal about it. "Any chance you have cameras set up that I didn't see?"

Roni shakes her head. "Should be here by one, and we'll have them in by dark."

Ames nods, "Gotta love Amazon."

They hear the forensics van pull up when Tuck's phone rings. "What's up, Katie?" He pauses a moment. "No problem, we'll be right there."

Ames changes his focus from Roni and looks at Tuck expectantly.

"They need us to move our cars," Tuck says, getting up from his chair, and walking toward the door with Ames following.

Tuck is waiting at the bottom of the steps. "Are you going to pull her?" he asks directly.

"What are your thoughts?"

"She was a little shaken up at first, but that's to be expected. She recovered well. I think she'll be fine."

Ames looks at him a moment longer. "Everything tells me to pull her."

"I know, Lieutenant, but to pull her now means I'll have to catch someone else up, and as you said, we must be close, closer than we think. Besides, he already knows where she lives. He's not going to just drop off the planet if she's off the case."

He thinks it over for a minute. "Okay, I've got to talk to the Chief tomorrow. I'll see what I can do." They move their cars so the forensics team can park and get to work.

Once they are back inside Ames says, "Novetti, until I talk to the Chief tomorrow, you're off the case."

"BUT LIEUTENANT!"

"I said until I talk to the Chief, and if I can get it by him, you may be back on, but only if you follow MY DIRECTION," he says, leaving no room for argument. "But for now, I'd like you and Angie to leave the premises."

"Bullshit, I'm not going anywhere! The son of a bitch isn't going to force me from my house!"

"Novetti, the forensics team is thirty seconds from walking in the door to do their thing. You will be in the way, and you know it. It's not up for discussion. I said I'd talk to the Chief, and I will, but until then, BYE! Tucker, get some black and whites to go door to door and get one of the IT geeks here by one o'clock to install the camera system. If it needs an upgrade, have them do it." The forensics team comes in as he says to Tuck, "I'm going back to my office. You've got the ball. Novetti, do you think you need a detail?"

"You're kidding right?"

"Not at all."

"You do realize I am a police officer, right?"

Ames looks at her for a long moment. "All right, no detail for now. Go pack a bag. Go somewhere, anywhere, but be gone in ten minutes."

Roni is about to argue when Angie grabs her hand and leads her upstairs. "Come on." Reluctantly, Roni allows herself to be led away.

In their bedroom, Angie asks, "You don't think Lindsay is in any danger, do you?"

Roni opens the lockbox in the closet, retrieves a pistol, puts it in her overnight bag along with her service weapon, and says, "Probably not. She's not involved in the investigation, and she only knows what Tuck and I feed her, so she's not the threat, but let's go talk to her and Victor, just in case."

"I've already called her. They're expecting us. She said she'd have Victor make Bloody Marys."

Roni reaches up and brushes Angie's cheek with the backs of her fingers. The realization of the situation dawns on her fully. "What about Tuck?" Angie asks, her anger rising again. "Will the forensics team head to his place when they're done fucking up our house? Did you forget we are hosting Thanksgiving in five days?"

Roni takes her hand and sits her down on the bed. "Sweetie, Tuck lives in a third-floor apartment in the middle of a gated complex. I doubt this guy went there. Even if he did, we'd never know it. Forensics is going to make a hell of a mess. They'll attempt to clean it up, as best they can, because of who we are, but we're probably going to have to cancel Thanksgiving here."

The disappointment at the thought of canceling their dinner causes her anger to rise even higher. "So how in the fuck did he find out where we live?"

"I don't know yet," Roni says in a calm voice, "but I need you to trust me when I tell you that we're going to find out. There are a lot of questions that don't make sense right now, but Tuck and I are very good at what we do. We're going to figure it out. For now, though, let's go have a Bloody Mary."

Once downstairs, Roni tells Angie that she needs to talk with Tuck for a minute and asks her to start the car. The forensics team is all over the outside of the house as Tuck finishes instructing the senior uniformed officer on the parameters for the door-to-door. "Do you think he's going to pull me?"

"Fifty-fifty," he says. "That will be up to the chief, but he'll put up a helluva fight. We will just have to wait and see. Now get out of here! I'll let you know if we find anything."

She grabs his forearm. "Thanks for everything," she says, giving him a gentle squeeze.

"GO!" he tells her, pointing to the door and winking at her.

41

"Of course," Lindsay says into her phone. "I'll have Victor make Bloody Marys. See you when you get here." She walks down the hallway, looking for Victor. She sees him through the living room window in the backyard with Shelby. He's picking up dog poop. She is following him around, acting like a little girl with her daddy. She watches them enjoying each other's company for a while.

Victor has said nothing about finding a counselor, but she has noticed a change in his demeanor lately. He's still not sleeping well, if at all, and he still runs at night, but he seems to be calmer, and less stressed. Roni had called her back the day after she'd asked her to see what she could find out about his childhood, but apparently, the records were sealed by the court. She said she knew a few people, and she'd make a few more calls, but without a court order, there wasn't much else she could do.

She opens the back door. "Sweetie," she calls. "Angie and Roni are on their way over. Would you make a pitcher of Bloody Marys please?"

Victor looks over at his wife in the doorway with a quizzical look and notices the slight shake of her head, indicating that she didn't want to say anything else in front of Shelby. Taking her cue, he answers, "Yeah, let me finish this up, and I'll get right on it."

"Thank you," she says and turns back inside.

Victor comes inside ten minutes later and finds Lindsay preparing the guest room. "What's up?" he asks.

She tells him about Angie's call and finishes by saying, "They're going to need a place to stay for a night or two."

Inwardly, Victor smiles.

"What?" Lindsay asks.

"Wha... What?" Victor says, turning away from his inner thoughts.

She looks at him with concern. "You just had a faraway look on your face, like you were somewhere else for a minute."

"Eh, did I?" is all he says before smiling at her and walking towards the kitchen.

"Victor?"

"Yeah babe?" he replies, turning back to his wife with a crooked smile still on his face.

She approaches him, tugs on the front of his t-shirt with two fingers, looks up into his face her concern still showing, and asks, "Are you okay?"

"Yeah, why?" He looks at her. His expression is now puzzled.

"I don't know. I'm just trying to get a read on you, and I'm having a hard time. You just don't seem like yourself lately."

Things just keep getting better, almost like someone had a plan. "What are you talking about? What could be better than my wife's best friend and her fiancé coming to spend a few days with us?" he says, trying to sound overly sarcastic.

"Uh-huh," she replies with skepticism still trying to read him as Shelby comes into the house after taking the dog poop bag to the trash bin.

"Can I go over to Abby's now?" she asks.

"That's a great idea baby," Lindsay says, turning away from Victor. "Angie and Roni are coming over, and we have some adult stuff to talk about."

"Roni is coming over?" Shelby's whole being brightens. She's been enthralled with Roni ever since she found out that Roni is a police detective.

"Yes, but as I said, we have some adult stuff to talk about."

"Can I wait till they get here before I go to Abby's house?"

Looking into her daughter's excited face, Lindsay says, "Sure Honey. That will be fine. They're going to be here for a couple of days, so don't wear them out as soon as they get here, okay?"

"A couple of days?" she asks, overjoyed as if it were more than her six-year-old mind could fathom.

"Yeah, there's some work being done at their house, and they need somewhere to stay."

"THAT'S GREAT!" she shrieks.

"Now, why don't you hop in the shower before they get here? You smell like dog poop," she says, wrinkling her nose.

"Okay Mommy," she says, turning down the hall and into the bathroom.

"Don't forget your towel!" Lindsay calls.

An exaggerated sigh comes from the bathroom as the door opens and Shelby stomps out, "I won't!" she says as she opens the linen closet.

Lindsay turns back to the kitchen as Victor comes in from the garage after putting the pitcher in the refrigerator to chill while they wait for their guests. "I'm going to take a shower as well. I probably smell a lot like dog poop myself."

"Listen," she says. "I appreciate your understanding here. I know it's a lot."

"Don't mention it, babe," he says, flashing the crooked smile she has always loved. "It's just life, and life sometimes gets complicated. We'll just do what we need to and deal with it."

"Did your counselor give you that little tidbit of advice?" she asks with her smirk.

"Nope... came up with that one all on my own," he says as he walks away from her toward their bedroom.

Complicated, that's putting it mildly. I can't think of anyone else whose best friend is coming to spend a couple of days because a forensics team is currently turning their house upside down because a serial killer, whom her fiancé is investigating, has somehow figured out where they live. Nope, the most normal thing in the world.

Shelby comes out of the bathroom with a towel wrapped around her chest, catches her mother's eye, and smiles. "Will you comb my hair for me, Mommy?"

"Of course, sweetie. Did you get all the shampoo out?"

"Yep!" Shelby says proudly.

"All right, go get dressed, and I'll brush your hair when you're done."

"Okay."

Lindsay smiles after her daughter, realizing how fast she is growing up and how well she has adjusted to life's changes over the last several months.

Ten minutes later, Victor and Shelby come down the hallway together, giggling like schoolgirls.

"What's so funny?"

"Dad just told me a joke," Shelby says.

"He did? Well, let's hear it."

"If April showers bring May flowers, what do May flowers bring?"

"I don't know. What?"

Giggling, Shelby shrieks, "PILGRIMS! Do you get it?"

Lindsay can't help but crack up at the joke. "Yes sweetie, I get it," she says as she looks up at Victor, who is grinning from ear to ear. "New Dad Joke page on Facebook?"

"You know it, baby. Stick around, I'll be here all night. I've got a ton of 'em."

She takes the brush from Shelby's hand and starts brushing her hair. Just then, the doorbell rings and Kona starts barking and wagging his tail. Victor tells Lindsay he'll get it as he walks towards the front door. As expected, he opens it to find Angie and Roni standing on the doorstep, each with a suitcase at their feet. "Ladies, please come in," he says. hugging Angie, then Roni. "Let me take your bags to your room."

"Thank you, Victor," they say in unison.

"Rough morning, huh?" he says, following them inside.

"RONI! ANGIE!" Shelby screams as they cross the threshold.

"SHELBY!" They both shout as they crouch down and open their arms to the little girl running towards their embrace.

Victor brushes past the trio, overnight bags in tow, and heads to the guest room while Shelby tells them how excited she is that they will be staying for a few days.

When he emerges, Shelby, Angie, and Roni are seated around the kitchen table and Lindsay is pouring glasses of Bloody Marys from the pitcher. Shelby has her best "big girl" face on and is carrying on, for a girl her age, a rather mature conversation with their guests. "Mommy told me that there is some work being done at your house, and that is why you will be staying with us."

Angie's smile remains while her eyes shift from Shelby to Lindsay, who gives a slight nod to her friend. "That's right, sweetie. Thank you so much for letting us stay with you."

"Mommy says it's what you do for friends..."

Hesitation hangs in the air as she attempts to drum her fingers on the table. "Is there something else?" Roni asks.

"Well... kinda."

"What is it, sweetie?" Roni encourages.

With a hopeful face and almost a conspiratorial whisper, she asks, "Can I tell people you're here?"

Roni reaches across the corner of the table, puts her hand on Shelby's forearm, and glances around the room as if looking for anyone listening. "We'd rather you not." Seeing the immediate look of disappointment on the little girl's face, she continues in the same secretive tone. "You see, I'm working undercover, and no one is supposed to know where I am right now, so it's really important that you not tell anyone, okay?"

Shelby's eyes get wide, and her hands cover her mouth as she takes in the enormity of the secret bestowed on her. "I won't tell, promise," she says as she crosses her heart with her finger.

"But there is something that you can tell if you want," Angie interjects.

Shelby turns from Roni and focuses her full attention on Angie. "What?" she asks expectantly.

"Well, have your mommy and daddy told you that Roni and I are getting married in a couple of months?"

"Yeah...?" she says, unsure of where this is going.

"Well, your mommy is going to stand up and be our witness, and your daddy is going to officiate."

"What's that mean?"

"Witness or officiate?"

"Both."

"Well, to witness something means that you saw it happen, and your mom is going to sign her name on our license saying that she saw it happen."

"Oh, and the other one?"

Thinking for a second before answering, Angie asks, "Have you ever seen a wedding on TV?"

"Yeah..."

"Well, the minister, or priest, or in our case, your daddy is the officiant. They are the ones who perform the ceremony."

"Oh," she says. It takes a minute to sink in, and when the gravity of what she has been told hits her, she exclaims, "Ooooh!" and looks over at her dad with renewed awe. "You can do that?"

"You betcha, pumpkin," he says, leaning down and kissing the top of her head, then adding, "Your Daddy can do anything."

"So," Angie says, recapturing Shelby's attention. "We'd like to ask you to do the most important job of all."

Still wide-eyed, Shelby squeals, "What is it?"

"We'd like you to be the flower girl."

Somewhere between excited and anxious Shelby asks, "Wha... what do I have to do?"

Lindsay brings over their drinks and a glass of orange juice for Shelby and says, "The flower girl is one of the most important jobs in a wedding. You'll have to get a new dress and some new shoes, so we'll have a girl's day to go shopping and get manis and pedis, and then, on the day of the wedding, you will hold their bouquets when they exchange their promises to each other."

"Up in front of EVERYBODY?" her excitement quickly overcame her anxiety. "I can't wait to tell Abby! Mommy, can I go over to her house now?"

"Sure sweetie," Lindsay says, smiling. "Victor, would you walk her over, please?"

"Sure, come on Shelby," he says, rising from the barstool.

"Um, Daddy... can Roni take me over?"

"Uh, it's okay with me if she wants to," he says, taken a bit off guard as he and Shelby look at her expectantly.

Roni, feeling flattered, chuckles and says, "How can I say no to that face? Come on, kiddo." Standing from the table, she takes Shelby's hand.

After they walk out the door, Victor looks at Angie and says, "She's good with kids, isn't she?"

"Yeah, she is," she replies, taking a sip of her drink. "Oh Victor, these are very good!"

"Thank you," he says, taking a sip of his own.

You need to be sober today.

I'm fine, back off!

They're both on edge and hyper-alert after your visit last night.

I've got it under control.

Do you?

I'm going to keep their drinks poured and nurse mine. I know what's at stake.

No slip-ups.

This is all going according to plan. Relax.

42

Lindsay looks across the table at Angie and asks, "How are you holding up?"

"Oh, I was shaken up at first, but you know me, Linds. I'll be fine. I'm more pissed right now, thinking they may take Roni off the case because now she's more than an investigating officer. The cocksucker has made it personal. Oh, and they're going to put a detail on me."

"A detail?"

"Yeah, can you believe it? I'll have a uniformed police officer as a shadow."

"Wow!" Victor chimes in. "Did they say anything about Lindsay? Are we in any danger?" Kona lifts his head and lets out a low woof.

"We don't think so," Roni answers as she re-enters through the garage door and takes her place at the table. "Lindsay only knows what we feed her, and this guy is smart enough to know that."

"How do you know?" he asks with what he hopes is an appropriate amount of irritation.

"He's been around a long time," she says, taking a long pull from her glass. "Damn, these are good."

Victor gets up from his chair and refills her glass. "Anyone else?" Lindsay and Angie both hold out their glasses to him.

"How can you be certain, though?" he inquires. "How can you be sure that he will not come after her or Shelby or even me? Do I need to buy a gun and take some classes?"

"Victor, relax. We know this because we've been investigating him for close to six months, and him coming to our house," she says, reaching over to take Angie's hand, "tells us we're getting close. He's not interested in you or your family. He didn't get into our house or hurt either of us. There are many ways he could have watched our house, unnoticed, and he probably has, to be completely honest. He wanted us to know that he was there. He wanted to scare us."

"Well, it's working on me," he says. "What do you know about him?"

"We know that he's a hunter, he's cautious, and he's patient. He probably follows a set of rules unknown to anyone but him."

"Rules? What do you mean by rules?"

"He probably doesn't kill anyone he knows; his victims are, more than likely, random people whom he encounters throughout his day."

"What sets him off?"

"Who knows, maybe something that's said, a smile, a laugh, maybe somebody cut him off in traffic. Hell, maybe someone reminds him of his mother, that part, we just don't know."

"We do know that he doesn't follow any patterns when it comes to his victims. He kills everybody: men, women, young, old, black, white, Hispanic… doesn't matter. He's an equal-opportunity killer except when it comes to kids; he doesn't kill kids. They would be too high a profile for him. He likes to lie low and blend in. He also doesn't rape or molest his victims, so we don't believe his crimes are sexually motivated."

"Also, his method of killing follows no pattern," she continues, taking another drink from her glass. "The weapons he uses are common tools that can be purchased anywhere without raising suspicion. He's used hammers, screwdrivers, ice picks, rope, tire irons, and knives. We think he buys the tools, probably pays with cash, scrubs them in bleach, and never touches them with his bare hands again. We believe he has a plan when he kills but is adaptable because sometimes shit happens. Once the hunt starts, he's committed. He leaves nothing at the scene except the victims and whatever he kills them with. Not a hair, a fingerprint, clothing fibers, or the smallest trace of DNA is ever left. Nothing, that is, except for prints from size thirteen and a half Caterpillar work boots that have no wear pattern. He probably wears Caterpillar boots because they're inexpensive, and he can buy them anywhere. He uses hairspray and sprays it all over himself and his clothes, and he most likely wears a hairnet, which is why there are never any hair strands or clothes fibers at the scenes. From what we can tell, and this is more of a hunch, he doesn't keep any trophies, and he gets rid of anything he wears and uses during the murders. He's too smart to keep any evidence. No, he's there for the kill. Nothing more."

"Do you believe this?" Victor asks. "This sounds like an episode of Forensic Files. I mean, if he's that smart, how do you know he's not wearing bigger boots with thick socks or that he doesn't have a shrine in his house full of pictures of his victims, or potential victims for that matter? Hell, Lindsay is always on TV, and her pictures are all over Channel 4's web page. It wouldn't be hard to download and print as many as he wants!"

Shut up, you idiot!

"I can see where you might think that, but this guy's been around too long. Tuck and I may be able to tie him to some unsolved murders that go back as far as twelve years," she says, fishing the pickle spear from her glass and crunching down on it, "which tells us he's slipping. He's getting sloppy."

Victor's attention is fully focused on Roni as he tries to figure out how to get her to elaborate. Then Lindsay, unwittingly, comes to his rescue as he once again retrieves the pitcher and refills their glasses. "Sloppy how?"

Roni focuses on her and can almost see the tape recorder in Lindsay's head turn on. "Don't go all reporter on me," she says with a semi-smile, "anything said here, stays here. This is off the record and between friends. I'm just trying to ease your mind and calm you down. The danger to you is minimal, Lindsay. Victor, for you it's almost nonexistent. Shelby has a better chance of getting hit by a bus than being on this guy's radar, but it never hurts to be safe. Do you have a gun in the house?"

"Yeah, I've got an old shotgun that I used for dove hunting on top of the closet."

"Is it in good condition?"

Victor looks at her like she has just kicked his dog. "Of course it is."

"What is it?"

"It's a Winchester model 24, double-barrel, twenty gauge."

"Side-by-side or over-under?"

"Side-by-side."

"Perfect for home protection," she says. "What's in it?"

"Right now? Nothing. It's empty, but I've got a box of birdshot shells."

"Okay, you might want to consider getting a box of slugs, a box of buckshot, and load the slug in the left barrel."

"Lindsay, how about you?"

"I... I don't have a gun. I've never even shot one."

"Would you like to?"

"I... uh... sure? Right now?"

Roni laughs at this. "No, sweetie. We're drinking, and guns and booze never mix, but if you'd like, we can go to a range this week, and I'll teach you."

"Do you think it's necessary?"

"In this instance, not particularly, but it might not be a bad idea."

"But I don't have a gun."

Undeterred, Roni replies, "Well, you have a couple of options. You can rent one from the range, and after you figure out what you like, you can buy it, or you can use one of mine until you buy one."

"Can we go tomorrow? Lindsay asks with piqued interest."

"Of course," she says, draining her glass again, "but I am going to insist that on top of what you learn from me, you take a CCW course."

"Arizona is an open-carry state, though," Victor says as he gets up and notices that the pitcher is empty.

"Yes, it is, but when it comes to firearms, there is no such thing as having too much training or being too safe. There's a lot to learn."

"I suppose so," he says, hoping to sound lighter than he feels right now. "Ladies, we're out. Should I make another?"

Angie speaks up, crunching on her pickle spear. "Victor, those were the best Bloody Marys I've ever had, but if I drink anymore, I see a bad case of heartburn in my future." The ladies agree all around.

"All right then, no offense taken," he says with a laugh. "What else can I get you? Mimosa perhaps?"

Angie's eyes brighten at the thought, and she quickly accepts, "Roni... babe?"

"Yes please," Lindsay says with a slight slur.

Roni thinks about it a moment longer, "Eh, what the hell, I'm in."

Victor makes three mimosas and suggests that they move to the back patio. "It's not quite pool weather, but we can light the fire table if we need to."

Once they are all comfortable on the patio, Roni resumes where she left off, "As I was saying, CCW classes are sponsored by the NRA, and are packed full of information. They focus on safety and the law. It's a good course and good knowledge to have."

"You've convinced me," Lindsay says. "I'm excited to go try it out."

"Works out great, since it doesn't look like I'll be going to work tomorrow anyway," says Roni.

"Listen, we need to lighten this up a bit," Angie interjects. "Roni and I were talking on the way over here — well actually, it was about the time we were getting kicked out of our house, but anyway," Angie begins—

"Ang..." Roni interrupts. "Now is probably not the time."

"Oh bullshit," she retorts, her temper flaring. "It's ruined, anyway. What's the worst that could happen? They say no?"

Roni shrugs slightly, purses her lips, and with a slight tilt of her head, turns her hands up in a half surrender gesture. This exchange has both Victor and Lindsay's full attention.

"What? What's going on?" Lindsay asks, the smile leaving her face as she looks at the group solemnly.

"Lindsay, Victor, I know that over the last couple of weeks, and especially after today, you will have every right to say no, but we have another favor to ask, and it's a big one."

"Well," Lindsay says, "you can't leave us hanging now. Let's hear it."

"Well, here's the thing," Angie says, losing confidence. "Thanksgiving is going to have to be canceled. The forensics team won't be done until tomorrow sometime, and the house will be such a mess that we won't be able to get it cleaned in time for Thursday."

"So you want us to have it here?" Lindsay asks, looking past Angie at Victor, who is already nodding.

"Oh, Lindsay, would you, please? It wouldn't even be a big deal except that we were planning on telling everyone about the wedding."

"We'd love to," Lindsay exclaims. "We'll do anything we can to help you," she says as she steps inside in search of snacks.

Victor interjects, "So, how many people are we talking about?"

"Thirty to thirty-five." Victor visibly gulps, and his eyes widen at her words.

Angie laughs and says, "Don't worry, Victor, we're having it catered. We wouldn't dream of putting you out that much," she says as Lindsay brings out a plate of chips and salsa.

"I told you they were having it catered, sweetie."

"Yeah, but I guess I didn't realize it was a service for thirty-five people."

"So it's settled then?" exclaims Lindsay.

Victor takes a deep breath. "Yep, I guess it is."

"Thank you so much, guys! This means the world to us. I'll call the caterers tomorrow and change the address."

"Yes, thank you so very much," Roni adds with a faraway look.

"Oh, I know that look," Angie says. "Something is bubbling on the back burner." She places her hand gently on Roni's arm. "Sweetie, stop thinking about work. We're with our friends; besides, you know they're probably going to pull you from the case."

At that, Roni blinks her attention back to the conversation. "I'm sorry," she says, glancing over at Victor. "I almost had something there for a minute, and then it was gone," she laughs. "I must need another drink."

Victor gets up and takes her glass. "Anyone else?" he asks, meeting and holding Roni's look.

"Not right now, thanks," Angie says.

"Yeah, I need to slow down a bit too," says Lindsay.

Victor takes Roni's and his glass inside for refills.

What the Hell are you doing?

"Back off. I know what I'm doing."

You're taunting her. Why not just confess and get it over with?

Victor smiles as he pours champagne into her glass and tops it off with orange juice.

"Don't tempt me..."

43

The next day, Victor arrives home from work to find Lindsay, Roni, and Shelby sitting on the back patio talking excitedly. Angie must not be off work yet. He turns back to the garage and grabs a beer from the fridge, opens it, and takes a long pull from the bottle before returning and joining them.

"DADDY!" Shelby screams, hopping from her seat and running into his open arms.

"Hey pumpkin, how was your day?" he asks, picking her up and hugging her, then setting her down with a kiss on the cheek.

"I went to the shooting range with Mommy and Roni!"

"You did?" he asks, looking at Lindsay with raised eyebrows before leaning in to kiss her lips.

"Yeah, Roni says that you're never too young to learn gun safety."

"She does, does she?" he says, shifting his gaze to Roni now with the same raised eyebrows. To which Roni tilts her head and bats her eyelashes in an obvious vain attempt at innocence.

"Yeah, I do."

"What did you think?" he asks, not wanting to take away from her enthusiasm.

"It was very loud."

"I bet. Did you have earmuffs on?"

"Yeah, but it was still loud."

"Did you shoot anything?"

After a slight hesitation Shelby replies, "No, I just watched, but Roni says when I get just a bit older, and if I pay attention, she'll show me how, if it's okay with you and Mommy. Please, Daddy! Can I please?"

Glancing at Roni, who is looking on with approval, he says, "We'll see, baby when the time comes."

"What did you think?" he asks, shifting his attention to Lindsay.

"Oh, my God! I was so nervous at first. I suppose that's to be expected, but I had a great time, and I learned a lot. Roni is a good teacher. She's very patient," she says, laughing in Roni's direction.

Shelby, at some point, moves over beside Roni, who wraps an arm around her. "Well, I will say, I had some pretty apt pupils," she says, smiling at the compliment.

"Tell me more. What exactly did you learn?"

Roni picks up on the edge in his voice. "Victor, are you okay with this?"

Glaring at her, but immediately catching himself, he says, "Can we speak inside for a few minutes, please?"

Caught a bit off guard, Roni says, "Sure." and gets up from her chair and walks past him to the kitchen.

Directly behind her, he picks up where she left off. "Am I okay with what? Taking my wife and daughter to a shooting range? Yeah, I'm just fine!"

"Victor, I am a certified instructor. It was very safe. Lindsay now knows the basics of defending herself with a firearm. I taught her about sight alignment, sight picture, and when and how to draw and aim her weapon. I showed her how to get into a tactical firing stance, and how to control her breathing and trigger control."

"You said yourself that you don't think she's in any real danger. Do you think she needs to carry a gun?"

"If you ask me, I think every law-abiding citizen should carry a gun if they have the correct training."

"But again, you said that you didn't think that she was in any danger from this guy."

"I still think that, but let's be realistic. This guy isn't the only weirdo out there, Victor. Lindsay is a woman with a made-for-TV face. She has a bubbly personality, both on and off-air, which makes her approachable. She drives, alone, to downtown Phoenix at two or three o'clock in the morning, and she has a growing fanbase. While ninety-eight percent of that fanbase are probably good and respectable people, there's always that other two percent that may have ill intentions, so another layer of protection is not a bad thing."

"The lot at the station is gated and patrolled by security," he argues, though he knows his lack of conviction is showing.

"Yeah, it is," Roni continues, as if she doesn't hear it, "but what if she gets a flat tire, or gets approached while she's Christmas shopping with Shelby? Wouldn't you rather her be able to defend herself if needed?"

"Yeah, I guess I would," he says, conceding.

"Victor, you, and I both know that Lindsay isn't going to brandish her weapon unless necessary. It's for defensive measures only. She has already signed up for a CCW course next week, at Bass Pro Shops, to further her training."

"Do you know the instructor?" he asks.

"Yes, I do. His name is Marty Packard, and he's a retired Marine Master Gunnery Sergeant. He stresses safety, responsibility, and the law. I've sat in on a few of his classes and he's very good."

"All right," he says, you've convinced me. What do we need to do to get her a weapon, and what kind do we get?"

"Well, I'm going to suggest she get a Beretta M9 9mm. It's what she shot today, and she likes it. It fits her hand like it was made for it, and for a beginner, she's good with it."

"Okay, so I can just go to Bass Pro Shops and buy it?"

"Kinda, can you guys get tomorrow afternoon off?"

"Lindsay is already, but I can't. I've got afternoon meetings all week. Plus, my boss will be in town the first week of December, so I've got to prep for that as well."

"Okay, the next afternoon you have off together, go see Marty. He usually works Monday thru Friday. His hours vary, but he's usually there in the afternoon. I let him know you will be stopping in at some point so that he'll be expecting you."

"All right..."

"Hey, you okay now?"

"Yeah, I am. Thanks, Roni. I appreciate it. If you'll excuse me, I need to use the bathroom."

The Demons are surprisingly quiet, Victor notices while washing his hands. He expected them to haunt his sleep last night, or at the very least, interrupt his day today, but they haven't said a word. "I'm not sure how I feel about this," he says to the smiling reflection as he dries his hands.

As Victor crosses through the empty kitchen, Roni's phone rings on the counter. Tuck's name and number appear on the screen. Memorizing the number, he picks it up, takes it to the patio out back, and hands it to Roni. She thanks him and immediately answers, "Hey Tuck," she says, getting up and walking back inside.

"Are you sure that you're okay with all this, babe?" Lindsay asks.

"Yeah, I just want you to be safe. I know that the gun thing was brought up yesterday, but I guess I thought it was drunk talk. I didn't realize that it had been decided. I was just caught off guard, and we all know how much I love that," he smirks.

"She didn't push me into it. It was all me. I started asking her questions this morning, and she answered them. She suggested we go to the range in the afternoon, so she could show me. I said no because I needed to get Shelby, but she said we could pick her up on the way. She didn't seem to think it was a big deal, so I didn't. She is very good with her, and Shelby adores her."

"Yeah, I know she does," he says. "How about you? Are you okay with all of this? Carrying a gun and all?"

"Well, I've never been against it. I just never thought I would."

"Yeah, me too..."

Roni opens the door and rejoins them on the patio with drinks in hand.

Victor looks from his wife to their guest and asks, "Well, what's the good word? Are we celebrating?"

"In a sense. The chief left it up to my lieutenant whether to pull me from the case, and Tuck went to bat for me, so against his better judgment, he agreed to let me stay on."

"Well, here's to that!" Lindsay says with a smile, raising her glass. "What did they find at your house?"

"At the house? Nothing except the boot prints. It seems he just wanted to say hello."

"I feel a but coming on," Victor says.

Roni's face breaks into a big smile as she says, "One of our neighbors has security cameras. We've got him on video."

That's just fucking great!

Oh, there you are.

Is this a joke to you?

Relax, it's under control.

They've got us on video.

We took precautions, relax!

Are you trying to get caught? Trying to go to jail?

No, I'm not! You know I followed the rules.

Fucking with a police officer who's investigating us isn't following the rules.

I parked over half a mile away and walked in. I was disguised with a beard, glasses, and a hat. Hell, I even put a pillow under my jacket so they wouldn't get an accurate description of me just for this type of situation. Relax.

You'd better hope...

I said relax. We're not going to get caught.

He rejoins the women on the patio, still deep in thought. Lindsay's voice snaps him back into the conversation happening on the patio. "Victor? Where did you go, sweetie?"

"Wha...? I'm sorry. I must have gone off with Captain Kirk there for a minute," he jokes.

Roni looks from Victor to Lindsay with unspoken questions all over her face.

"It's what he says when he spaces out for a minute or two," Lindsay says.

"Yeah, sorry about that. It's one of my loveable quirks," he says, laughing it off.

Kona lets out a bark from inside as Angie enters the garage with her phone to her ear.

Glancing around the patio, she says, "Give me one second please," and mutes the call. "The caterers want to start setting up on Wednesday evening around four. Is that all right?"

Lindsay and Victor look at each other and shrug.

Angie goes back to her call. "Yes, that will be fine, and you'll be here at eleven on Thursday to set up for dinner service at two? Oh, I see. No, four should be just fine. Of course, I understand, and that's dinner service for forty, correct? Great, can you humor me, and go over our menu one more time just so I know we are on the same page? And what address do you have? Perfect! We will see you Wednesday at four, then." She hangs up and says, "Okay, we're all set for Thanksgiving! Again, thank you both so much." She leans in and kisses Roni and hugs everyone else before going back inside to pour herself a glass of wine. When she returns, she asks the group, "How was everyone's day?"

44

Tuesday morning, Tuck walks into the squad room at his normal time to find Roni at her desk, going through the case file. "Hey, you're here early."

"Yeah, take a look at these," she says, handing him a stack of pictures.

Tuck takes the stack from her hand and flips through them quickly. "Yeah, so?"

"What do you see?"

"What do you mean?" he says irritably. "I see the same thing you see, boot prints from size thirteen and a half Caterpillar work boots."

"Look harder."

"Roni, what am I looking for?"

"Just hold on a second," she says, looking at the screen on her computer. "Here." she says, turning the screen so that he can get a better view.

"Okay, a different set of boot prints? Is there something you're seeing that I'm not?"

"The first set is the picture from my house. The second and third are images I found on Google. Pay particular attention to the toe."

Then he sees it. The toe in the print from Roni's flower bed is slightly raised as if the weight distribution were different from the similar picture on the internet. "Okay, I see the raised toe. So what?"

"Now look at these," she says as she clicks the mouse, and the pictures on the screen are placed next to the crime scene photos of the carpet in Riley Duncan's apartment and the prints left in the closet at Lauren and Ash's house. The same raised toe is barely noticeable on the carpet, but once seen, it is clear.

"Roni, I see what you're seeing now, but I don't see the significance. Beat cops, the military, hell, anyone that stands in one place over long periods will shift their weight on their feet to keep them from falling asleep."

"Now look at this," she says, clicking the mouse again. Photos of the patio from Lauren and Ash's house pop up on the screen. In these photos, the toe in the prints is barely notable.

This gets Tuck's attention, but he stays silent about it for the moment. "Where are you with this?" he asks, looking up from the screen. "Why are you paying so much attention to the boots?"

"Something Victor said the other day. He was concerned for Lindsay's safety, after what happened at my house, and I was trying to calm their nerves about it. I briefly went over what we know, and where we are in the investigation." Tuck raises an eyebrow. Her look turns to an icy glare. "No Tuck, I didn't divulge anything. I didn't say anything more than what we've already told Lindsay."

"Relax Defense," he says dismissively. "What did he say?"

"He said it sounds like an episode of Forensic Files and started asking all kinds of questions about how we know this or that, and then he asked how we could be sure that he wears a size thirteen and a half boot. That maybe our guy is wearing extra thick socks and bigger boots to throw us off. I heard him say it, but it didn't register at first. It kinda went to the back burner if you know what I mean."

"I do," he says. "When did it boil over for you?"

"Yesterday at the range."

"Anything in particular?"

"No, not really... just kinda had a flashback of the conversation while I was showing Lindsay a tactical shooting stance. I was showing her how to place her feet."

"You're teaching Lindsay how to shoot?"

"Yeah," she says with a smile.

"How did she do?"

"Not bad after she got some trigger control and stopped closing her eyes. Shelby was the one that surprised me."

"Shelby?"

"Yeah, Lindsay and Victor's daughter."

"Wait, you're teaching her as well? What, isn't she like seven years old?"

"She's six," Roni says, smiling, "and no, but she was there, and she was paying as much attention as Lindsay was and may have been comprehending even more."

"Hmmph, start 'em young, I guess. How was he about it?"

"Reluctant at first, but I suppose that's to be expected. I guess it's hard for a man to realize that he can't always be there to protect his family if need be, but after a while, he was fine."

"And that has led to this conversation about boot prints?"

"Yep."

"Let's look at the video."

At first glance, the video turns out to be a grainy and blurry black-and-white video clip about twenty seconds long. It appears to show a heavy-set person walking down the sidewalk dressed in dark clothes and a ball cap. There is a glint of light that flashes below the brim of the cap, indicating that the subject may be wearing glasses.

"That's it?" Roni asks with disappointment evident in her voice.

"Yep, that's the original doorbell cam footage from your neighbor's house three doors to the west of you," Tuck says, clicking the mouse on his computer. "This is after the IT guy enhanced it."

She can see that this video is a bit clearer, and it's more obvious that the subject is a man. He is wearing a ball cap and has a dark beard. He has a bit of a belly and has an easy stride. "Is this the only video we have?" Roni asks.

"It is, why?"

"And this was captured by my neighbor three houses to the west?"

"Yeah, the Claymores," Tuck says, looking through his notes. "Steve goes by Hoss and his wife is Nichole. Nice folks."

"Yeah, they are," she says as an afterthought. "And the tracks left in the dew in my grass came from the east and moved west from my house?"

"Yeah, what are you getting at?"

"The west end of my street is a cul-de-sac; a dead end, so where did he go?"

"He must have hopped the wall."

"Did you see his belly? The fence in front of the Claymore's is three feet high. That puts our guy at five-eleven, six feet at the max. The wall at the end of the street is seven and a half feet high, so he didn't just hop the wall."

Roni's phone rings, "Novetti."

Tuck turns his attention back to the video and watches it again.

"I'm sorry who? Oh, Jamie, I'm sorry I couldn't hear you at first. Thank you for calling me back." She sits down at her desk and starts doodling on a notepad as she listens. "Can you email it to me? How about faxing it? Jamie, please don't make me remind you that you owe me. Yes, we'll be even, but I'll give you one better. I'll owe you—Just put my name on the cover sheet. The fax number here is (480)726-0026. Thank you, Jamie."

She ends the call, and Tuck calls her over to his desk. "Take a look at this Roni." She crosses over and sits down in his chair as he starts the video again. She's not sure what she sees but knows that something isn't quite right and says as much to Tuck. "Watch it again," he says. "This time, pay attention to the way he walks." He clicks the play button again and watches over her shoulder as she concentrates on the footage. He smiles to himself as she clicks the mouse and watches three more times.

"I see... something, but I can't put my finger on it. What am I supposed to see?"

"Does he walk like a fat guy?"

It finally dawns on her. He doesn't walk like he's used to carrying the extra thirty to forty pounds like he's trying to portray here. He doesn't have the strut of a heavy-set man. This guy has a laid-back, easy stride... A runner's stride. This guy is in shape and is trying to hide it.

She looks up at Tuck. "Think the beard and glasses are fake too?"

"I'm only guessing here, but yeah, I think so."

"He's a smart son of a bitch, isn't he?"

A uniformed officer comes by their desks and hands Roni a stack of papers. "This was on the fax machine for you, detective."

"Thanks, Pat," she says, putting the stack in the locking drawer in her desk. Tuck gives her a look with a slight tilt of his head.

"A favor for a friend. Don't ask if you don't want to know," she says in response.

"As in, it is better if I don't?"

"For now."

Tuck turns his attention back to the video and watches it again. "Something about this guy…"

Jenkins from the lab comes into the squad room with the flash drive from Circle K. "Here you go detective. It's clean. Sorry, it took so long. We have been backed up in the lab."

"Yeah, I guess it's better to be safe than sorry, huh? Thanks, Pal." He says as he inserts the drive into his computer and waits for it to download. "Have you played with this at all?" He asks the lab tech.

"Yeah, the first block you see there is from the twenty-third between four-thirty and seven like you asked. The other blocks are about two-hour increments for the rest of the day with a thirty-second overlap on each.

"Have you watched it? Did anything stand out to you?"

"Only while I was breaking it into the blocks, and unless the store was being robbed at gunpoint, nothing would have stood out to me." he chuckles.

Yeah, I guess so." Tuck concedes. "Thanks, Mike." He says turning his full attention to his computer screen. He clicks on the first block and begins to watch. Thirty-seven minutes in, something catches his eye. He stops the video, rewinds it, replays the segment, and confirms that indeed it is Victor Powers he sees casually pulling the door open, striding over to the cooler, grabbing a bottle of water, and waiting in line to make his purchase. Once his purchase is made, he walks back out the door with the same easy stride. Unsure of what is clicking in his head, he watches it three more times before going back to the doorbell camera and watching that video again.

"Circle K video? Anything on it?" Roni asks.

"Not much. Victor Powers went in and bought a bottle of water a little after five," he says, watching for her reaction.

"What? Anything about that strike you as odd?"

"I'm not sure. It's on the back burner for now."

"You can't possibly think Victor could have anything to do with this. Come on Tuck. He happened to buy a bottle of water."

"That's right Roni. He just happened to be in a store buying a bottle of water from a kid who was murdered that same night. Of the six billion people in the world, the only ones I know for a fact that didn't do it are you and me!" He snaps at her.

"Jesus Tuck," she says, "this guy has gotten under your skin. You, okay?"

"Yeah, I'm fine. I just can't put my finger on it. When it boils, I'll let you know."

"Hey," she says with compassion, "what's going on Tuck?"

He takes a deep breath and lets it out slowly. "I'm just frustrated. We've been on this guy's trail for almost six months and aren't any closer to knowing who he is than we were when he killed the Duncans, but he seems to know exactly who we are. He was at your house just saying, 'Hi' for fucks sake. We're just missing something right under our noses."

"Believe me, I get it, but Victor? I think you're grasping here."

"Yeah, probably." He says with a tight-lipped nod.

45

On Thanksgiving morning Lindsay wakes at eight to an empty bed, which is hardly uncommon anymore. She smells coffee and bacon, accompanied by the sound of laughter coming from the kitchen. "Well," she says to the empty bed, "I suppose there are worse things to wake up to." She reaches into the closet to find one of Victor's button-up shirts and pulls on a pair of his boxers as she pads out of the bedroom barefooted, enjoying the sound of her family making breakfast. She pauses in the hallway and watches them together and makes a mental note to get some flowers for Isabel Cruz who volunteered to cover her shift at the station this morning so that she could enjoy the morning with her family before everyone shows up for dinner. The caterers had come yesterday afternoon and brought in tables and chairs to the backyard. They will be back at two to finish up. *Service for forty. Good Lord, Angie, what were you thinking?* Angie and Roni will be here around ten, which in "Angie time" is more like nine-thirty. Nine forty-five at the latest, which gives them an hour and forty-five minutes tops to eat breakfast, clean up, shower, and enjoy themselves as a family before the mayhem begins. Their guests are due to start arriving at two-thirty. Victor had spent yesterday getting the backyard mowed and cleaned up and getting the pool ready. Not that they planned on anyone going swimming, but you never know.

"Mommy!" Shelby's call snaps her back to real-time.

"Hey sweetie," she says, smiling at her daughter as she makes her way to the kitchen, where Victor hands her a cup of coffee and kisses her.

"How'd you sleep, babe?" he asks.

"Not bad," she says, accepting the mug. "You?"

"Slept in till six," he says with a smile.

"Really?"

"Yeah!" he says with a chuckle. "It was kinda nice."

Leaning down and kissing Shelby, she says, "How about you, kiddo? How did you sleep?"

"Pretty good. I'm so excited for today, so I got up early."

"You did?"

"Yeah, I was up before Daddy!" she says with a nearly toothless grin.

"You were? How much earlier?"

"Just one show."

"She was watching Tom and Jerry when I got up, so I'm guessing about a half-hour or so."

"We're making you breakfast," Shelby says, her excitement oozing.

"I see that. What's on the menu?" she asks, snagging a piece of bacon off the plate.

"Bacon, eggs, toast, and orange juice," she replies with the same toothless grin.

"Egg whites, for milady, of course," Victor interjects with a terrible rendition of a British accent. "It should be done in about ten minutes?"

"Sounds amazing!"

Angie and Roni arrive promptly at ten. Shelby comes running down the hall as Lindsay answers the door. "RONI! ANGIE!"

"SHELBY!" They shriek in unison as Roni bends down to embrace her.

"Is that a new dress?" Angie asks.

"Yes, it is," she says, twirling so that the hem balloons upward. "Mommy bought it for me for today. Do you like it?"

"It's beautiful. Your sandals are pretty, too."

"Thank you," Shelby replies, relishing in the attention.

"Victor should be out of the shower any minute. What can I get you?"

"Coffee if it's made," Roni answers.

"Yeah, that sounds good," Angie agrees.

"Coming right up," Lindsay says as she moves toward the kitchen.

"Linds, I can make it, Angie says. Don't put yourself out any more than you already have."

"Don't be silly. I was just about to put on a fresh pot. How's the house?"

Roni excuses herself to the bathroom while Angie sits down at the counter and says, "Oh, good Lord, it's awful. Fingerprint dust was everywhere. They trampled all over the yard, and some bonehead spilled plaster all over the driveway. We were up after midnight cleaning it up. We'll still probably have to have a cleaning service come in next week."

"Plaster?"

"They took casts of the boot prints in the flower bed, but apparently, they are training a new guy who spilled the first batch."

Lindsay laughs. "Well, he was working at the house of one of the lead newscasters at Channel 4, and a homicide detective from the Phillips PD, whose partner was overseeing everything, not to mention a police lieutenant waiting by the phone for any updates. Perhaps he was nervous?"

Angie looks blankly at her for just a moment and then bursts out laughing. "Yeah, I guess he probably was."

Roni joins them at the counter as Lindsay pours them coffee and then pours cups for herself and Victor, whom she hears emerging from the bedroom, a cup. "I thought I heard you, ladies. Thank you, babe," he says as he picks up the mug. "Are you ready for today?"

Angie looks over at Victor with a straight face. "Why is something going on today?"

"Cute," he says. "You are still planning on announcing your nuptials, I assume?"

"Of course we are. We're so excited," she says, beaming.

Victor looks at the two of them for a moment, saying nothing.

"What's on your mind, Victor?" Roni asks.

"It's nothing."

"You're not backing out, are you?"

"What? No, of course not. I got my credentials in the mail last week. I do have a question, but I'm not sure if it's my place to ask."

Roni laughs. "Now there's so much intrigue that you have to ask."

"Okay but understand that this question is not meant to offend either of you in any way."

"Victor, just ask for Pete's sake."

Taking a sip of his coffee, he takes a deep breath. "Could your marriage impact either of your careers?"

"Victor!" Lindsay hisses.

Unfazed, Angie answers first, "It's fine, Lindsay. We don't take it maliciously, do we?" She looks at Roni who shakes her head and watches thoughtfully as Angie takes her hand. "We know where you're coming from. My manager asked me the same thing when I told him."

"And?"

"And yes, it could, but it probably won't. It's not 1952 anymore. Most people don't care, and besides, my personal life is none of the management or the viewer's business."

"Well, aren't you considered, for lack of a better term, a top commodity?"

"I am, but I'm also not an advocate. I don't preach and normally don't give my opinion on the air. We just live our lives and try to be the best people we can be."

"Exactly," Roni says, tagging in. "In this day and age, why should it matter?"

"There may be a few Neanderthals who take offense to us being married, but in the end... fuck 'em! Let them turn the channel," Angie continues.

"Is it that simple?" Victor asks.

"Yeah, it is. Life doesn't always fit neatly into a box. I mean, I guess part of me has always known that I'm gay, but I didn't realize it until we met," she says, looking at Roni. "I'm happier than I've ever been. I'm content. We both take marriage very seriously and see it as a lifetime commitment to each other. We're not sure how that affects anyone else's life or marriage."

Victor smiles leans in and kisses each of them on the cheek. "I am thrilled for both of you. Since we have some time, and we're all here, let's go over a few things if you don't mind." Pulling a spiral notebook and pen from a drawer, and then walks to the dining room table.

"Sure," Roni says, placing her arm around Shelby, who has come up and wrapped her arms around her. "What do you want to know?"

Eyeing his daughter as he writes both of their names at the top of the page. "It's been a while for me, so let's keep it simple for now. Have you set a date?"

"We're thinking about the second Saturday in January."

"Okay, do you know how many guests you will have?"

"For the ceremony or the reception?"

Victor chuckles. "Sure."

"Well," Angie begins, "the ceremony itself is going to be very small and intimate. Just the five of us, plus Roni's dad, my parents, and Tuck, who may or may not have a plus one?"

She looks at Roni, hoping for an answer. Roni shrugs and says, "I'm not sure. We will ask him when he gets here."

"How many is that?" Angie asks.

"Nine, maybe ten," is Victor's immediate reply.

"Okay, then there are a few colleagues from the station coming, and Roni has a couple of friends driving up from Tucson," she says, counting in her head. "So, let's just say less than twenty for the ceremony, and we'll at least triple that for the reception."

"Perfect," he says, jotting the information. "Where are you thinking? Do you have a venue picked out already?"

"We're thinking one of the greenbelts on the Lakes at Ocotillo."

"Ooh, very nice!" Lindsay exclaims.

"Yeah," Angie smiles. "We were having a picnic there one day when I realized that I was head over heels for the first time in my life."

"What kind of ceremony do you want? Short and sweet, long and drawn out, or somewhere in between?"

"Somewhere in between, I think... babe?" She looks at Roni, who nods approval.

"Are you going to write your vows, or would you like me to come up with something?"

Angie and Roni share a lingering look. "Let us get back to you on that," Angie says.

"Okay, I guess that's all I need for now," Victor says, closing the notebook and sticking the pen in the spiral wire. "When you figure out what you want to do with your vows, let me know."

"Where are you having the reception?" Lindsay asks, with anticipation.

"Well, Tuck is taking care of that for us," Roni says. "The clubhouse at his apartment complex is beautiful, and it has everything we'll need: a DJ booth, a bar, and they can move a dance floor in. There is even a small kitchen for the caterers."

Victor pulls the pen from the notebook and opens it back up. "And where is that?"

"The San Marcos Luxury Villas off Phillips Boulevard," Roni says.

"Oh yeah," Victor says as he writes the address. "That's a very nice place."

46

The caterers arrived at one forty-five. Part of the crew discreetly takes over the kitchen while others move to the backyard to set up the tables and chairs for the dinner service. Victor goes to the store and gets flowers for Isabel before the guests arrive and he returns to find the ladies on the patio having a glass of wine. He grabs a beer from the refrigerator in the garage and joins them.

The first to arrive are Ted Payne, Angie's handsome co-anchor, and his wife Monica. Lindsay makes introductions. Victor recognizes her immediately from the "old days," and from the surprised look on her face, she recognizes him as well. She gives him a pleading look and a quick shake of her head. He picks up her cue. "Monica, it's a pleasure to meet you. Welcome." Her look changes from fear to relief in an instant and is not seen by anyone other than Victor who smiles to himself.

"Thank you! You have a lovely home. Happy Thanksgiving," she says.

I guess your past always comes back to haunt you at some point. **You would know...**

An hour later, all the guests have arrived, and everyone seems to be enjoying themselves as they intermingle. The caterers have everything ready on schedule, and the wait staff is keeping the appetizer trays stocked and everyone's glasses filled. Angie and Roni are drifting from group to group, thanking them for coming. Lindsay is on the back patio making small talk with one of the producers from the station. Shelby is playing tag in the yard with the other kids. Victor notices Tuck standing by the fireplace with Janice McKinny, his standing plus one. It appears that Janice is doing all the talking, while Tuck seems to smile and nod at the appropriate times. They make eye contact across the room.

Victor smiles and nods, while Tuck just holds the stare a moment before leaning to Janice, who looks over at Victor and smiles. Victor walks over and greets Tuck. "Detective Tucker, it's good to see you again," he says, extending his hand.

"Victor," he says, shaking his hand. "Please call me Tuck. Have you met my dear friend Janice McKinny?"

"No, I don't believe I have. Ms. McKinny, I'm Victor Powers. It is a pleasure to make your acquaintance."

"Victor, thank you for having us. Happy Thanksgiving, and please, call me Janice."

"Janice, very well," he says with a slight nod of his head. "Thank you for coming."

"It was very good of you and Lindsay to have everyone here, especially on such short notice," Tuck says with all sincerity.

"No trouble at all. Angie didn't have to ask twice. She and Roni have been great friends to us. Angie and Lindsay have been friends since college, and there's no doubt that she and Roni and hell, even you have jump-started her career more than anyone could imagine."

"Still," Tuck retorts, "it's big of you. Today means a lot to Roni."

Victor leans forward in a conspiratorial way and whispers, "Between you and me, Tuck, having Thanksgiving here means more leftovers, so I'll be making sandwiches all weekend." The three of them laugh in unison at the joke as Victor continues. "The funny thing is that you think I'm joking!" he says, laughing harder.

"I understand congratulations are in order as well," Janice says.

"Oh?" Victor replies, confused.

"Yes, Tuck tells me you made a great call on the boot prints."

Victor's expression changes from puzzled to complete anticipation as he looks at Tuck.

"Boot prints?" he asks with caution.

"Yeah, because of what you asked Roni the other day, you know, about the killer wearing boots that might be too big. We took a closer look at the boot prints, and it turns out you were right. He wears boots that are at least three sizes too big. Good call!"

"Thanks, I guess," Victor says, the hairs on the back of his neck standing up.

"So, you watch a lot of 'Forensic Files' huh?"

Careful!

"I used to," Victor says on edge. "I thought it was fascinating."

"Uh-huh, the only show on TV that teaches you how to kill people and not get caught."

He's fishing.

Still wary, Victor looks at Tuck. "Yeah, but they always get caught, Tuck. If they didn't, there wouldn't be a show."

"Hmm, I suppose you have a point," he says smiling.

"Roni told us you've got the guy on video?"

"Yeah, from a doorbell camera. The quality isn't very good. All we can see is a guy walking down the sidewalk and not much else," Tuck says, disappointed.

He's lying, there's more...

I know.

"Anyway, I don't want to talk shop here if you don't mind," he says with the same easy smile.

Victor smiles at him. "Of course, I don't blame you."

After watching the entire exchange in silence, Janice chimes in. "Wow, this is some spread they're putting on. I'm going to ruin my diet."

"Yeah, Victor chuckles while taking a sip of his drink. I know what you mean. I'll have to run a few extra miles myself next week."

"Oh? You're a runner? How long have you been running for?" Tuck asks.

"Off and on all my life. I picked it up again earlier this year. It helps me sleep."

Tuck shares a look with Janice, smiles, and places both hands on his stomach. He shakes them up and down a couple of times. "Doesn't hurt to get rid of this either, I'm sure."

Victor leans back a bit as he laughs. "Yeah, doesn't hurt at all."

"Excuse me, Victor, can I steal you away for a moment? There's someone I'd like you to meet," Lindsay says, appearing in front of them.

"Of course," he says, nodding at Tuck and Janice, "If you'll pardon me?"

They both nod back in unison. "Sure," Tuck says, taking a sip from his glass.

After Victor excuses himself, Janice leans over and says, "He's got a pretty flat stomach."

"You saw that, did you?"

"Yep."

After dinner has been cleared, but before dessert is served, Angie stands up from her place at the center of the front table and taps her wineglass with her fork. "Folks? If I could have your attention for just a moment, please?" The guests stop their current conversations and politely focus their full attention on their host. "First of all, thank you all for coming. I would like to give a special note of thanks to our hosts, Victor, and Lindsay, for opening their beautiful home to us. If not for them, today would not have been possible." She looks across the table at them, tips her glass, and says, "Thank you! Thank you so very much!" The guests applaud, showing their appreciation. When the applause dies down, she continues. "The main reason you were all asked here today is so that Roni and I can share some news with you all." At this point, Roni rises from her chair and takes Angie's hand. "We want to let you, our friends and coworkers, know that we've decided to get married." More applause erupts from the tables as all the guests rise from their seats to deliver a standing ovation.

"Thank you all so much! It means the world to us to have such love and support from you all. Please, let's all take our seats and enjoy the rest of our meal." They share a kiss before they both sit down amid the dying applause. The staff immediately brings dessert trays to each table, allowing everyone to choose their pies and cakes. An hour later, there is a procession line as everyone waits their turn to congratulate the couple and thank them for dinner.

Thirty minutes after that, Angie and Roni are saying goodbye and thanking Lindsay and Victor for hosting Thanksgiving and preparing to leave the Powers family to their own devices when Angie asks, "Lindsay, would you mind if I wait for Roni here?"

"Sure?" Lindsay answers, looking at her friend like she has two heads.

Seeing the questioning look on Lindsay's face, Roni clarifies, "I've got to go back to my office to get a file that I need to read over this weekend, and Angie doesn't want to go downtown."

"Oh," Lindsay replies, "sure, no problem. I'm shocked that you think you need to ask."

47

The following morning, Victor is lathering his face in the steamy mirror. Hot water runs over his razor in the sink.
The cop knows.
"Maybe."
He knows!
"If he doesn't, he suspects."
You know what you need to do.
Victor doesn't reply but picks up the razor and smiles inwardly as he shaves.

He continues getting dressed and grabs his keys from the hook. Lindsay is on the television. She and Isabel banter back and forth about what they each are thankful for this year before reporting what went on in the world since yesterday's broadcast. He finishes dressing, turns off the TV, and leaves the house. Shelby is across the street until either he or Lindsay returns home from work unless there is a sleepover, which will probably be the case, he thinks as he starts his car and backs out of the driveway.

The Demons are screaming at him as he turns up the car radio to block them out. He's sweating profusely despite it being late November, so he turns the car's A/C up to high, trying to maintain a calm demeanor despite his white-knuckle grip on the steering wheel. He briefly debates stopping to grab a pack of cigarettes but decides against it after catching his reflection in the mirror. *"Good Lord, Victor! You look strung out. Get it together!"* he tells himself.

Victor makes his way to Phillips Boulevard and drives past the San Marcos Luxury Villas. The gates on both sides of the driveway are closed. A keypad at the entrance will unlock both sides simultaneously, but he doesn't have the key code. *No big deal,* he thinks to himself. *There's always a way.* He makes a mental note of the address and continues. When he reaches his office, he parks his car in the gated parking lot and enters the building. He logs onto his computer and checks his email. There is a message from Jarod about recognizing his "act of heroism" at the Christmas party that will be held at a local banquet hall on the fifteenth of December. Eddie is to be recognized as well for fixing the plant's magnet that same night. There isn't anything pressing and nothing that needs a reply today. He closes his email, opens Google Maps, types in the address of the San Marcos Luxury Villas, clicks on the satellite view button, and studies the screen. Twenty minutes later, he grabs the keys to one of the fleet pickups parked at the back of the lot and exits the building.

The pickup has been in the lot for a little over a month. It's used as a spare truck if needed. It's very dirty and needs a wash. The good thing about it is that it's kept in top running condition, and it's unmarked. It's a basic run-of-the-mill half-ton pickup that blends in with the ten-thousand others on the road. The first place he goes is to the drive-thru car wash a mile away and gets the deluxe wash. As he's vacuuming the truck, he happens to glance across the parking lot to the convenience store across the street and sees Detective Pete Tucker pull out of the parking lot and turn south on Arizona Avenue, and back towards the downtown area.

Not believing his luck, Victor hangs up the vacuum hose, gets in the truck, and follows, always staying two cars behind. He reaches into the back seat of the truck, grabs a ball cap he'd found in the back seat while cleaning the truck, and pulls it on.

48

Roni finishes reading the file, tosses it on the bed, and shakes her head in disbelief. "Holy fuck!" she says aloud.

"What's up, sweetie?" Angie asks as she towels off from the shower.

"What does Lindsay know about Victor's childhood?" she inquires, staring at the closed file in disgust.

"As far as I know, just what she told you. His father left when he was ten or so, and his mother died when he was in his teens. Afterward, he was in foster care until he turned eighteen. He joined the Job Corps, learned a trade, and moved here shortly after. Why?"

"Well, a couple of weeks ago Lindsay asked me to dig into Victor's past because they had an argument and she realized how very little she knows about his childhood. His records have been sealed by the court, so I called in a huge favor from an old friend."

"And that's what you have there?" she asks, pointing to the file.

"Yeah... I really need to talk to Lindsay."

"Did you find something bad?"

"That's one way to put it, I suppose," she says, getting up from the bed. "His mother died when he was twelve because he cut her head off."

"Oh my God!" Angie says, covering her mouth with her towel.

"Yeah, apparently his father was a trucker who spent a lot of time on the road. He left when Victor was ten because he had come home and walked in on his wife and her lover on the couch. His mother just laughed at him and kept on doing her thing. Victor was in his room at the time; his father turned and walked out without a word."

"Oh, that poor kid."

"Just wait, it gets better." Going into full cop mode, Roni recites the file in a monotone voice. "According to the court transcripts, Victor's mother spent the next year trolling the bars and leaving Victor to his own devices. She had different men who came and went almost nightly. Then one evening, after a rough and drunken session with one of her lovers, she decided to 'Make a man out of her son' and called him to her."

"Oh my God!" is all Angie can say as she listens to the horror story being bestowed upon her.

"It goes on to say how Victor had found a machete in the garage earlier that day and decided he was going to try to 'scare her straight.' When she and her 'date' got home that night, Victor confronted them at the front door. The guy laughed at him, took the machete, tossed it aside, brushed past Victor, and started fooling around with his mom as if Victor weren't there. Victor attacked them with his bare hands; pounding their backs and kicking them in the sides, he screamed for them to stop. The guy laughed, backhanded him, and he flew across the room."

"And his mother did nothing?" Angie asks, shocked.

"No, she just laughed and said something along the lines of him being just as big of a wimp as his father, and then she went down on the guy."

The horror on Angie's face is obvious as a tear runs down her cheek.

Roni continues, "The couple ends up taking it to the bedroom, where her 'date' slaps her around some as they continue going at it. Victor followed a short time later and watched them."

"Did they know he was there?"

"I don't know about the guy, but she did. After they were done and he left, she called Victor to her bed and told him it was time he learned how to be a man," and asked if he liked what he saw.

Tears are streaming down Angie's face as Roni continues in her monotone voice. "He had brought the machete with him when he snuck into the room."

"Oh, Jesus, Roni..."

"The transcript states he swung it with both hands, as if a baseball bat, and caught her at about the middle of her left ear, effectively chopping her head off above her lower jaw. He put her severed head on the dinner table like a centerpiece, then walked to the neighbor's house covered in her blood. There is nothing about him being in foster care, but he was admitted to the pediatric ward of the state mental hospital, where he responded well to intensive therapy, and on the approval of his team of doctors, was released by the court six months after his eighteenth birthday with his records sealed."

"His father?"

"His father drank a bottle of whisky, swallowed a handful of pills, then passed out and drowned in his own vomit two weeks after he left his family."

"Dear God, poor Victor!"

"The rest of his story is pretty on point. He joined the Job Corps, learned a trade, and with his psychiatrist's approval, he put Santa Fe behind him and started over here. I've got to talk to Lindsay."

"You can't. She's on the air all day, and you can't tell her this during a commercial break."

"You're right, I know. I'll give her a call tomorrow. Ang, please don't say anything to her about this. It needs to come from me."

Angie sniffs and wipes away the last of her tears. "Don't worry. I don't think I could repeat that if I were forced to."

"How do you think she'll take it?"

"What, that her husband of seven years and the father of her daughter spent seven years of his childhood in a psych ward for killing his mother when he was twelve years old and never told her about it? I'm sure she'll be fine with it."

"Yeah, I'm sure she will be..."

49

Victor waits in the parking lot at Walmart two rows away from where Tuck parked his car before going inside. The Demons are quiet, as they always are, at the beginning of the hunt. He waits with the patience of a skilled hunter, knowing that everything happening right now is breaking the rules; he's hunting someone he knows, and that someone is a cop.

This whole ordeal is too close to home, and he knows the Demons are right. If Tuck doesn't already know, he has to at least suspect. It's his own doing, he knows. Roni was right when she said, 'He's getting sloppy.' He's made too many mistakes, and now Detective Pete Tucker must pay for those mistakes with his life.

And his partner?

He stares at his reflection in the rearview mirror for a long moment... "*Yeah, her too, if necessary.*"

His phone rings. It's Jenny. "Fuck, now what?" He answers the phone. "Hey Jen, what's up?"

"Sorry to bother you at work, Victor, but I just took Kona to my brother-in-law's office. He's a vet."

"Oh, no!" he exclaims. "What happened?"

"Well, I took the kids to the park, and while the girls were playing with him, he stepped on a piece of glass. It's pretty deep. Jake's going to keep him overnight."

"Okay, thank you. Are you out of pocket for anything?"

"No, it's fine. He's my brother-in-law, so he probably won't charge you at all."

"Okay, thank you again, Jen," he says and hits end.

Tuck strolls out of Walmart, pushing his cart in front of him and scanning the parking lot. It's a habit he's had for so long that he's not even aware that he's doing it. He notices a nondescript white pickup backed into its parking spot with the daytime running lights on two rows over. Someone is in the driver's seat wearing a ball cap pulled low covering his eyes and seems to be looking down at his phone. "Haven't I seen that truck all morning?" he asks himself. *Jesus, calm down Tuck. It's just a guy waiting for his wife.*

As he approaches his car, he pops the trunk with his fob. While he's unloading his cart into his car, he glances up at the truck in time to see the driver's head drop back to his phone. After he empties the cart, he closes the trunk and pushes the cart across the lane to the cart corral. The driver of the truck hasn't looked up. Tuck crosses back to his car, gets in, and starts it. Using his mirrors, he backs out of his spot and sees the driver of the truck raise his head. Something about the movement registers a faint recognition in Tuck's mind as he pulls toward the exit.

He turns west into traffic on Warner Road and catches the red light. As he waits, he checks his mirror. The white pickup pulls out of the lot and turns west onto Warner Road and is now stopped at the light about four cars behind him. *Probably a coincidence, there are only two ways he could have turned. Is he still alone?*

Tuck checks his passenger-side mirror but doesn't see the truck. The results are the same in the rearview. The driver's side view shows just enough of the truck that he knows it's there. Had he not seen the truck pull out when he did, he doubts he would even know it was there. *So, either this guy has had experience in surveillance and knows how to not be seen..., or his wife came out and he's driving home. Jesus Christ Tuck, are you getting paranoid in your old age?* The light turns green, and Tuck continues west on Warner Road. "Well, there's one way to find out," he says, flipping the right turn signal and changing lanes while watching the mirror. The car directly behind him follows. Three seconds later, the white pickup does as well.

The general rule for spotting a tail, Tuck knows, is four right turns. If they're still behind you after four right turns, they're following you. He turns his turn signal and turns north on Dobson and watches the mirror as the car makes the same turn, followed by the white pickup.

"There's one." Staying in the right lane, Tuck continues north on Dobson Road for one mile and catches the green light as it turns yellow and turns right onto Elliot. He watches the mirror, when he can safely, and counts three cars turning right off Dobson onto Elliot. He does not see the truck. Tuck slows his vehicle as he approaches a stoplight, keeping an eye on his mirror, he catches a glimpse of the truck one lane over and four cars back. "Two," he says.

Fighting the urge to just pull into the next parking lot and see what happens, Tuck follows protocol and continues east on Elliot for two miles until he gets to Arizona Ave and then turns south, and watches as the white pickup does the same, always staying three to four cars behind.

"Three. This is bullshit!" he says as all doubt leaves his mind, and he reaches for his phone. It's not in the cup holder where it usually is. *It must have fallen between the seats when I got in the car back at Walmart. It's okay,* he thinks as he recalls part two of the four-turn rule, to end up at the police station. He continues driving south on Arizona Avenue for four miles, watching the truck keep its consistent three to four-car lengths behind him until he gets to the entrance to the underground police parking garage. He parks his car in the first available spot, which happens to be the parking spot for the Phillips Chief of Police, then exits, leaving his door open and the engine running. Tuck runs up the slight ramp at the street entrance and stepped behind the pillar as the pickup cruised past. Due to the tint on the window, he can't tell anything about the driver except that he appears to be a male between twenty and forty. Something about how he's holding his head seems familiar, but he can't quite name it. "Four," he says, straining to see the license plate before the pickup turns out of view.

The garage elevator doors open as Tuck reaches the bottom of the ramp and Jenkins from the lab steps out. "Mike, I need a favor."

"Sure, Tuck, what's up?"

"I need you to trade cars with me. Wait here for ten minutes and drive my car to my apartment. When you get there, park in my spot, number 125 in the southwest section of the complex. Don't hurry, but don't take your time either."

"Okay... but?" he says, fishing his keys from his pocket.

Exchanging keys with the confused tech, Tuck says, "I'm sorry, Mike. I don't have time to explain. Ten minutes, then head to my apartment. The gate opener is on the visor. I'll be right behind you. Where are you parked?"

Confusion still evident on his face, he points to the white Corsica on the ramp, as Tuck pushes the fob button, flashing its lights. "Thanks, Mike. I owe you one," he says, running to the elevator. "Ten minutes!" he yells as he checks his watch and the doors close. He pushes the button for the fifth floor and waits.

He steps out, expecting to see Roni at her desk, but it's empty, so he looks to the lieutenant's office. The door is closed, and the lights are off inside. It's Thanksgiving weekend, and the squad room is empty. He reaches into his pocket for his phone and remembers that it's stuck between the console and the seat in his car. "Fuck," he says, looking at his watch. Eight minutes have passed since he left the garage. "Well, I guess I'm on my own for a bit," and hurries back to the elevator. The doors open immediately, and he presses the G as he steps inside. The doors open again just in time for Tuck to see his car pull out of the garage and turn left onto the street. He hurries up the ramp while watching his car at the light. As he pulls out of the parking spot and turns toward the exit, he is not surprised to see the white pickup fall in three cars behind Jenkins.

Tuck pulls onto the street two cars behind the white truck. Jenkins follows his instructions perfectly to the letter. He does the speed limit and takes the most direct route to Phillips Boulevard. The white truck gets closer but stays two cars back. Tuck, in turn, keeps his distance. Jenkins pulls into the center lane and waits for traffic to clear before turning. To Tuck's surprise, the truck does not follow. Instead continues west down Phillips Boulevard and takes the next left into the adjoining neighborhood. Now Tuck must be very careful to avoid being seen, so he turns at the next street, does a U-turn in the neighborhood, and backtracks to follow the pickup.

He knows that there is a wide utility easement on the other side of the wall behind the golf course that surrounds the backside of his complex and is not surprised to see fresh tire tracks in the dirt at the head of the alley.

Wishing he had his phone or radio, and knowing he is breaking department protocol by proceeding on his own, Tuck parks the car, draws his service weapon, and continues down the alley on foot until he sees the truck sitting empty. He crouches down to ensure no one is hiding beneath it, and following his gut, he rushes the truck, points his gun into the empty bed, and then into the empty cab. He climbs into the bed of the truck and peers over the wall in time to see the shape of a man move into the oleanders across the golf course from him. *Something about the way this guy moves...*

Tuck's apartment is along the fourteenth fairway, and he wonders, as he goes over the wall, how long has this guy been watching him? He crosses the fairway focused solely on where he saw the shape disappear in the bushes when, from his right, he hears someone yell, "FOORREE!" right as a golf ball whizzes behind him. He instinctively points his weapon toward the golfers, realizing that he's crossing a fairway, he puts his gun back in its holster, raises his badge, and jogs in their direction while waving them toward him. They comply and drive their cart to him. "I'm Detective Pete Tucker with Phillips Police. You're in a police situation, and I need you to clear the area. Go to the clubhouse. When you get there, I want you to call my partner, Detective Veronica Novetti," he says, as he pulls his card out of his breast pocket, grabs a score pencil off the cart, and scratches Roni's number on the back. "Tell her where I am and that I think I've got our guy. She'll know what you're talking about. Now Go! Go! Go!"

50

Victor is moving with as much stealth as possible through the oleanders along the fence that separates San Marcos Luxury Villas and The San Marcos Golf Club. He is sure that he hasn't been seen. He thought he'd blown it in the parking lot at Walmart after the roundabout way Tuck took to the police station, but ten minutes later he headed home. Now he's presumably putting away the items he bought all comfy in his apartment without a care in the world.

He's quite impressed with the quality of Google Maps on his phone. It shows the slight maintenance breezeway between the fence and the oleanders along the course. When the time comes, he'll be able to move around relatively unnoticed. Ahead, he can see Tuck's car parked in the covered parking. Behind him he hears one of the drunk golfers, he'd seen tee off earlier, yell, "FOORREE!" at whom he assumes to be another drunken idiot that has stumbled onto the fairway. He chuckles to himself. Moving forward, he sees what he was hoping for: a maintenance valve for the course sprinkler system that is wide enough for him to crouch or sit in but still allows for a complete view of the front of the building and the parking lot. The ornate fence is low enough that he can easily hop over it in the cover of darkness and remain unseen. He hears a twig snap behind him as he's contemplating the kill zone and instantly freezes not knowing if he's been seen or if it's a greenskeeper doing his job.

"Hello Victor," Tuck says, pulling the hammer back on his pistol and aiming it at Victor's crouching body. "I want you to do exactly what I tell you and do it very slowly. Do you understand?"

Trying to bide his time, he says, "How long have you known?"

"Don't give me any of your bullshit, Victor. I am locked and loaded on the back of your skull. DO YOU UNDERSTAND?!" Tuck screams, shifting his stance in the uneven undergrowth.

"NOW GET ON YOUR FACE AND PUT YOUR HANDS OVER YOUR HEAD!"

In for a penny...

"DO IT NOW VICTOR! MOVE!"

In for a pound...

Victor slumps his shoulders, hoping he's giving Tuck the impression that he's going to give up as he pulls the knife from his boot, turns, and simultaneously springs at Tuck's waist. Tuck fires his weapon, but in the close quarters of the brushy area, his bullet misses its mark. He feels Victor's full weight hit his lower chest, instantly knocking the wind from his lungs as he falls backward. He can't move and then feels a sharp burning sensation in his lower abdomen as Victor's face fills his vision. Struggling to knock Victor off him and trying to breathe, Tuck comes to the painful realization that his situation is hopeless. He tries to point his gun at his attacker for another shot, but his arm is too heavy. As his vision blurs, he sees Victor smile.

"I'm sorry it was you, Tuck," he says pulling the knife up to the sternum, twisting it, then pushing it down to follow Tuck's lower ribs. The sharp knife, slicing through his body and into the dead sticks and leaves below, gutting him. "I always liked you."

"Fuck you, you puke!" are Tuck's dying words as his internal organs spill onto the ground beside him.

"Shhh," Victor says as he kisses the top of his forehead and watches the life fade from Detective Pete Tucker's eyes. He wipes the knife off on Tuck's shirt, puts it back in its sheath, then hops over the fence, ducking between the buildings, intending to circle back to the alley.

You're slipping!

"Fuck off!"

Sirens blare in the distance and are coming closer. He knows it will take some time for them to get to the alley, but not long. He doesn't have time to get back to the truck and escape, but he must get back to it. It holds too much evidence.

You weren't prepared...

"I didn't have any choice but to kill him. He had a gun to my head if you recall."

You took too big of a chance. Are you trying to go to jail or get killed?

"I told you, we're not going to jail."

So you're trying to get killed...

"I didn't let him kill me, and right now I just need to get out of here, so I can keep my promise of not going to jail, SO BACK OFF and let me handle this!"

That was too close, and you know it...

"Right now, I need to get us out of here, so if you don't mind… SHUT UP!"

For now…

After realizing there is no way back to the alley, Victor hops back over the decorative fence and runs along the maintenance path to the spot that he came over before, leaps up, climbs over the wall, and jumps down, landing in the truck's bed. Hopping over the bed rail, and quickly opening the cab, he frantically searches the inside. Hearing the sirens coming closer, he knows they are closing on the country club entrance as well as the gate to San Marcos Luxury Villas. It won't be long before they find the alley. Not finding what he wants, Victor rips his shirt over his head and tears off a sleeve. He then unscrews the gas cap and stuffs the sleeve of his shirt as deep as it will go leaving about six inches protruding from the opening. Reaching into his pocket, he retrieves his lighter, lights the tail end of the would-be fuse, and runs. He must get out of the alley and at least onto a paved street before the explosion. Making it to Phillips Boulevard would be preferred, *you don't want to go that way,* but that would be beyond hope.

His arms and legs are pumping in unison, his lungs heaving, but he is controlled. He can keep this pace all day if he must, but right now, he needs to get to the street, not only to avoid the concussion but to blend in with the crowd and make his escape. He lengthens his stride, reaches the street, turns north, and is halfway to the next corner when the fuel tank explodes. The strength of the concussion, from this distance, surprises him. *I guess thirty gallons of gasoline makes a helluva boom.*

As a crow flies, Victor realizes the offices for Little General Recycling are less than half a mile from the San Marcos Luxury Apartments and Golf Club. Changing course, he zigs zags through the neighborhood and turns it into a two-mile trek. When he gets to the office, he checks the building to ensure that he's alone. He strips down to his underwear and takes what his mother used to call a whore's bath' from the sink in the bathroom. Seeing his reflection in the mirror, he laughs.

I'd love to know what is so fucking funny!

"What are you so worried about? I'm doing what you wanted... I'm killing people."

The kill is a part of it, yes, but you know it isn't just the kill.

"I didn't have any choice."

You took it too far; you got cocky, and you let him sneak up behind you. You were supposed to be following him, remember?

"Yeah, yeah, yeah..."

Don't yeah, yeah, me Victor. You killed a cop! You killed someone you know.

"It was unavoid—"

NO! Don't give ME your excuses! You were not prepared; you did not follow the rules; you did not know his routines, his habits, hell you barely knew where he lived. You had no escape route, and you did it in broad daylight, and you didn't bring a change of clothes. We are in a helluva mess. Do you hear the helicopters?

Victor strains and hears the drum of helicopter rotors flying around the surrounding neighborhoods searching.

"Relax, I've got clothes in the car. You know, he did have a gun to my head. I didn't have a choice. When do you think he spotted me?"

Probably Walmart... That's when he started acting funny, going out of his way by taking the scenic route to the police station. You should have pulled off.

"That's easy to say now," Victor says to his reflection. "I don't seem to remember hearing you pipe up then," he says, drying his face.

We're in a helluva mess. What about the truck?
"What about it?"
How long do you think it will take them to find out that it's registered with Little General Recycling, and that you happen to be the regional manager of that company?

Victor puts on his pants, goes out to the car, retrieves his gym bag from the trunk, and changes his clothes in his office. He grabs the remote off his desk and turns on the TV just as his phone rings. Lindsay.

"Hey, babe. What's up?"

"Are you watching the news? There was an explosion over by your office, and now it's a police situation, but they won't let our choppers anywhere near the scene. Did you hear it?"

"Maybe," he says. "I've been inside all day, and I just turned on the TV. A commercial is on right now. What's going on?"

"I don't know yet, but it's right by your office. I was kinda hoping that you could tell me. Isabel is doing the on-scene report, but they won't let her within a half-mile of the scene. I gotta go," she says and hangs up.

The commercial ends and Lindsay is sitting at the NEWS desk with an aerial view of the scene on the screen behind her. The truck is still engulfed in flames and billowing black plumes of smoke. The BREAKING NEWS tape is running at the bottom of the screen as she looks into the camera. "This just in, an explosion rocked a neighborhood close to downtown Phillips about thirty minutes ago, and firefighters are having a hard time getting their trucks on the scene. Scott, you've probably got the best view from NEWS CHOPPER 4. What can you tell us?"

"Not much Lindsay. We are about three miles from the site, and that is as close as Phillips PD will allow at this point. I'm able to zoom in on what appears to be a burning pickup truck, but that's all I can tell you. As you mentioned, fire units are not on the scene yet. We do see some activity at an adjoining apartment complex, though. The police presence is growing by the second Lindsay. We will keep you informed as we find out more about this developing situation."

51

"NOVETTI!" Lieutenant Ames calls for the third time, walking toward his detective.

Roni, deaf to the outside world, stares down into her partner's lifeless face. Tears are flowing down her cheeks as she chokes back the bile that rises in her throat when she sees the severity of the gash that opened his stomach. At that moment, her emotion switches from grief to anger and then rage. She takes his hand in hers as the lieutenant crouches behind her and places his hand on her shoulder.

"Roni," he says, his voice full of compassion. "Let him go. We've got to take him now. Come on now," he says gently, urging her up from her partner. She looks at the man before her, dazed, as if she'd never seen him before when it all comes crashing back... the call from the drunken golfer that she almost didn't answer because she didn't recognize the number, how she'd almost hung up after hearing his slurred speech, and how she was on the verge of pushing the end button when she heard him say, "Detective Tucker told me to call you."

"The golfer," she says to Ames as a member of the coroner's team approaches. "We need to talk to the golfer that called me."

"Did he give you his name?"

Searching her memory of the call, she says, "I don't think so, but I have his number on my phone."

"I'll call him in a minute," he says gently, taking Roni by her shoulders and turning her towards him and away from Tuck's body. "Go home, Roni."

Anger flashed across her face. "No!" she says, struggling to unlock her phone. Ames reaches out and takes the phone from her hand.

"Lieutenant, he told me that Tuck was following 'Our guy.' That means Tuck figured out who he was and got killed for it. This is as close as we've been to this guy. The golfer may know something more."

"I know," Ames says dropping her phone into his shirt pocket, "but he's not going to tell you because you're going home."

"There is no fucking way I'm going home, Lieutenant! This son of a bitch killed my partner!"

"Novetti, we don't know that yet. All we know for certain is that someone killed your partner. I've read your reports and nothing at this scene indicates that it's tied to your investigation. You are NOT investigating the death of your partner. You are too close and cannot be objective, and as of right now, you are on three days of bereavement."

"Then fuck you! I quit!"

Ames glares at her and growls as he walks toward her, backing her up slightly. "Fine Novetti, quit! Quit and you'll never get to the bottom of this. That is unless by chance or some dumb luck that this guy walks into the station and makes a full confession. Quit, and if I ever see or hear of you nosing around this, I will have you arrested for interference and obstruction of a police investigation. I'm not putting you on a desk... yet, but you ARE taking a couple of days off to grieve the loss of your partner and friend. Roni," he says his tone softening. "There is nothing you can do for him here, and damnit, you're just going to be in the way. I want you to go home, call his family, and take the next three days off. You can come back on Monday. I'll take your statement then."

"You're not putting me on a desk?"

"Novetti, as I said, we don't know if this investigation will tie into yours. Until we do know, you're still working on your case. If it does tie in... well, we'll deal with that when and if the time comes. For now, though, you're going home. Please offer Jeff and Krissy my condolences and let them know that I'll be calling them a little later."

"Who's picking up this case?" she asks.

Ames looks at her for a long moment. "Greene," he says. "Now go home!"

Knowing that he's right doesn't make her feel any better as she turns and finds her way back to her car. She looks back over her shoulder as the coroner's team zips up Tuck's body bag and lifts him to the gurney. She notices the smoke in the alley has changed from black to white and figures that the fire dept must have finally found their way back there to put the fire out.

"I've got to call Angie," she says to herself, reaching for her phone and remembering that Ames has it. She turns back looking for the lieutenant so she can retrieve it when she notices two men who look like they just came off the course standing outside of the crime scene tape, well away from the scene, but not going anywhere.

She looks around, and all the officers are working diligently at their various jobs. *Of course, they are. One of their own has been killed.*

"What the hell," she says, turning toward the men on a hunch. She approaches them. "Gentlemen, I'm Detective Novetti," she says digging in her pocket for her nonexistent notebook. "Which of you is Mr....?"

"I'm Mark Connelly," says the larger man, wearing a yellow Izod, as he extends his hand. "I'm the guy that called you."

"Thank you for that, Mr. Connelly. I appreciate your call. Can you tell me exactly what Detective Tucker said to you?"

"He's dead, isn't he?"

Roni looks at him with a tight-lipped stare. "Mr. Connelly, please. It's very important that you tell me exactly what he said to you."

"There wasn't much. He said that we were in a police situation and told us to clear the area, and then he said I needed to call you when we got to the clubhouse. He wanted me to tell you where he was and that he thinks he's got your guy and that you'd know what I was talking about."

"And that's it? Did he say a name or anything like that?"

"No, I'm sorry."

"Did you see anything else... like the guy he was following?"

"Nah, fourteen is a par five, and we were on the fairway." He says as if that were explanation enough. "Hell, Bill here almost hit your detective with a ball. We didn't see anyone else."

Turning slightly to his buddy, she asks, "Is that about how it went down Bill?"

"Yeah, pretty much. It's the fourteenth hole, Detective. We'd had a few beers. I'm sorry."

"Yeah, me too." She fishes two cards from her breast pocket and hands them to the two men before her. "If you think of anything else, please give me a call. Thanks for your time and for sticking around," she says turning from the men.

"Sure thing… Detective?"

She turns back, her eyebrows raised, "Yeah?"

"I'm sorry about your friend," Mark Connelly says.

"Thanks," she says, turning back towards the parking lot.

Halfway to her car, she sees Lieutenant Ames and Detective Chad (Chip) Greene talking to Mike Jenkins in the covered parking. From what she can tell, Ames is asking Jenkins questions and Greene is scribbling notes as fast as he can. Ames looks up from the questioning and notices her approaching. "Fuck, Novetti, I thought I told you to get out of here until Monday."

"You did, Lieutenant, but you also took my phone. I need it."

He reaches into his pocket and retrieves her phone. Handing it over, he says, "Do I need to tell you not to call the man who called you?"

"You have my word. I won't call him," she says with a smirk.

"Novetti…"

"Lieutenant! I said I wouldn't call him, and I won't," she says, taking her phone from him.

"Get out of my crime scene, Novetti, and do it now." His tone is uneven but serious.

"Lieutenant, I've got a lot going on back at the lab. Do you have anything else for me here?" Jenkins asks.

Ames is still staring down at Roni, who is holding his glare with equal ferocity. "Greene?" he asks without shifting his gaze.

"Yeah, we're done here, Mike. I'll get your statement in the morning," Greene says.

Jenkins continues to stand there fidgeting and shifting his weight from one foot to the other.

Ames looks away from Roni. "What Jenkins? You're cleared to go. Now go!"

"Um... Lieutenant, I drove Tuck's car here. I need a ride."

"Novetti was just leaving. She'll drive you back to the station."

In the car, Roni says, "So Mike, Tuck asked you to trade cars with him and drive to his apartment?"

"Uh, yeah," he replies. "He came flying into the garage and almost knocked me over. Then he asked me for my keys and told me to drive his car to his place."

"Why?"

"He didn't say, but he was in a hurry, and he kept looking up at the street like he was—"

"Like he was being followed?" Roni interrupts. "Mike, do you have access to the station cameras?"

Jenkins looks over at her and smiles. "Officially? No."

Playing along and trying to hide her irritation at his trying to be coy she smiles back "But...?"

"Roni, I'm a geek, a super geek. If the truth were known, I can hack anything."

"Can you cover your tracks?"

His smile changed to a smirk. "Don't insult me, of course, I can."

"Are you sure? I mean, a hundred percent sure?"

He chuckles and offers a genuine smile. "Roni, I've still got my job, so yeah, I'm pretty sure."

"Good to know. Would you mind letting me take a look at a few things?" she says as she pulls into the police parking garage.

"Yeah, I've got some time I can give you... considering the circumstances."

52

Fifteen minutes later, Roni is leaning over Jenkins's shoulder as he taps the keys on his computer terminal. The dual monitors show images from eight cameras for ten-second intervals, then change to different cameras throughout the building.

"All right, let's see the garage entrance from about ten minutes before you and Tuck traded cars."

"Okay, coming right up." The left monitor expands to one camera view as Jenkins clicks the mouse. Almost as an afterthought, Roni asks him to put the camera view from inside the garage on the right-side monitor. "You bet," he says tapping more keys and the right monitor expands with the requested view.

"There's his car," Roni says, pointing to the left monitor as Tuck's car enters the frame. It shows him coming down the street and turning into the garage. Roni peers at the image on the screen, hoping to see Tuck's face through the windshield. Her disappointment is evident as they both shift their gazes to the right monitor in unison. The view from above the elevator door shows Tuck's car as he pulls inside and parks abruptly. They watch Tuck get out of the car, run to the top of the ramp, and step behind the pillar. The camera does not show what he was looking at or looking for. A few seconds later, he's running towards the elevator doors and reaches them right as they slide open and Jenkins steps out. They watch the conversation in silence; Roni studying Tuck's every movement. The men part ways as Jenkins turns towards Tuck's car and Tuck rushes inside.

"Do you want me to follow him in?" Jenkins asks.

"No, I know where he went. He went to the squad room. He was looking for me," she says as a pang of guilt wrenches in her stomach. "Actually, can you…" she shifts her gaze.

"Way ahead of you, Detective," he says, tapping the keys again as the left monitor runs backward in slow motion. They watch as a white pickup backs up the street in the choppy frame-by-frame. As it backs around the corner on the screen, Tuck's car backs out of the garage and up the street, and around the same corner.

"All right," Roni says, "take it from there."

Jenkins clicks the mouse, and the video moves forward, as Tuck's car once again turns the corner, and drives down the street before turning into the garage. Eight seconds later, the white pickup comes around the same corner and continues to the stop sign at the end of the street.

"Can you zoom in on the driver?" Roni asks.

"I don't think with any more clarity, but let's see," he says tapping the keyboard. The ghostly image behind the windshield becomes more distorted as the pixels morph beyond their capacity.

"SHIT!" "How about a license plate?"

"That I can get for you," he says. Tapping the keyboard some more, the screen zooms in on the back of the pickup as it passes the garage entrance.

Roni writes down the plate number on a notepad and does a double take. "Mike, this is a commercial plate. Can you get into the DMV?"

He looks at her with a mock hurt on his face that shifts into a toothy grin. "Detective, why must you insult me so?" The screen on the right-side monitor changes to the Department of Motor Vehicles page. "Looks like the truck, or the plate anyway, belongs to Little General Recycling."

"What? Did you say Little General Recycling?"

"Yeah, they're one of, if not the biggest, recycling companies in the state. Surely, you've heard of them."

"Yeah, I have. I know a guy that works there," Roni says, tapping her pen on the desk and fading off into space half-listening to what Jenkins is saying, and only realizing, too late, that he had stopped talking and was waiting for her to reply. "I'm sorry Mike, I was lost in my thoughts. What was the last thing you said?"

"I said that they're such a big company and have so many vehicles that they might not even know it's missing."

"Yeah, probably. Listen, can you take the clearest image that we have of the guy in the truck, enhance it, and email it to me? I've got a few things I've got to check out."

"Uh, sure, I can get it to you first thing in the morning."

She looks at him blankly. "I need it in an hour."

"Listen, Roni, we're not supposed to be doing this, to begin with, and besides that, I've got pla—"

Her icy glare cuts him off. "Fine," he says, caving in. "You'll have it in an hour, but you owe me."

Collecting her purse and jacket she says "Yeah, I'll owe you huge."

"Listen Roni, I know my timing sucks, and believe me when I tell you how sorry I am about Det. Tucker..."

Irritation flares on her face when she realizes that he's about to call in his favor.

Her expression stops him mid-sentence. "Never mind..."

Roni closes her eyes, takes a deep breath, and lets it out over the space of five seconds. "No, come on Mike what do you need?"

"Well, I...uh..."

"Mike, I'm in a bit of a rush here, spit it out or we'll have to talk about it later." She says waiting a moment longer before turning to leave.

"I applied for a job as an officer in the department."

Roni can't hide her surprise at this. "Mike are you sure?"

"Yeah, it's something I've always wanted to do, and well, I figured now's the time."

"Well, I'm thrilled for you, congratulations. How can I help? I can't pull any strings at the academy if that's what you're thinking."

"No, nothing like that, I'd never ask anything like that."

"Then what?"

"I can't shoot." He says as he hangs his head.

"What?"

"I can't pass the academy if I can't shoot right?"

"When do you start the academy?"

"January 9th."

"Okay, that's plenty of time, we'll go to the range a few times, and when you get there pay attention to the instructors, and you'll be fine."

"Thanks Roni."

53

She walks into the squad room and takes a seat at her desk, opens her laptop, sees Tuck's coffee cup on his desk, and loses the last of her control. The tears come rushing as her sobs echo throughout the lifeless room. Her chest is heaving as she blows her nose into a tissue. Her phone rings in her purse, but whoever it is can wait. She needs this time. She needs at least a few minutes alone to just be sad. She knows that there will be more later, but right now a few minutes is all she has.

Ten minutes later, she blows her nose a final time and goes to the lady's room to wash her face. Looking at her reflection in the mirror above the sink, she says aloud, "Okay Roni, get your shit together."

Back at her desk, she turns on her computer and searches the police department's internal database for recent stolen vehicle reports. Nothing from Little General Recycling has been reported to Phillips PD in the last three months. Suddenly remembering that Victor had told her at some point that he also has an office in Prescott, she expands the search to cover the state. Again, nothing reported in the last three months. She jots a note on a post-it note next to her keyboard to call Victor and absently puts a question mark behind his name. Next, she opens her email and opens the video of her neighbor's Ring doorbell.

She flashes back to the first time she'd seen it. Tuck had been obsessed and watched it repeatedly. *What was it he had said?* Thinking back to that day, his words come back to her. He had said… 'Something about this guy?' She reaches for her coffee cup, takes a sip, sets it back down next to her keyboard, and stares at it for a moment. It's partially covering the post-it note she'd written to herself earlier. Victor-? peeks out from beneath the cup.

She turns her attention back to the video. Tuck had seen something… *Maybe in the way the guy walked?* There is no sound to the video, so it must have been something along those lines, she reasons with herself. Something familiar… "Maybe," she says under her breath. "What did you see, Tuck? What got you killed?"

They had decided that the guy had gone to some length to hide his appearance; a ball cap, glasses, perhaps a fake beard, and more than likely, he had a small pillow or padding under his shirt to give the appearance of extra girth. 'Because he doesn't walk like a fat guy…' "That's it!" she said, slapping the desk.

Her computer dings and she sees that she's just received an email from Jenkins. She checks the clock on the wall. Forty-five minutes had passed since she'd left him in his lab. "Good job Mike! I still owe you one." She opens it and sees that there are two pictures attached along with a note confirming that Little General Recycling had not reported any vehicles stolen recently, but they do indeed have four white late-model F-150s registered in the state.

She opens the first picture, and the back of the pickup fills the screen with the license plate visible. The second picture is disappointing, as the only thing she can make out about the driver is that he's wearing a ball cap and sunglasses. She clicks back to the Ring doorbell video, glances down at her coffee cup again, and sees the post-it note... Victor-? Remembering the circle K video, Victor was there and interacted with the victim the night he was murdered. As well as how her conversation with him about the boot prints, had given them a new direction in their case, because 'He used to watch Forensic Files on TV', makes her pause. "Jesus Roni, you're reaching." *Are you?* '*Go all the way through it.*' She hears Tuck's voice in her head. He had always encouraged her to listen to her gut but to think it all the way through before deciding on anything. "Go all the way through it," she says, as she gets up from her desk and paces the room, talking her way through her thoughts.

She looks at the computer screen with the Ring video frozen on the clearest still shot of the man walking past her neighbor's house, then down again at the coffee cup partially covering the post-it note. Searching her memory, she flashes back to the first time she met Victor. He was coming in from the garage with two beers in hand. "He's lost a few pounds since then." She mutters aloud.

Her phone buzzes on the desk. Lindsay's name and number flash across the screen. "Hey Lindsay, what's up?"

"Are you working?"

"Yes," she says, grabbing the remote and turning on the squad room TV to Channel 4. A commercial selling New Balance running shoes is on.

"Can you comment on what is going on at the golf course?"

She takes a deep breath as tears fill her eyes, and she sniffles a bit before answering. "Lindsay, if you're calling me as a Channel 4 reporter, I have no comment."

"Roni, are you okay? Roni..."

"He... If you're calling as my friend, no, I'm not okay. The son of a bitch killed my partner."

"What! Tuck's dead? Oh my God, Roni! I am so sorry. When?"

"About an hour, an hour and a half ago."

"That explains all the police at San Marcos Apartments. I called Victor to see if he had heard the explosion from his office...."

"Victor is working today?" Roni interrupts.

"Yeah, he said he had some last-minute preparations to tie down for his company Christmas party on the fifteenth."

"Hmmm," she says looking at the post-it note again, then shifting her gaze back up to the TV that is showing an aerial view of the area, and then back to the computer screen.

"What?" Lindsay asks.

Roni shifts back into "cop mode" without realizing it. "So, he's in the area of the explosion?"

"I suppose so. His office is only about a half-mile away. Roni, what's going on? Something in your voice just changed."

"What? Nothing, just curious." *What about a Christmas party is so important that it had to be handled on a holiday weekend?* "Sorry, Linds, just the cop part of my brain asking random questions. I'm kinda all over the place right now."

"I'm sure. Is there anything I can do?"

"No," she says her gaze shifting from the post-it note to the computer screen and back. "Hey, I've got to let you go because I need to call Angie and Tuck's kids."

"God, that's going to be a hard call to make."

"Did he hear it? The explosion I mean?"

"Who, wha... Victor? No, he said he didn't. He's been inside the office all day. Listen, after you make your calls, go home, clean up a bit, then come over to our house for dinner and drinks. I'll call Victor and let him know about Tuck."

"Yeah, that sounds good, but do me a favor if you would? Let me tell Victor. I know they liked each other, and I'd just like to be the one to tell him."

"Oh, sure, I guess that makes sense."

"Listen, Lindsay, I've got to go! Thanks for calling, AND for keeping this off the record." "Sure, no problem, and Roni, I'm so sorry."

"Thank you, Lindsay. We'll see you in a couple of hours," Roni says and hangs up.

54

Gathering her laptop and digging in her purse for her keys, she clears her desk and walks toward the elevator. Once she reaches the garage level, she presses the send button on her phone to call Angie but sees a figure in the garage lurking by her car.

Dropping her phone in her purse and reaching for her gun, she sees the figure raise his hands in surrender. "Don't shoot! It's me, it's Buddy Laird. I'm looking for Tuck."

Lowering her weapon, but not re-holstering, she says, "Get out of here Buddy I don't have time right now."

"Detective Novetti? Where's Tuck? I need to talk to him."

Closing the distance but keeping the car between them and her gun at the ready, she says, "Tuck's not available right now Buddy, what do you need?"

"I saw the guy."

"What guy?" she asks, exasperated.

"The guy that blew up the truck in the alley by the golf course. I saw him."

Roni's phone rings in her purse. "Get in the car, Buddy," she says, answering. "Ang, I'm going to have to call you back." Her eyes never leave Buddy Laird as she continues, "I'm fine, not really, but for now, I am. Call Lindsay. She'll fill you in, but right now I've got to go," she says ending the call.

Buddy gets in the passenger side as she gets in the driver's side.

"Are you fucked up?"

"No."

Roni looks at him blankly.

"I was," he says, scratching his neck and face. "I was burning a rock when I first saw him running out of the alley, then I heard the explosion. Hell, I was close enough to feel it, but I'm straight now. Tuck will never talk to me unless I'm at least semi-straight. I had to wait a while."

"Tell me what you saw."

"Twenty bucks," he says, trembling.

"What?" she asks, her irritation becoming more prevalent by the second.

"Tuck always pays me twenty bucks."

Leaning closer to him, she says, "Buddy, my first thought is to knock what teeth you have left in your head out."

He flinches and tries to cover his face and head. "Nooo, please Detective Novetti, don't do that. I never pass bum scoop, and I'll tell you, just don't hurt me."

Realizing that she was being too harsh on him and that she was still carrying a grudge from almost two years ago, she let up. "When was the last time you had anything to eat?" she asks, shifting back into the driver's seat.

"I don't know. I can't remember."

She starts the car and backs out of the parking spot. "Buckle up. If I get you something to eat, do you think you'll be able to hold it down?"

"I don't know."

"Okay," she says, taking a deep breath. "I'm not Tuck, and I won't ever give you money. From now on you're going to be dealing with me. Do you understand?"

"No deal."

Continuing as though he hadn't spoken, she says, "I will see that you get into rehab. I will give you my private number that you can call twenty-four-seven, but only if you're in the program, and I will get you off the street. This is a one-time deal, and the offer lasts for another twelve seconds."

"And if I say no?"

"Then I will knock the rest of your teeth out of your head, and you'll tell me what I want to know, anyway. Then I will out you as a CI. Good luck getting your next fix. The same goes if you drop out of the program."

"Jesus man! Why are you so hard on me?"

"Listen, Buddy, I'm not sure why, but Tuck had a soft spot for you, and right now there's no line of people waiting to give you a better offer."

"Had?" he asks with eyebrows raised.

"Had," she says flatly.

"Fuck an A, man..."

"Five seconds."

"All right, deal."

"Okay," she says, pulling her phone from her purse. "Do you recognize anyone in any of these pictures?"

"Yeah," he says smiling. "That's you, and the lady beside you is Angie Keller from Channel 4."

"That's good, Buddy, and these?" she says, swiping the screen on her phone.

"That's the new girl on Channel 4, and Ted, what's his name? Do you know them? Is he as big of a prick as he seems on camera?"

"Focus Buddy."

"That's him! That's the guy!" he says, pointing at the next picture.

"Buddy, that's Tuck."

"Not Tuck, the guy behind him in the background. That's the guy I saw running out of the alley."

Swiping again, she asks him, "This is the guy you saw?"

He takes her proffered phone and looks closely. "I'm not as sure with the close-up, Detective, but the guy in the last picture, standing behind Tuck was the guy I saw today."

"Okay Buddy, thank you. I need you to take me to where you were when you saw this guy and tell me everything you saw in as much detail as you can." She watches as he leans back in his seat, smiling like a child who had just been praised.

"When you pull out of the garage, turn left." Roni follows his directions to the field at the mouth of the alley. "This is where he came out when I first saw him."

She stops the car and gets out looking for footprints but is not surprised when she doesn't see any. All the police and fire units have destroyed any footprints he would have left. "Where were you?" She asks, getting back in the car. Buddy points to a dirty tent pitched across the field along the eastern fence. "And that's where you live?" He nods. "And where did he go?"

"He ran through that neighborhood." he said, pointing to the nearest group of houses, "but then I saw him again as he was cutting back to the north."

So, he zig-zagged out in case he was seen. Good thinking Victor. "Your camouflage is almost perfect. If you hadn't pointed it out, I never would have seen it."

"That's the idea," he says with some amount of pride.

"Take a good look, Buddy. Burn it into your mind because this is the last time that you will ever see it."

"You mean our deal starts now?" he asks in disbelief.

"I mean, our deal starts now. We are going to Circle K, and I'm going to get you a sandwich, some chips, and a Coke. Then we are going to a rehab center that I know in Gilbert where we'll check you in. It's a long-term treatment facility that specializes in cases like yours."

They drive to the closest Circle K in silence. Roni gets out and goes in alone. She returns with her purchases in a plastic bag to an empty car. "Shit!" she says, then she spies him across the parking lot sitting on the curb, appearing to be contemplating the turn of events in his life. She walks across the parking lot and sits beside him on the curb.

"Egg salad is all they had," she says, handing him the bag. "Eat slowly to see if you're going to keep it down."

"I almost ran." is all he says.

"But you didn't."

"Will you tell me what happened to him?"

"Not today."

"Why are you doing this, anyway? I mean, you and I aren't exactly on what you would call the best of terms."

"Truth be told, I'm not sure, but I made a deal with you. Tuck was one of the best men I've ever known, and he, for whatever reason, saw some good in you, so I'm going to call in a favor at this treatment facility in Gilbert. You will be admitted voluntarily, but I swear to God Buddy if you check yourself out before completing the program you'd better go south until you find penguins because I will hunt you the rest of your miserable life if you make a fool out of me and taking advantage of my good nature."

At this, he laughs as he reaches and pulls the sandwich container from the bag. "Yeah, your good nature. Why take the chance?"

"Buddy, we're not friends, and frankly, I don't have time to sit here with you and discuss your life's choices. I'm doing this because we made a deal, and you had the chance to run and didn't. You know this is the best opportunity that you might ever get." She pulls a card and a pen from her jacket pocket and scribbles on the back. "This is my card and personal cell. As long as you are in the program, you can call it twenty-four-seven, and I will be available to you." She stands up and looking down at him says, "Now, get back in the fucking car and let's go."

55

It's a trap...

"What makes you think so?"

You haven't talked to Lindsay since early this afternoon. Roni hasn't called you to let you know that the burning truck belongs to your company or to arrest you...

"I told you that we're not going to jail."

It's a trap...

"Lindsay's car is there."

Pull around the block. Go in from the back.

"I will not. There is no reason. Lindsay's car is in the driveway. There is nothing out of the ordinary. Why do I need to take extra precautions at my own house?"

Because you killed a cop, and you weren't smart about it. You didn't follow the rules. Roni is smart. She'll figure it out soon enough if she hasn't already...

"We've got time."

It's a trap...

Victor opens the garage door and parks his car in the driveway. Coming into the house from the garage like he always does, he calls, "Babe? I'm home!"

"I'm back here! He hears Lindsay call from the bedroom. Victor, what in the hell is going on?"

"What do you mean?"

"Well, I spoke with Roni earlier, and she and Angie are supposed to come over for dinner and drinks tonight, but now Angie has no idea where she is and is very upset. Have you heard anything?"

"What did you and Roni talk about?" he asks with panic creeping into his voice. "When did you talk to her?"

"Victor, honey, what's wrong?"

"WHAT DID YOU TALK ABOUT AND WHEN?" he screams.

"Jesus Victor." She says surprised at his outburst. "I called her about a half-hour after I talked to you. I wanted to see if she knew anything about what was going on over by the golf course."

"The fucking story..."

"Victor, Tuck is dead. Roni wanted to be the one to tell you because you two were getting close..."

"Of course she did."

It dawns on her at that moment. "Wait, did you know about Tuck? Victor, what is going on?"

Roni bursts through the garage entry at a crouch with her weapon held in both hands straight out in front of her, clearing the room as she moves. "LINDSAY? ARE YOU HERE? VICTOR? WE NEED TO TALK. WHERE ARE YOU?"

In the bedroom. Lindsay crosses the room and calls to her, "We're back here Ron—Hey!"

Victor pulls his knife and snatches her into his grasp by her hair. He holds the knife to her throat and pulls her close, holding her in front of him. "There's no other way out, baby. I'm sorry," he whispers in her ear.

"It's you?" she asks through her sobs.

"Sorry, babe," he says with a maniacal grin as he pushes through the bedroom door. "Here we are, Roni. Now I need you to put your gun down and let us pass you," he says, closing the distance between them slowly.

"Not a fucking chance. Victor put the knife down and let her go."

"Not going to happen," he says taking another step.

"Victor, stop! Don't make me shoot you." Her voice is calm and even. "You can't possibly think that I'm going to let you walk out of here holding a knife to your wife's throat after all the people you've killed? Is that the knife you used to kill Tuck, you bastard?"

Victor's smile widens. "Well, yes, it is," he replies, taking another step.

"DON'T FUCKING MOVE, VICTOR!"

He chuckles. "Funnily enough, Tuck said the exact opposite right before I gutted him."

"Daddy?"

Shelby's voice from behind surprises him so much that the blade presses further into the skin on Lindsay's throat enough that a trickle of blood runs down her neck. "Baby, I want you to go into your room and grab your Boo Bear, and put some clothes for tomorrow and some jams' in your backpack, okay? We're going on a little trip."

"Roni, why are you pointing your gun at my Daddy?"

"Roni and I are playing a little game right now, and when it's over, you and me and mommy are going on a little trip. Now, go back to your room and do what I asked."

"Why is Mommy crying?"

"SHELBY DO WHAT I TOLD YOU TO DO AND DO IT NOW!"

Roni is trying to move into a better position. "Uh uh," he says. "Move again and I'll cut her throat and take my chances with you. SHELBY, GO!" He hears her sob as she runs back down the hall and then slams the door.

"Great," he says calmly. "Another woman is pissed at me. Roni, it seems that we've reached an impasse. Now either put your gun down and stand aside or I will cut this bitch's head off and hand it to you as I bury this knife in your heart."

"Lindsay, he's bluffing. He's not going to hurt you."

"Try me," he says, hearing the bedroom door open and taking another step toward Roni.

"Ready, baby?" he asks as he sees Roni's eyes grow slightly larger.

She lowers her gun and screams, "SHELBY, NOOO!" as she dives for cover.

Victor makes a quarter turn as the boom from the gunshot echoes in the hallway. The bullet enters his body under his right arm, destroying his right lung, then passes through his heart and left lung before exiting his body and lodging itself in the armoire less than a foot from Roni's head had been moments before. Instantly dead, Victor releases Lindsay unharmed and hits the floor at the same time as the pistol that Shelby shot him with, and the knife that he held to Lindsay's throat does. Blood trickles from his mouth as his eyes glaze over and stare up in wonderment at his daughter sobbing over him.

"Sight alignment, sight picture, right Roni?" Shelby asks through her sobs.

"My star student," Roni replies, kicking the gun and knife out of reach before making sure he is dead, then checking on Lindsay and ushering her and Shelby away from Victor's body.

Epilogue

Ten months later, Lindsay is picking Shelby up from her therapy session. She's responding well to her therapist and is dealing as well as can be expected, considering that she'd killed her father last year.

When Victor yelled at her to go to her room and pack her backpack, her instincts kicked in, and she ran to her parent's room and hid instead. She hadn't wanted to make Victor angrier by crossing the hall, so she sat by the door and listened to his hateful words and cried. She had seen Lindsay's purse lying open on the bed. She'd known that Lindsay kept her gun there and grabbed it after hearing her father admit to killing Tuck. She knew it wasn't a game then.

This is her last weekly session, but she will continue with monthly sessions for as long as needed.

The TV station treated Lindsay wonderfully in the aftermath. They did not insist on an on-screen interview. They had buried the story on their end as much as they could out of respect for her and Shelby. The other channels did, as well.... to a degree.

Roni got a commendation and was promoted to Senior Detective. She also got a new partner. They seem to be working a few things out.

Victor, it seems, had at some point taken out a phenomenal life insurance policy from an agency that she'd never heard of. It's a Chinese Company whose name roughly translates to Kim Lee Appreciation Agency. It seems he was in the right place at the right time when he took out the policy. She and Shelby had sold the house in record time, all things considered. It seemed that their life insurance agent had an aunt that was looking to buy in the area and fell in love with the house.

While packing his things up she had found two letters from Victor. One for each of them. She hasn't had the heart to read either one yet. And isn't sure if she ever will.

Lindsay's parents had come for the first month or so and had practically begged her to move back to San Diego, but she declined. Phoenix is her home now. She and Shelby are still in the Phoenix area but no longer in Phillips. She misses Victor so much that it hurts sometimes, but she has a daughter to raise, so she does her best to push those thoughts from her mind and focus on her and Shelby's healing.

She walks into the office and greets the receptionist. "Hi, Kay."

Kay looks up from her computer screen. "Oh, hi Lindsay, take a seat. They're almost done." Lindsay sits in a lobby chair and waits for Shelby to come out.

"MOMMY!" Shelby screams in her hushed inside voice.

"Hey baby," she says, taking her in her arms in a huge bear hug. How's Dr. Haely?

"He's good. Today is my last session for a whole month!"

"I know! Are you so excited?" she asks, taking her hand and turning to the door. The Dr. will call her tomorrow after reviewing his notes from today's session. "I've got a surprise for you tonight."

"What is it?" she asks, fidgeting. Shelby is very leery of breaking from routine since her father.... died. She doesn't talk to Lindsay about him at all. She does talk to Dr. Haely about him, though. He's a wonderful therapist who was recommended by her life insurance provider of all people. He tells Lindsay that it is normal for Shelby to feel guilty for killing, not only her father but her mother's husband as well. Though she has never spoken of that day at all, he feels that she's coping as best as she can, and it will just take some more time. He also feels that with the anniversary of Victor's death approaching, she could open up at any time.

Outside of the building now, and walking to the car, she thinks to herself, that she does hear her talking to Victor sometimes though, through her closed door.

"Well, Roni and Angie want to take us out to dinner. How does that sound?"

"Can't we just stay home and order a pizza? They can come over if they want to."

"Sweetie, we're going to have to start living our lives again sometime. We have a new house, in a new town, you're in a new school, we have new lives, right?"

"I miss Daddy though," she says with tears welling in her eyes.

"Ooh, I know baby. I do too, and it's okay to miss him. It's okay to love him still. I know I do, and I know that you do, too."

"You do? Even after... that day?"

"Of course I do baby," she says crouching down and getting eye level with her daughter.

Roni had given her Victor's file the following weekend. She's read through it a dozen times, hoping to make sense of it all. She has to read it in segments, or she has nightmares, and not just about the night her husband was going to kill her. "

Baby, I don't know what was going on with your Daddy when he died, but never doubt that he loved both of us very much. He had some problems, and there at the end, he got overwhelmed by them, but promise me you will never doubt that he loved you... loved both of us, very much."

"Is that why I have to talk to Dr. Haely? So that I don't stress out and..., do what Daddy did?"

"Ooh sweetie, no! You went through a very traumatic experience... one that most people never have to go through. You talk to Dr. Haely because we want to make sure that you're coping with everything alright."

"Okay Mommy, but do we have to go tonight?"

"No baby. I'll call and get a rain check."

"What does that mean?"

"It means that we'll go next time."

"Okay, thanks, Mom."

Later that night, after pizza and a movie, Shelby gets out of bed to get a drink of water. She checks in her Mommy's room and makes sure that she's sleeping soundly. She hears her Mommy crying sometimes late at night when she's supposed to be asleep. It worries her.

She's fine, she's just sad right now. Just like you.

"I know, but I still worry about her."

She's going to be okay. The important thing is that you never tell anyone about our conversations, right? Not your Mommy, or your friends, and especially not Dr. Haely, okay?

"Okay."

If someone hears us talking, just tell them that you're talking to your Daddy, okay? They'll believe that.

"Are you my Daddy?"

Kind of... I knew your Daddy when he was a little boy... You can call me Daddy if it will make you feel better... Remember, tell no one....
"Okay," she says as she fills her cup at the sink.

Turn the page for a sneak peak of the sequel to
DEMONS

HEIRESS
DEMONS II

DARREN OWENS

1

"SHELBY NOOOO!..." Shelby snaps awake, the gunshot still echoing in her ears from the dream that she can almost remember. She's wide awake as she struggles to get her breathing under control. The dream occurs more frequently now than before. Not a dream really. More like a suppressed memory. She knows her role in what happened to her father. She can find more than enough information through a simple internet search. Her therapist, Dr. Haely, told her it's natural that she doesn't remember everything, both because it was a little over twelve years ago, and because she was only six years old when she killed her father.

She checks her phone for the time and watches as it turns from 2:24am to 2:25am. "Eh, what the hell," she says, swinging her legs out of bed. After listening at her mother's closed door for a moment, Shelby goes to the kitchen and makes a pot of coffee. As the coffee brews, she hears her mother's alarm go off, pours creamer into another cup, and waits.

"Why are you up so early, Sweetie?" she hears Lindsay ask as she pours a cup for them both.

"I just opened my eyes and was awake. When I saw the time, I thought I'd get up with you," she says, turning and handing her mother the steaming cup. Walking around the counter and sitting on a barstool, she looks at her mother for a long while, saying nothing. As she gazes at the lines on her mother's face, she realizes how hard the last few years have been on her. She's still beautiful, but she's aged harder than most do in the same amount of time.

Considering that she was married to a serial killer, and that her daughter killed him while he held a knife to her throat would cause a few gray hairs on anyone.

I suppose... I'm still not talking to you...

Lindsay pulls a stool across the counter from Shelby and takes a sip from her cup. "Mmm, thank you." She says, smiling. "This is nice."

"What's that?" Shelby asks, still looking in her mother's face.

"We haven't had morning coffee together in a long time."

"We haven't, have we?"

"No, how are you?"

"I'm good..."

"How's Danny?" she asks with a sly smile.

"Mom... we're... he's fine, we're friends that's all." she snaps harder than she intends.

"Shelby, what's going on? Did you have another dream?" she asks as she gets up and drops an English muffin in the toaster.

"I don't know. When I woke up, I almost remembered everything, but the more I tried to hold on to it, the further away it slipped. Do you still love Daddy?"

Unable to hide her initial shock from the question, Lindsay turns back to her daughter. "Of course I do. Why would you ask that?"

"Well, he killed a lot of people, and nobody really knows how many people he killed. How do you love someone like that?" she asks, with tears welling in her eyes.

"Well," Lindsay says swallowing. "Your dad had different sides to his personality, and one of them was despicable and killed people, there's no doubt, but the other one, the one we knew and loved was a loving, caring, wonderful human being. He loved both of us very much. It's important to remember that."

"Do you hold it against me?"

"What?" she asks in surprise. "Shelby, look at me." As Shelby looks up from her coffee cup, Lindsay continues. "What happened to your father was not your fault, you know that, right?"

"Yeah... I still don't remember what happened that day. Do you think he would have killed us?"

Unconsciously Lindsay's hand reaches to the small, almost invisible scar on her neck as her mind flashes back *'Move or I'll cut this bitch's head off and hand it to you before I stab you in the heart,'...* "No baby, he never would have hurt us. You know that."

"But..."

"No buts. Your father loved us and would never hurt us, so forget about that."

"I'll try." She says, reaching for the nearby box of tissues, "It's just so hard. I want to remember him the way you do, and I try to remember that day, but I can't. I see the true crime documentaries on TV, and that crazy bitch on YouTube, and it's like I can almost..."

"God Damnit, is she calling you again?"

"No mom, she's not, but the court order doesn't stop her from talking about it on her podcast, that whole First Amendment thing, you know?"

"Yeah, that pesky thing." Lindsay scoffs. The toaster pops, and she turns to the refrigerator to get the butter out. "But that doesn't mean you have to watch. Do you want to make an appointment with Dr. Haely?"

"No, I haven't talked with him in what? Two years?" she asks, furrowing her brow before giving her mother a serious look. "I think I'd rather talk to Roni. There's a lot I don't know and so much bullshit that's out there. I just want to know the truth."

Lindsay puts the muffin on a plate and drops another in the toaster before handing the plate to Shelby, saying nothing.

"Mom, she was the investigating officer. She knows more about that side of Daddy than anyone else. I'm eight-teen years old, and I think it's time... I need the truth."

"I know you do Sweetie, it's just..." Lindsay pauses and looks across the counter at her daughter as she remembers the six-year-old version of her. The sweet innocence of childhood that was taken from her. *She looks so much like you Victor.* She thinks.

"What? It's just what?" Shelby pleads. "Mom, I want to know about Daddy. Roni can tell me things you either don't know or won't tell me."

The toaster pops again, Lindsay turns to retrieve her muffin and tops off her coffee. "OK, listen, I'm going to call Dr. Haely this morning when the office opens and make an appointment..."

"Mom..!" Shelby interrupts.

"An appointment for both of us," she continues, "to talk with him. I want to get his opinion about this and if he thinks it's a good idea, then I will make the final decision."

"Don't I have a right to know about my father?"

"That's not what I said. You've been through a lot Sweetie," she says as she reaches across the counter to brush the hair out of Shelby's face, before continuing. "I want to avoid causing you more trauma than you've already had. After we talk to Dr. Haely, and he gives us his opinion, I am going to make the final decision and that's the end of it. OK?"

Shelby scoffs and rolls her eyes.

"Don't you roll your eyes at me, young lady." She says, sounding more like her mother than she ever thought she would.

"I'm sorry, Mom, but I'm eighteen, and I don't want to talk with Dr. Haely again."

"Sweetie, I'm just looking out for you. I don't want you hurt anymore."

Trying to hide her exasperation Shelby replies, "I love you Mom, but I need to know, no matter what Dr. Haely might have to say, I'm not going to another appointment with him."

"I love you too, Baby, and I know that you're frustrated, but I'm still going to call him this morning to get his opinion." She looks at the clock. "Oh shit, I'm late. I have to get in the shower. We good?"

"Yeah Mom, we're good, but..."

"But what? Come on, what's on your mind?"

"What about before he met you? What about the people he killed then? Then he just stopped? Could he control it? Just turn it on and off?"

"Sweetie I've asked myself that very same thing. I've even asked my therapist, and done my own research on the subject. I've done a lot of soul searching. as well. The truth is, I just don't know. He was a tortured soul, and his childhood was just this side of horrific..."

"What happened?" Shelby interrupts.

"Well, that's exactly what I'm talking about. I need to discuss the best approach with Dr. Haely.

"What? You don't think I can handle it?" Shelby scoffs.

"Hey, easy there Defense. This is me, remember? It's not that I don't think you can handle it. I want to handle this correctly. I don't want it to traumatize you further than you already have been. He may have ideas on how to handle this properly. It's not exactly a chapter in the parents' handbook, you know?"

Shelby smiles, "Yeah, I'm sure it's not. You can call Dr. Haely if you want, but I'm not going. I want to know the truth about my father from those who knew him. Not what's on the internet."

"I get it." Lindsay says as she finishes her muffin, puts the plate in the sink, kisses Shelby on the cheek and says "I've got to get in the shower Sweetie, I'm on the air in a little over an hour. I'll think about it more this morning and we'll figure it out, OK?"

"OK Mom." Shelby says as Lindsay walks toward the hallway. "Mom?" Lindsay turns to her. "Thanks."

Lindsay winks at her and smiles, "Sure thing, Kiddo, I love you."

"Love you too."

2

Detective Sergeant Veronica Novetti answers the phone ringing on her hip without looking at the caller ID, "Novetti."

"Hey Roni, got a minute?"

Checking her watch, she says "Oh hey Linds, sure, what's up?" as she sits at her desk in the Detective's squad room at the Phillips Police Department.

"Hey, just a heads up. Shelby might give you a call today, or maybe tomorrow."

"Okayyyy, so?"

"I'm sorry, that came out wrong. She asked me about Victor this morning over coffee and said that since you and Tuck were the detectives on the case, she wants to talk to you, because you know more about that side of him."

"Oh, OK... well, what do you want me to say to her if she does?"

"I offered to make an appointment with Dr. Haely for both of us, but she refuses to talk to him and wants to talk to you. She wants to hear it from you. I told her I was going to call Dr. Haely and get his opinion on how to best go about it, before I decide. But you know how impatient and headstrong she is. I'm just heading her off at the pass, so to speak."

"Gotcha, no problem."

"You're the best Roni, thank you."

"No worries." As they hang up, Commander Ames walks through the squad room, nods at Roni on his way to Lt. Damian's office, and closes the door. Mike Jenkins, Roni's partner of the last six months, looks up from his computer screen. "What do you think that's about?"

Roni shrugs and scoffs simultaneously, "No idea." She looks across her desk at Tuck's coffee cup sitting beside her computer. *Jeez, Tuck, it's hard to believe you've been gone this long. You weren't supposed to die, fucker.* She gets lost in her thoughts about her former partner whenever she talks to Lindsay or Shelby. She loves them both too much to blame either of them for what happened to Tuck.

"Hey, Roni, where're you at?" Jenkins asks, snapping his fingers in the air to get her attention.

She looks up unapologetic that she had zoned out for a minute, but says, "I'm sorry Mike, what did you say?"

"Just that Ames has been spending a lot of time in the Lieutenant's office lately, and I would kinda like to be a fly on the wall." His fingers fly over his keyboard.

"Don't do it Mike," she says.

"I've gotta keep my skills sharp." He says with a sly grin.

"Hacking the Lt's computer camera to listen in on a conversation he's having behind closed doors with Commander Ames isn't the way you want to keep them sharp. Damian might let it slide if he finds out, but Ames will can your ass."

The Lieutenant's door opens, and Lt. Patrick Damian sticks his head out, gives them a two-finger point, and waves them to the office.

Jenkins logs off his computer and locks it before hurrying behind his partner.

Inside the office, Lt. Damian is already behind his desk, and Commander Ames is leaning against the filing cabinet with his arms folded across his chest. Damian gestures to the two chairs opposite his desk.

"Sgt. Novetti, Detective Jenkins." Ames greets them in his typical gruff voice.

"Commander." They say in unison.

Damian looks at them both and lets out his breath. "Listen." he says, "That crazy internet bitch is here again." The annoyance in his tone hangs in the air.

"Here, as in...?" Roni asks.

"Here as in inside the building." Replies Commander Ames. "Novetti, you're not going to like this, but upstairs wants you to do the interview." Holding up his hand in anticipation of an argument, he's surprised there is none. Roni sits back in her chair and scoffs but says nothing. "I don't know why," he continues, "but Victor Powers has picked up some kind of an online cult like following, and Lori Collins is leading the charge."

"Why me? Don't we have a whole Public Relations Division that is supposed to handle 'the press'? she asks, putting air quotes up with sarcasm.

"You're correct, and they have decided that we should appear cooperative with the press. Besides, I don't recall you being camera shy." He says with a grin.

"If you're referring to my wife, you're right, I have no problem with the press, or doing a live interview. If you're also referring to Lindsay Powers, no, I'm not shy at all. They are legitimate press."

"Novetti, do you know what it takes to be considered legitimate press?"

"Yeah, an iPhone, an audience and a willingness to throw blood in the water."

"Exactly."

"Does my marriage to one of the most popular newscasters in Phoenix, and my personal relationship with another, have any impact on this decision?"

"On the record? Of course not."

"Can I get out of it?"

"Not likely."

"Well, that's bullshit, and you know it. Why am I getting hit with doing an interview about a case that was closed over ten years ago?" She pauses for a minute, collecting her thoughts. "Fine, you want me to talk to this... reporter? On the record I will, I won't be happy about it, but I will. I will not deviate from department policy, and I'll do it with a fucking smile," she says, trying to keep her anger in check.

Damian looks across the desk at Ames and raises his eyebrows as if he'd just asked a question. Ames gives him a slight nod, with no emotion in his eyes.

"It's a closed case." Roni continues. "He's been dead for over ten years. He killed my partner, for fuck's sake. Why is this coming back now?" She asks, more to herself than to anyone in the room. Ames crosses the room and stands behind the desk beside Lt. Damian, and looks down at her, still seated in front of the desk.

"Officers," he says, his gaze held on Roni, "if you will excuse me." He walks out of the office and closes the door behind him.

"Mike, would you give us the room please?" the lieutenant asks.

Jenkins gets up and leaves immediately.

Damian rises from his chair and comes around the desk and perches himself on the edge and asks, "What's going on Novetti?"

"Nothing.... I'm just getting hit from all sides with Victor Powers. Lori Collins is trolling me online, and just happens to show up when I'm in public." She says, putting air quotes up as she speaks again. "This so-called reporter hasn't been to my house yet, but I'm sure she's not above it. She sat outside the TV station waiting for either Lindsay or Angie to come out. They both have escorts to their cars now. The minute she turned eighteen she camped outside Shelby's school, not so much to get an interview with her but to take pictures of her for her show. After that Lindsay got a restraining order against her. That helped, but she just turned up the heat on her podcast. She's a bottom feeding wannabe journalist, hiding behind the First Amendment. Frankly, I'm shocked that you and Ames are making me do an interview with her to save the department's reputation, all because some junkie used my name in an interview."

"Is that all?"

"Professionally? Yes, that's all."

"And personally?"

"Personally, is not your concern," she says, glaring at him.

Holding her glare, he says nothing but leans back slightly on the edge of his desk and folds his arms over his chest to wait her out.

"Listen, Lieutenant...."

"Bullshit."

Taken aback, she looks at him with a semi shocked expression. "Excuse me?"

"You're deliberating on what about your personal life you're willing to share with me. You don't know me from Adam, and you certainly don't trust me. I've only been here three months, and I'm sure you'd rather be talking with Commander Ames, but you're stuck with me and I need you to trust me. You are my squad's ranking detective, and the others follow your lead. I'm not asking you about your personal life. I only want to know how it affects you professionally. Let me tell you what I know… I know you are a brilliant detective. I know that you've got a hot temper on a short fuse. I know that you've been through five different partners since Det. Tucker was killed. I know that you're married to Angie Keller. I know you are friends with both Lindsay Powers and her daughter. I know that relationship extended to her husband, who her husband was, and that he killed your partner. I also know that you've got a big heart, and that you care about the job. I need the assurance that my best detective's personal life won't affect her job."

"Of course. It's not like it's my first day on the job, sir. I need to handle a couple of things that have been happening lately.

"Alright, then get a handle on them and do it as soon as possible. I'll push back on the Chief. Take a few days to prepare for it, just in case."

Her phone rings, and Roni looks down at the screen. "I'll think about it… If you'll excuse me, Lt. I've got to take this," she says, looking at him expectantly.

He meets her gaze, "Go."

Getting up and walking to the door. "Novetti." She says as she grabs her purse from her desk and walks toward the elevator, leaving the lieutenant still sitting on the corner of his desk without another word. Once inside the elevator and the doors close, she hangs up the phone and pushes the button for the garage. Jenkins is waiting in the car and unlocks the passenger door for her as she exits the elevator. "Thanks Mike, I owe you one." She says, climbing into the car and shutting the door.

"I figured you'd be about ready for lunch."

3

Mike holds the door for Roni at The Edgy Egg. "How many?" the hostess asks as they approach.

"Two please." Roni replies.

"Make it four, and on the patio, please." A gruff voice comes from behind them. They turn around together to see Commander Johnathan Ames rising from the row of chairs along the wall beside the door. Roni looks at her partner, her face full of suspicion. Jenkins shakes his head with a slight shrug of his shoulders.

"Table for four then. If you'll follow me," the hostess says as she grabs four menus from the cubby behind the hostess stand, turns and walks toward the patio. Once there, she shows them to their table, waits for them to take their seats. Roni sits directly across from Ames and Jenkins sits beside her across from the empty chair. The hostess hands them their menus. Roni first and then the men. "Stephanie will be your server and she will be right with you." She lingers for a moment before walking away.

Roni and Ames lock eyes while Jenkins considers his menu options. A few lingering moments pass before Jenkins chimes, "I guess I'll break the ice," from over the top of his menu. "To what do we owe the pleasure, Commander?" Roni tilts her head somewhat and raises her eyebrows while keeping eye contact.

Ames looks at Roni a few moments more before he starts, "A couple of things." Hardening his gaze, he turns to Jenkins. "First, I know that you've been accessing secure inner department systems, files and laptops, without authorization, and you need to stop."

The corners of Jenkins mouth turn up somewhat before he replies, "Commander, I'm not sure what you're trying to imply, but if I were doing that, I would be sure to cover my tracks. Unless of course I wanted you to know that I'd been there."

"I'm not implying anything Jenkins. I'm flat out telling you I know you are, and I'm giving you the opportunity off the record to knock it off before it comes to a formal investigation. You're a brilliant hack, and I know that we, as a department, use your skills to our advantage when it's authorized. What you're doing can lead to both termination and imprisonment."

"Understood Sir." He replies with a smile and goes back to his menu.

To both Roni and Jenkins' surprise, Lt. Damian is escorted to their table by the hostess. "All right," he says in a casual voice, "wanna catch me up?"

"I held off until you got here." Ames says as he shifts his gaze back to Roni.

Stephanie, their server, appears beside their table to take their drink order.

Ames and Damian each order a Coke, while the junior officer's order iced tea.

"Very good. I'll have that right here."

Puzzled, Roni shares a look with Jenkins and asks, "What's going on here?"

"Well," the Lt. replies. "While we were in my office, we were on the record. I was a lieutenant, and Commander Ames here was a commander, but here we are colleagues discussing a work problem over lunch."

"And that problem would be?" Roni asks.

"Don't get your hackles up Novetti," Ames says. "The problem the Lt. is talking about is Lori Collins and the Chief breaking protocol by wanting you to do an interview with her."

"You said there was no avoiding it."

"I did, but that was in my office."

Roni looks over at Jenkins and shrugs as he drops his eyes back to his menu. "You must have something in mind for us to be enjoying your company."

Ames takes a deep breath and lets it out with deliberation. "Department policy states that we cannot comment on an ongoing investigation."

"I'm aware of that." She says as Jenkins looks up from his menu, watching without comment. "But Victor Powers is dead. He has been for over twelve years." Ames and Damian are quiet as they both look at her across the table. "You want me to reopen a closed case on a dead suspect that, had he lived, would be sitting on Death Row down in Florence as we speak?"

Ames and Damian say nothing but continue watching her debate the question at hand.

"How would I do that?" She asks, more to herself than to anyone else. Her mind flashes back to the day she and her former partner, Detective Pete Tucker, or Tuck to his friends, had met Lindsay, then a rookie reporter on her first actual story, for coffee and an interview.

Afterward, she and Tuck met with Janice McKinny down in The Vault and got a stack of thirty plus unsolved case files. She remembers asking Janice, "These are all related?"

"That I can't tell you." Janice replied. "What I can tell you is these cases fit the criteria that you asked for over the last ten years. Where there was little, if any, evidence left behind except the murder weapon." The sight of the stack of case files that could be linked to their guy overwhelmed her, she remembers. Later, Janice expanded her search to fifteen years at Tuck's request and came up with even more.

Her eyes grow wide and her speech speeds up as she realizes Ames' suggestion. "Victor Powers could be responsible for a significant number of those unsolved cases."

Ames' expression matches Roni's as he sees she is getting it. "And?"

"Solving these cases is our responsibility to the other victims' families." Jenkins pipes up, surprising them both.

"Exactly." Ames says as Stephanie, their server appears at the table with their drinks and takes their order.

4

Shelby sits in the passenger seat of Danny's truck in front of the house where she once lived in Phillips, Arizona. The house where she killed her father all those years ago, straining to remember. A for sale sign swings in the front yard close to the sidewalk.

"Anything?" Danny, her not boyfriend, but more than a friend, asks from the seat beside her.

"Yeah," she says, smiling. "I remember a lot about this house." Her voice takes a faraway tone as her eyes peer at the front of the house she used to call home. "I remember the happiest times of my life happening in that house. My Dad and I would go on these Daddy-Daughter Day adventures, never anything huge looking back, but at the time I thought we were having the time of our lives."

Danny smiles at her. "Yeah? What kinds of things did you do?"

Shelby turns her head and looks at him like he had just appeared from thin air, then regains her composure. "Well," she says smiling, brushing her hair from her face, "we always started out with breakfast at either IHOP or Waffle House, and we'd talk and laugh. He had all these stupid Dad Jokes I thought were hysterical. Even though I was only five or six, he cared about and listened to my thoughts and perspectives." She says as she wipes the tear running down her cheek with her finger before continuing. "After breakfast, it was up in the air. Sometimes we went to museums, or roller skating, one time we went ice skating, but he said it hurt his ankles, so we only did that the one time. Sometimes we went to Bass Pro Shops and played hide and seek in the campground upstairs. He even took me fishing a couple of times. We always ended up at the frozen yogurt place around the corner." She says, gesturing with her hand in a northwestern direction. She takes the proffered tissue from him and wipes her eyes. Shelby is lost in the nostalgia of her story when someone taps on her window. She jumps in her seat, startled as she turns to look at who had interrupted her thoughts. She sees a semi-familiar face peering through the window.

"Shelby? Oh my God, it is you!" Jen says as Shelby rolls down her window.

Shelby looks into the woman's face, searching her memory for a name. "Mrs. Langston?" her face breaks into a smile as she opens the truck door and gets out. "Is that you? My God, how are you? I had no idea that you still lived here." She says, embracing the older woman in a tight hug. "Where's Abby and Joey?"

"Sweetie," she says, pulling out of their embrace. "You can call me Jen, and Abby and Joey are at their dad's this weekend." She says with a touch of sadness in her voice. "Bill and I got divorced about five years ago."

"I'm so sorry. I didn't know."

"Of course you didn't. How would you?" She says, smiling as she places both hands on Shelby's shoulders and holds her at arm's length. "How are you? How's your mom?"

"Well," Shelby replies. "Mom's still the morning NEWS anchor at Channel 4 and still loves it."

"Yeah, I guess I knew that. I used to watch her every morning, but since the divorce, I just don't find the time anymore."

"Can I ask what happened? I'm sorry, I'm sure that's out of line and none of my business."

"No, it's OK, it's not such a big deal now.... I just didn't like his girlfriend." She says with a shrug and a tight-lipped smirk. "Who is this handsome guy?" she asks, changing the subject.

Shelby turns and notices Danny now blushing at the compliment and leaning against the fender of his truck. "Oh, uhm, this is my bo... my friend Danny." she blushes, stammering through the introduction.

Danny leans forward and offers his hand awkwardly. "Mrs. Langston, it's a pleasure."

"Well, Danny, it's nice to meet you." She says, shaking his hand. "Would you two like to come inside? I can get you a soda or water...?"

"Uh, yes, please." Shelby replies for them both.

Once inside, Jen gestures towards the living room, Shelby and Danny sit on the sofa while Jen turns toward the kitchen to get the drinks. "So, what'll it be guys? I've got Coke, Dr. Pepper or water."

"Coke will be fine, please."

"Danny?"

"Coke please."

Danny looks over and questions her with his eyes.

Shelby leans close to him. "Her daughter Abby was my best friend when we lived here."

Jen returns with two cans of soda and a bottle of water, handing over the soda. "It's great to see you again."

"I was just explaining to Danny that Abby and I were best friends when we lived here."

"Oh, dear Lord, yes, you were. She'll be so disappointed that she missed you. I'll have to get your number before you leave. Do you have plans for college after high school?"

"I applied at U of A for their School of Veterinary Medicine. My school councilor seems to think I'm a shoe in, so I'm waiting for the Letter of Acceptance I guess." Shelby looks around the living room. It's mostly the same, with a few minor differences from what she recalls. "It's hard to believe you're still here after all this time." Shelby says as she looks around the room, memories of her and Abby replaying in her mind.

"Well Sweetie, this is our home. Even after everything that's happened over the years, Bill and I bought this house to raise our family. It's still a great neighborhood, even after… Oh Honey, I'm sorry, I didn't mean that to sound horrible."

"You're fine, that's actually part of why I, er, we are here. I have such wonderful memories of that house and you guys," she says, staring at the wall closest to her former home. "Of my dad and our life here. We really were happy, weren't we? I mean, it was real, wasn't it?" Shelby asks with tears welling in her eyes.

"Oh, I think so. Bill and I wondered if there was anything we missed after you and your mom moved, and concluded that we didn't. We both remember your family fondly, the backyard bar-b-ques, the pool parties, Halloween, New Year's. God, there's just so much. Shelby don't ever doubt his love for you, or your mom. That was real. He doted on you both. Sometimes he would zone out for a few minutes at a time, like he was in deep thought or had something else on his mind, especially for the last six months or so. That was when your mom got the job at the TV station and he got promoted. We assumed he was just stressed about work, or something. But then he would pop back as if nothing happened, saying he must have gone off with Capt. Kirk."

Shelby listens with a smile as memories resurface. She and Abby learning to swim in each other's pools, riding their bikes around in the cul-de-sac, the sleepovers. They were thrilled when her mom announced she would be reporting the news on TV, thinking she would become famous. Their dads standing around the grills beers in hand on weekends, while their wives lounged by the pool, and the kids played in the pool or on the swing sets. "Yeah, I guess we were really happy, weren't we?" she says to no one in particular.

After a moment Jen says, "Yeah Sweetie, you really were."

"What do you know about that day? Will you tell me?"

Jen looks at the young woman leaning forward with her elbows on her knees sitting on her couch and reaches across the coffee table. She takes Shelby's hand and squeezes it for just a moment before sitting back in her chair. *She is such a perfect blend of her parents...* "It's not much, but I'll tell you what I know." She takes a deep breath and lets it out slowly as she recalls her memory of that day. "It was the day after Thanksgiving. Your mom had to work at the station, and your dad called and asked if you could come over for a few hours while he went to his office for a bit." She smiles at the memory. "Of course, Bill and I had no issues with that. You were almost a second daughter to us. Anyway, we ended up taking Kona up to the park. We were playing Frisbee with him when he stepped on a piece of glass. We had to take him to the vet, and I called your dad..."

"What did he say? Looking back, did you have any clue?"

"Like I've told you Sweetie, I've gone over it in my mind several times, and I don't think so. He sounded somewhere between concerned and annoyed now that I'm saying it out loud. But, at the time, I didn't give it any thought at all." She is silent for a minute before continuing. "Then your mom came to pick you up when she got home from work. Everything seemed fine. I told her about Kona, and she asked if he was alright, and where he was. Come to think of it, I did think it was odd that your dad hadn't called her about it, but I figured he was into whatever he was working on. So, I told her where my brother-in-law's clinic was. And that's really about it. You guys went home and about a half hour to forty-five minutes later, police cars, fire trucks and ambulances filled the cul-de-sac."

"Thank you." Shelby says, the tears rolling down her face.

Handing her a tissue, Jen asks "Are you all right? Is that not how you remember it?"

"I don't remember leaving your house. I remember you talking to my mom in the doorway and the next thing I know, my mom and I are in a hospital room. My therapist says it's a normal thing for someone not to remember something as traumatic as... what happened. But it was over twelve years ago, and I'm so frustrated that I remember everything about that day except killing my father, and whatever happened directly after. I really thought coming here would trigger something, hell, anything, but it doesn't. It's like I can almost remember everything if that makes any sense, but it's just.... It's like reaching for something that's just beyond your grasp."

"I understand." She says, handing another tissue across the table.

Danny drains his soda and stands. "Mrs. Langston, may I use your restroom please?"

"Of course you can, Danny." She points towards the hall. "It's the first door on the right. And please, call me Jen."

"Thank you, and yes ma'am."

Rising from her chair, Jen smiles as she collects the empty can from the table. "He seems like a nice boy. Is he?" she asks as she crosses to the kitchen and drops the can in the recycling bin.

Shelby blushes at the comment. "Yeah, he is." She says rising from the couch and following.

Remembering the awkward introduction, and seeing the acute shyness come over the girl, Jen touches her arm. "I'm glad that you have a friend like him you can rely on."

"I'm not sure what he is. I like him. More than a friend, I think, but I'm just not sure."

"That's fine too." She winks. "You two just go at your own pace."

Danny enters the room. "We should, uh, probably get going, don't you think?"

"Yeah, it's about that time, isn't it?"

"Well," Jen says, picking up her phone, "let me get your number before you go. I'm sure Abby will want to call you." Shelby recites her phone number to Jen, and she plugs the number in her phone and pushes send. "Now you have mine. Please give it to your mom for me, or you can use it if you ever just need someone to talk to."

Jen walks them to the truck, to say goodbye. Shelby says, "Listen Jen, I think you should know that there's a wanna-be newscaster with a video blog trying to make a name for herself off of my dad. It won't be long before she finds this place." She says, gesturing to her former home.

"Oh, you mean Lori Collins?" she scoffs. "Yeah, she's been here already. I told her to go to hell."

"You're the best Jen, thank you."

"Remember, call me anytime you need to and give my number to your mom." She waves as they drive away.

5

Shelby is rummaging through the fridge when Lindsay comes through the garage door into the house. She leans against the doorjamb, watching her for a moment before Danny greets her from the living room. "Hey Mrs. Powers."

"Hi Danny." She says, smiling at the boy. She likes Danny. He's polite, has good manners, and he treats Shelby like a lady. She doesn't think that they have gone farther than kissing yet, if that. Shelby insists, to her anyway, that they are just friends. "Hey Kiddo." She continues as she crosses into the kitchen.

"Hi Mom." Shelby says as she closes the fridge and turns to kiss her mother's cheek. "How was your day?" Danny joins them and pulls a bar stool up to the counter and sits.

"Same as always, I guess. How about you?"

"It was OK. We had an early release day."

"I forgot about that. What did you guys do?" she asks as she grabs a glass and fills it with water.

"Well, we uh," Shelby stalls, looking down at the counter. "We, I mean Danny, uh..."

"Shelby," Lindsay says, trying to ignore the images of writhing, naked, teenage bodies that flash through her mind, "come on, out with it."

"We went over to the old house in Phillips." She states finally.

Taken aback and relieved for a moment, she scoffs, "Oh, all right, I guess I'm not that surprised. Has it changed much?"

"Not really. It's for sale. Jen says hi by the way."

"Oh, how are they? Did you see Abby? I bet little Joey is getting big."

"No, they were at their dad's."

"Oh no, Bill and Jen got divorced? That's too bad. I wonder what happened."

"Apparently girlfriends have that effect on a marriage."

"Oh Bill, you dumbass." She says in disgust. "How's Jen?"

"She's good. She said it was hard at first, of course, but it's better now. She and Bill power through all the bitterness and resentment during the holidays and birthdays for Abby and Joey. She told me to give you her phone number, and that she'd love to hear from you."

"Cool, thanks. Anything else?"

"Mom, she told me what she remembers about that day..."

Lindsay takes a deep breath and lets it out. "All right, what did she say?"

"Nothing that I didn't already know," disappointment hangs in the air after she says it.

"Shelby, there are only three people who know what happened in that house, and you're one of them. I've told you, and Roni has told you the same story, that you don't remember is nothing to worry about, and normal..."

I've even told you what happened...

Like I'd believe you GO AWAY!!

"...he thinks you'll be able to handle it without any issues. He said it may even help."

"I'm sorry Mom. What was that?"

Lindsay furrows her brow at her, then smiles. "I said that I talked to Dr. Haely about it this afternoon, and he thinks you will be fine and able to handle knowing everything about your father. He asked me to make an appointment in a month to see how you handle it, but he's confident you'll be able to. So, here's our plan. We're going to call Roni and ask her if she will share what she and the police know about him. Then we'll ask her if she would mind talking to us about it."

Now it's Shelby's turn to furrow her brow. "Why wouldn't she?"

"Sweetie," she says, grasping Shelby's arm, "We aren't the only ones that have to live with that day. Roni went through a lot too, and from what Angie tells me with all the bullshit Lori Collins is spewing, she's really closed up over the last month or so."

"Yeah, I guess so," she replies, even more disappointed now than before.

"I tell you what, it's been a while since we've seen them outside of work. Why don't we invite her and Angie over for dinner this weekend and see how it goes? Danny, you're welcome to join us if you'd like."

"I, um," he stammers at the unexpected invitation. To tell the truth, he was thinking they had forgotten he was here. Both Lindsay and Shelby are looking at him, waiting for his response. His gaze lingers on Shelby longer than necessary, her hazel eyes gazing at him in expectation. *Good Lord, she's beautiful.* Shelby blushes as if she'd read his thoughts and smiles. "I, I'll have to check with my parents, but I'd love to. Thank you." He finally manages.

"I'm not going to ambush her." Lindsay says turning her attention back to Shelby, "I'll run it by her, but if she doesn't want to talk about it, I'm going to drop it, and I don't want you calling her and hounding her about it."

"Why would I do that?"

Lindsay looks at her daughter with a slight tilt of her head and raises her eyebrows. "Really? I'm surprised you didn't call her today."

Shelby straightens her arms and interlocks her fingers, stretches her hands backwards, then bats her eyes as she tilts her head to one side, and asks. "Who me?"

Lindsay scoffs, "Yeah, you young lady. I'm serious though. I'll bring it up when I think the time is right."

"What's the big deal, Mom? It's not like it's a secret, is it?"

"Oh Honey," Lindsay says concerned, "you know better than that, don't you?"

"Yeah, I do. I'm sorry. I'm just frustrated, I guess."

Lindsay comes around the counter and hugs her. "I know, Honey, and I'm sorry. It'll come."

Seeing Danny over her mother's shoulder, Shelby gets a case of self-consciousness at him seeing her this vulnerable. She pulls away from her mother's embrace. "What do you want for dinner?"

"Oh, I saw a new recipe for Chicken Parmesan that I want to try."

Shelby smiles at her.

"What?"

"I'm talking about tonight."

"Oh, how about pizza?"

About the Author

DARREN OWENS IS a loving husband, father of five, and grandfather of two. He was raised in central Wyoming and currently lives in the Phoenix area. He served his country in The United States Marine Corps and was deployed to Operations Desert Shield & Desert Storm. He has worked in the telecommunications industry for almost thirty years. He has been an aspiring author and storyteller for most of his life. Other than his family, he enjoys solving the world's problems with his friends, over a cold beer and a good cigar by the fire.